AN AMERICAN IN NAGALAND

Robert Donovan, an American academic, travels to India in 1991 with Meniu, an Indian student with whom he is having an affair. Meniu is from the Konyak tribe in Nagaland, a people who practiced headhunting as recently as the 1950's. Unknowingly, Donovan has violated a tribal taboo by having a relationship with Meniu. Meniu's father learns of his daughter's affair and vows to take revenge. Cultural differences, the threat of violence, sexual tensions, and unexpected plot twists make the story an engrossing one.

AN AMERICAN IN NAGALAND

Tom Farrell

INDIALOG PUBLICATIONS PVT. LTD.

Published in November 2004

Indialog Publications Pvt. Ltd.
O - 22, Lajpat Nagar II
New Delhi - 110024
Ph.: 91-11-29839936/29830504
Fax: 91-11-29834798
www.indialog.co.in

Copyright © Tom Farrell

10 9 8 7 6 5 4 3 2 1

Printed at Print Tech, Noida, UP.

All rights reserved. No part of this book may be reproduced or utilized in any form or by any means, electronic or mechanical, including photocopying, recording or by any information storage or retrieval system, without the prior written permission of the publisher.

ISBN 81-87981-77-6

To my wife,
Eileen

In the hills, among the Karen, the Kachins, and the Nagas, there was another world. Nearly all of these tribes took heads, and until a man had shown himself a man by bringing home the head of an enemy, he did not easily find a wife.... These were tribes that went entirely naked and tribes among whom money was unknown. It was a primitive half-savage world remote from ... India's highly developed Aryan Civilization.

(*The Men Who Ruled India*, Philip Mason)

PROLOGUE

1952 – The Naga Hills.

The boy joins the other young children on the outer fringes of the circle imitating the movements of his father and the other hunters inside the circle. The hunters dance a repetitive sequence of steps in which they bend their knees forward, hold their shields to their chests, and raise their machete-like daos to the striking position. They chant in rhythm to the thudding beat of the great log drum and its call. Elaborate white-striped tattoos cover each hunter's face and chest, and each has a headdress of multi-colored hornbill feathers. They wear only loin cloths below their waists.

On this morning, the boy wishes with all his being that he was old enough to be with his father inside the circle. A few days earlier, his father had fashioned him a makeshift wooden spear, and showed him how to put stripes on his face with a mixture of mud and clay. The spear and the markings on his face give him courage. He thumps the spear into the ground and tries to look as fierce as his father. Lost in his boyish imagination, he strays too close to the circle. It is his mother who scoops him up in her arms to save him from being trampled by the hunters who become more agitated as they dance.

Soon, his father gestures to slow the tempo of the dance, a signal that it is time to leave. The elders, who had once been great warriors, step off to the side. The drums, the chanting, and the dancing stop. A great quiet falls on the village. Without any farewells, the silent hunters file down a narrow path that exits through the fields. The boy is proud his father is not only the chief of the village, but the greatest hunter of them all.

Those who remain in the village busy themselves preparing the feast that will celebrate a successful hunt later that day. It has been some time since such a hunt has taken place. Pigs are killed and cooked, large pots of rice-beer boiled over smoky fires, and heavy balls of rice steamed to be served on banana leaves dipped in taro mash. Pan leaves are prepared with chalk and sweet-smelling bark to be chewed after the meal. There is much to be done. The boy is given no special status or privilege. He works along with the other children doing the small chores that the elders tell them to do.

The father, however, has given him a special task, one which the other children envy. On this afternoon, just as the sun reaches a certain point in the sky, he runs to the edge of the village where an ancient banyan tree spreads over a large area, its aerial roots contorted in sinister shapes. The tree has long been used as a lookout to warn the villagers of a raid by unfriendly neighbors. The boy climbs until he finds a comfortable perch from which he can see great distances across the fields. To pass the time, he picks at the scarlet fruit that hangs on the shafts of the leaves.

His friends pester him from the base of the tree. "Do you see anything, Chingmei? Tell us when they are coming so we can run to the village.... Can we climb up and help you watch?" He ignores them and concentrates on his responsibility as the mid-afternoon light begins to dim. Finally, he spies movement through the tall reeds of a distant field. Soon he sees a thin line of men turn a corner on to a path that heads to the village. His father leads the hunters who are moving at a slow trot. They are too far away for the boy to hear if they are chanting. He is able to make out the bamboo poles they hold high above their heads. The hunt has been successful. He calls down to his companions below who run screaming to the village wanting to be the first to deliver the good news.

Word of the hunters' return spreads through the village and an excited crowd gathers to greet them. An old man who had been in the circle earlier breaks into a frenzied dance, swinging his dao in the air as he jumps wildly from side to side. He is ecstatic that the hunters are bringing back trophies. It has been too long. Shouts ring out as the hunters dance into the village. The boy's father extends his arms to elevate the bamboo pole so all can see the human head that is impaled on its tip. It is one of three head-trophies taken this glorious day from the evil village of Pangsha, the same Pangsha whose men recently ambushed a young warrior from the village and then took his head.

Before the celebration can begin, there is a ceremony that must be performed. The boy watches with the other children as the oldest men of the village smash a raw egg over each of the captured heads. The egg's magic blinds the relatives of the dead so they will not be able to take revenge. Next the elders pour rice-beer into the mouths of the heads as they pray they will have other opportunities to take more Pangsha heads. Finally, the boy's father and the other hunters take the heads to the central hall and hang them from the ceiling.

Now the celebration begins. It will last until morning. Every villager will stay up except the children who try but eventually succumb to fatigue. The boy fights sleep as long as he can, thinking, until his last waking moment, what it will be like when he can join his father in the circle and then go on the heroic, great hunt.

PART ONE

1

1991. The most powerful man in the district of Mon was Chingmei Konyak, Minister of Public Roads and Highways in the territory of Nagaland in northeast India. His authority came only in part from his ministerial position and from the fact that he had served three terms in Lok Sabha. His real power came from being the "Great Ang" of Mon, a tribal chief of the Konyaks who was thought to have the undiluted sacred blood of Naga chiefs in his veins. Chingmei had married Sipra from his own Great Ang clan, keeping the blood pure and passing on the royal clan status to their only child and daughter, Meniu.

When the Congress party lost the general elections in 1989, Chingmei and Sipra left the government home in the capital city to return to their plantation in Mon. Here they worked at nurturing and refining the indigenous tea that grew on the low, sloped lands that covered much of their property. Someday, Chingmei believed, the teas of Nagaland would be as desired as those of Darjeeling.

The couple did not return to New Delhi until two years later when they went back to mourn the death of Rajiv Gandhi with many of their old friends in the Congress party. Gandhi was killed while campaigning in a suburb of Madras by a woman who triggered a bomb concealed beneath her dress. Sixteen other people died in the bombing. Oddly, the blast decapitated the assassin, but left her face intact. "This country has gone mad," Chingmei said to his wife as they watched the former prime minister's body being carried in procession across the city to the banks of the Jamuna River. Here Gandhi's body was cremated. It was May 24th.

Before taking the flight home to Dimapur, Chingmei obtained an Entry Permit to Nagaland from the Ministry of Home Affairs for Robert Donovan, an American sociology professor at the University of Rhode Island, the school where Meniu had just completed her bachelor's degree in International Business. Meniu had written praising Donovan, stating that the scholar wished to study firsthand various aspects of tribal culture among the Naga people. Chingmei knew what that meant. As with others before him, Donovan was likely drawn to Nagaland by the fact that as recently as the 1950's, disputes among the nine tribes that lived in the Naga hills were resolved by bands of headhunting warriors. The victors would display human heads with bamboo spikes thrust into the eye-sockets above the portals of their thatched huts. At forty-seven, Chingmei was old enough to remember the V-shaped tattoo of a headhunter on his father's chest. Though he had been too young to participate in a raiding party, he could still picture the wild excitement in the village, the shouting and dancing and brandishing of weapons, when the older men returned with captured heads. But that was in another earlier time, gone now except in the interest of men like Donovan, or in the memory of those old enough to have lived in the head-hunting culture who could recall its brutal ferocity. The "Great Ang" of Mon was such a person.

All his life he had struggled to separate himself from the primitive savagery of his father's world. Education, travel, his political success, and the unexpected accumulation of modest amounts of wealth had transformed him into a man with many modern sensibilities. But as much as he fled the past, it was always there, filling up the interiors of his mind with its darkness. Try as he might, he could never escape it.

Both Chingmei and his wife were glad to leave New Delhi after the funeral. It seemed as if the city, indeed the entire country, was in turmoil. The pre-monsoon heat had been oppressive, and violence surrounding the first round of voting had taken more than two hundred lives across the country. Following the assassination, the next rounds of voting were postponed until mid-June. India seemed about to come apart, unable to withstand the pressures of economic decline, separatist violence, and political instability. More were certain to die.

They flew first to Calcutta where they transferred to a late morning flight to Dimapur. They were happy to be heading home. The minister and his wife relaxed in the comfort of the first-class section. They were an attractive couple whose features were more South-East Asian than Indian. Chingmei's black hair was streaked with gray, his round face punctuated with broad high cheekbones, a flat nose, and narrow Mongoloid eyes. His rugged five foot eight body hinted of a stoutness to come.

Sipra was a few inches shorter than her husband with a shapely figure that made her appear younger than her forty-five years. Straight black hair fell to her shoulders, framing a face of exquisite oriental beauty that had attracted Chingmei to her twenty-four years ago. Their life together had been a series of constant challenges and adjustments, the journey from the villages of the Naga Hills to the halls of Lok Sabha in New Delhi an arduous one. They had depended upon each other to survive, and their marriage had grown stronger as a result.

"You made the right decision not to run for office this time," Sipra said to her husband, "it is much too dangerous now. Let others risk their lives. You have done your share."

Chingmei nodded agreement. "Our elections will be more unstable this year." Except for the states of Jammu and Kashmir, and Punjab, Nagaland elections were the most notoriously violent in the country.

"The guards will keep us safe. They always have," Sipra said. "Let's talk of happier things. Meniu will be home in two weeks, bringing her professor with her."

"She has done well. We can be proud of her."

"You will have to plan things for Professor Donovan to see and do."

"I don't mind. Perhaps if he tastes our tea, he can tell the world what is to come." Chingmei welcomed the change in the direction of the conversation. Though hardened by many political battles, he was tired of India's political chaos and the inability of the Indian people to make democracy work peacefully. He wanted stability and quiet, simple things such as his beautiful dark-haired daughter's return home.

As his mind drifted, he imagined a future in which Meniu gradually took over the management of the plantation. She would apply all the new things she had learned at the American university to be successful. She would marry in the clan, and there would be one or maybe even two grandchildren. A boy and a girl would be ideal. In this way, he and Sipra would be able to make up to their daughter for all the time they had been away when she was a child, all the years she had gone away to private schools.

He fell asleep with the image of Meniu's face in his mind.

2

After landing at Dimapur, Nagaland's only airport, Chingmei and Sipra still faced the five-hour journey across the territory northeast to Mon. They drove in a government-owned Tata Sierra, a 4x4 all-terrain vehicle complete with a driver and bodyguard. Although the Tata Sierra was well-suited for the bumpy roadbeds, they found the trip fatiguing.

The two lane state highway, still being constructed under Chingmei's supervision, rose out of the plains into the hills, cutting through the dense sub-tropical forests. The couple warmed to the familiar sights of the terraced rice fields and, later, workers tilling the maize, millet, and tapioca crops on the steeper, hilly slopes. Each landmark brought them closer to home; the scarred hillsides of the Western Borjan coal mine, the worker training centers, the plywood factories and, finally, the convergence of the Tejan, Yangnu, and Dikhu rivers which bordered the district of Mon.

Invariably, these sights reminded Chingmei and Sipra how different Nagaland was from the rest of India. If it weren't for the constant presence of the Indian military as well as the countless government bureaucrats who administered the assistance programs, one could easily consider Nagaland a separate nation. In fact, separatist groups working for an independent state of Nagaland had been active since the mid-1950's when negotiations with Nehru, the then Indian prime minister, ended with the violent suppression of the Naga nationalists.

Some of Chingmei's teenage comrades had never stopped fighting for independence, operating across the border eluding both the troops of the Burmese military junta and the Indian army. Chingmei had chosen to work within the system to better the lives of the Naga people, and his efforts in Lok Sabha had resulted in a number of beneficial programs, especially in education and job-training. Over the years, he had quietly maintained communications with some of his old friends and, though he knew some of the younger separatists did not trust him completely, he had the respect of their elders.

Dusk gave way to darkness as the Tata Sierra entered Mon, a collection of villages whose residents lived in a combination of traditional Naga bungalows as well as more recently constructed government, pre-fabricated housing. The three-room bungalows were built high above the ground on long wooden pillars, and all had small sitting platforms or veranda on the back. Palm-thatched roofs covered the bungalows. Some of the roofs were crowned with crossed wooden horns, the same symbol once used as a chest-tattoo by headhunting warriors.

By contrast, the Indian government had built rows of small box homes on flat ground, each identical to the other. When the homes were first built, villagers competed to be eligible to live in one of the new structures. Now, interest in the homes had decreased and the old bungalows had regained their lost status. So marked was the difference in the two styles of housing that first-time visitors to Mon often remarked to Chingmei that the newer houses intruded on the natural harmony of the village, that they seemed not to belong. At such times, Chingmei would shrug and comment that progress was always a double-edged sword. That was something he believed.

The great house of Chingmei and Sipra was the largest of all the houses. Gas lanterns lined the road up to the house, casting shadows that were shaped and reshaped by the evening breeze which blew through the trees. As was the custom, the entire plantation staff stood casually around the front entrance, ready to welcome the Great Ang and his wife. They were as pleased by their arrival as the couple was to be home.

The peace that Chingmei and Sipra sought following the public anguish of the Gandhi funeral lasted only a few short days. The arrival of the morning mail on Friday, May 31, disrupted the calm. Sipra brought a pack of envelopes to Chingmei as he sat in his library reading progress reports on the construction of the state highway system.

Only a few houses in Mon had libraries. Chingmei's library reflected not only his present status, but also the past that had formed him. An oak bookcase filled with records of his years in Lok Sabha as well as with current documents from the Ministry of Public Roads and Highways covered one wall. Glass cases sat on tables displaying body ornaments such as brass bangles, necklaces, and earrings, the kind that now were worn only at festival time or by village elders. Spears, bows and arrows, daos, shields and helmets made of cane, and a crudely made rifle, hung from the walls. Two gaily-colored shawls draped over a soft armchair in a corner brightened the room.

Chingmei had positioned his large desk in front of a window which afforded a view of the fields below. A cluster of framed photographs stood at one end of the desk. There was one of Chingmei and Sipra on their marriage day, another of Meniu at her highschool, and a few showing the couple meeting with various leaders of the Congress party in New Delhi. The smallest photo had clearly been taken many years ago, its original black and white now fading into a soft brownish hue. In it, the young adolescent Chingmei stands bare-chested between his parents. White stripes are painted on his mother's cheeks and she smiles out from a mouth of blackened teeth. His father is a study in contrasts, a pensive, thoughtful face looking down at his son. His lean muscular body is naked from the waist up and, on his chest, he wears the crossed horns tattoo.

"There is news from Meniu postmarked Bombay. She must have arrived on schedule. And this is for you, from the US." Sipra handed him an envelope that had been sent airmail. It was marked "Confidential." "It looks important."

Chingmei said nothing as he opened his letter, listening as his wife read the short note from their daughter.

"Let's see, if this is Friday, they are now in Madras. They leave for Calcutta on Sunday, spend two days there, go on to New Delhi June 5th, and then fly to Dimapur arriving at 2 o'clock on June 7th. We shall meet them at the plane."

Chingmei nodded understanding as he began to read the letter he had received from his trusted friend in Los Angeles, Abhi Chandra.

"Listen to this," Sipra said. "You won't believe it. Over two hundred people came to hear the professor lecture in the Taj Hotel in Bombay. When he was done, Meniu spoke to them about her experience as a student in the United States. The university's admissions department paid her airfare home; in return, she assists Professor Donovan."

When there was no response from her husband, Sipra glanced up, and immediately knew something was terribly wrong.

"She used to be so shy," Sipra continued. "She never would have ... Chingmei, what is the matter? Why do you look that way?"

Her husband's face had flushed, the usual soft, round shape chiseled hard, his black eyes narrowed to a slit, the high cheekbones taut with fury. "Leave me," he said. When angered, as he was now, he exuded power. Sipra started to say something and thought better of it. She wanted to say that whatever it was, they would face it together, overcome it together as they had done so many times before. She left the room, not sure if Chingmei would tell her what was wrong after his anger had settled. He shared many things with her, but there were also things he kept to himself.

The letter from Abhi Chandra sent the Great Ang of Mon into a rage he had not felt for years. But his years in politics had taught him to be thorough and cautious before acting. He reached for the telephone and began the process of placing a call through the ponderous long-distance system with its considerable potential for mishap. The expected delay allowed Chingmei to steady his breathing. As he waited, he picked up his daughter's photo and held it before him. Finally he heard Chandra's voice at the other end.

"Hello Abhi, Chingmei here. I received your letter today."

"I have been expecting your call. I am only sorry that I had to bring you such bad news."

"You have looked after my daughter as I asked you, my friend; you are not responsible for her actions."

Chandra did not reply, a habit of his that Chingmei remembered. If there was nothing to say of consequence, silence was preferable.

"Let me see if I understand what you have told me. Meniu is

sleeping with a man more than twice her age, a man who is older than me, her father. You are certain of this?"

"As certain as I can be of anything. The investigative agency I retained to check these matters provided me with the evidence that is included in my letter."

"This man is Robert Donovan, a professor of sociology at the university where Meniu studied?"

"Yes."

"She was a student in his sociology class? And this has been going on for over a year?"

"It appears to be longer than that. Some of my earlier letters mention what I thought was a change in Meniu's behavior in February of 1990."

"Is this man married? How old is he?"

"He is fifty-four and has a wife just slightly younger. They have been married twenty-six years. Her name is Paula. They have no children."

"And this abuser of my child has had the gall to write me and ask for help obtaining an Entry Permit to enter Nagaland, which I have foolishly obtained for him thinking he was sincerely interested in studying the cultures of the Naga tribes."

"He is a respected professor who has published some articles in prestigious academic journals."

"He is not interested in the Naga culture. He is interested in having sex with my daughter under her own father's roof, perhaps even on her childhood bed." Chingmei's voice rose as his rage escalated again.

"Perhaps you should have his Entry Permit revoked."

"It is too late for that."

Silence.

"If he knew anything about our tribal culture, he would know

Meniu is of the Great Ang clan and must not be contaminated by an outsider."

Still, Chandra did not reply.

"If he expects to find savages in Nagaland," Chingmei thundered, "that is what he will find. He will not be disappointed. He will come to know what savage means."

"Be careful, my friend, you have accomplished too much in your life to ruin it by some irrational act of revenge."

"I will think of your advice Abhi. Good-bye for now."

3

After twelve days in India, Robert Donovan was six pounds lighter, physically fatigued, and psychologically battered by the human calamity he had witnessed. He had not been caught up in the mystical appeal of the country that had drawn the imagination of so many westerners before him. Instead, he had been alternately appalled and angered by what he saw, particularly the sight of small children begging in the traffic jams of the cities, their frail, half-clothed bodies barely as big as the truck tyres under which they risked being crushed. It had been Meniu who kept his spirits up, soothing him with her soft words at night. But still he could not forget the images of packs of people crawling into the back of a broken-down garbage truck in Bombay to fight over scraps of food they found in the filth.

Now, with university business finished, he and Meniu were en route to Dimapur, the stopping-off point on the way into Nagaland. From the time Meniu first urged him to learn about the tribes of the Naga hills, Donovan recognized there might be a career opportunity for him to research and write something significant about cultures that had been generally overlooked in western sociological and anthropological literature. His focus would be on the transition from a violent primitive culture to a more modern one. The motif of cultures changing from what sociologists called "gemeinschaft" societies to "gessellschaft" was a dominant theme in twentieth-century sociological literature. What would differentiate Donovan's work was his decision to examine the impact that Christian missionaries and the intrusion of the Second World War had on the Naga people. In particular, he would try to understand how the tribes came to give up headhunting as a way of life.

Certain factors encouraged his planning. A computer search of the literature indicated scholarly books on Nagaland were few and limited in scope. To Donovan, this meant a chance to do original work in a subject area not already trampled over by fellow academics, a small miracle in itself. This was what had been missing in his career. He had not found a niche or specialty as so many other university faculty had. In his own department, a relatively nondescript professor had suddenly emerged as the national expert on domestic violence. Grant money poured in to support his work, and he was in great demand on local and national television programs. Donovan wanted all of that.

When the university's international admissions department announced they were looking for a faculty member to do a speaking tour in India on their behalf, he was the first and only volunteer. The decisive factor was Meniu offering to ask her father to obtain official permission for him to enter the protected territory of Nagaland, access that would otherwise likely be denied.

The fact that the trip afforded an opportunity to travel with Meniu added to its appeal. Donovan wanted to try to better understand the world that had shaped her. Two weeks was not enough time to accomplish anything definitive, but it was long enough to assess the potential for a longer return visit. It was time now to begin the work.

As with all Indian Airline flights, the process of boarding the plane from Delhi was more like a rugby scrimmage, an exercise in survival of the rudest. Donovan guided Meniu through the shoving tide of dark faces, his hands gently pressing on her thin shoulders as he steered clear of imminent collisions. They made a most unlikely couple, with their evident disparity of age – he, at six feet, towering over her by almost a foot. This, and the fact that he was the only blue-eyed Caucasian on board, attracted the stares of the other passengers.

"Are you ready to meet my parents?" Meniu asked as they settled into their seats.

"I am ready as long as you remember I am one of your professors and nothing more," Donovan replied.

She squeezed his arm affectionately. "Don't worry. They would never think anything else."

"I hope you're right," Donovan's stomach rumbled as the plane taxied toward the runway.

"I thought your Delhi belly was better?" she laughed and leaned against him, closing her eyes so she didn't have to see the takeoff.

"My stomach is just bidding good riddance to your nation's capital city," Donovan said. He resisted the urge to put his arm around her to draw her closer and instead smiled politely at the Indian couple across the aisle who were no doubt trying to figure out the relationship between the older gray-haired American and his younger Naga companion. Donovan turned to stare out the window. He too needed to sort out the meaning of what had taken place between them.

They first met when he was randomly assigned to be Meniu's faculty advisor in the fall of 1987. Their affair had begun during the Christmas holidays of 1989, more than two years after Meniu arrived on the Rhode Island campus. Donovan remembered it clearly, the way people often remember unexpected events that shape part of their lives.

He was driving Meniu back to the house she rented in Narragansett after a pleasant dinner at his house with Paula and two Swedish students. The party had been gay and festive, livened by the singing of Christmas carols in different languages. When the Swedish students left, the mood turned quiet. Donovan noticed the disappointment on Meniu's face when Paula suggested it was time to drive her home.

Once in the car, she began to cry softly.

"What's the matter?" he asked. "I thought you enjoyed the evening."

"Oh, I did, I did," she said. "It's just that it seems that all my life I've been leaving the people I care for, always being sent away somewhere else."

Donovan understood the reference. In more than one of their many long conversations, Meniu had told him that she had been educated in private schools, first in the mountain resort of Darjeeling for her grammar school years and then in the international high school in Hyderabad. She had only spent vacations at home with her parents. It was a part of her life that periodically saddened her. Donovan said nothing as she continued to cry.

He thought about turning the car around and bringing Meniu back to his house. Paula would understand. Meniu was not the first international student to become lonely and homesick. But some basic male instinct that he recognized kept him from doing that.

"Are your roommates at your apartment?"

"No, they have gone home to their families for Christmas."

"You are all by yourself?"

"Yes, but that is okay. I will be fine."

"Do you want me to keep you company for a while?"

"That would be nice. I think there is some wine left in the refrigerator."

That was how it began, she turning to him inside the apartment, before they took off their coats, before she offered him a glass of wine. She rushed into his arms, and he was not entirely surprised.

"Please just hold me," she said. "I just need you to hold me."

"It's okay," he said, pulling her close, gently patting her back. "Everything will be okay." She pressed her small body against him and, as her sobbing quieted, she raised her tear-stained face to be kissed.

Even though Donovan had been involved with many women during his twenty-six years of marriage to Paula, he never before had had an affair with a student. There had been opportunities, but until now, he knew student-faculty affairs to be a violation of professional ethics, a code he took seriously. Ever since his sexual initiation at thirteen with a twenty-year-old Welsh domestic, he had developed a theory about love-making as a behavior that was essentially good, as long as it was based on mutual affection and consideration. Except for a brief infatuation with Roman Catholicism during his sophomore year of college, the morality of pre or post-marital sex had never been an issue. For the most part, Donovan accepted eight of the Ten Commandments, totally disregarding the other two.

Now as he bent down to kiss Meniu's tears and then her mouth, Donovan knew he was about to break his self-imposed rule against affairs with students. He knew as soon as they kissed and she moved against him that she had made love before and was not a virgin. What surprised him that first time, and still fascinated him, was the extent of her experience and the heat of her sexual passion.

It was she who unbuttoned her blouse so he could see she was not wearing a bra over her small, pink-ringed breasts. He stared somewhat foolishly, not knowing what to say, as she stepped back from their kiss to take off her skirt. The sight of her flawless brown body contrasted with the pink panties she wore stunned him. All his years of sexual experience were little help as this petite twenty-year-old descendant of savages took his hand and led him into her bedroom.

"Meniu, I care for you very much, but I can't take advantage of you." It was a line and Donovan recognized it as soon as the words were out. He knew they were going to make love; it was already too late to stop.

"I am taking advantage of you," she replied, "and besides, when I am with you, I am happy and not lonely anymore." He first sat down on the edge of the bed and then stretched out full length, his head on the pillow. She stepped out of her panties, and then crawled on top of him, her hands deftly undoing his belt buckle. She has done this before, Donovan thought, many times but with whom?

"My beautiful, naked Naga," he said as she smiled and expertly guided him inside her.

"And you are my professor, my Professor Donovan, who has been so good to me and now makes me so happy."

They began to make love slowly, getting comfortable with each other's touch and rhythm. To his surprise, it was Donovan who lost control first and, recognizing his need to climax, Meniu quickened her movement to both help and join him.

"I can't believe it," Donovan said afterward.

"What can't you believe?" she whispered, her soft voice barely audible.

"That this happened and that it happened the way it did."

"You are not mad at me?"

"No, not at all."

"Will Mrs. Donovan be worried that you are not home?"

"I'll call her."

Donovan got up from the bed and walked to the living room to call his wife. He wore a sweater over a sports shirt and a pair of blue socks, nothing else. He told Paula that Meniu's roommates had invited him in for a drink before they left for the holidays. She was already in bed and asked him to wish the girls Merry Christmas and be careful driving home.

Donovan went back to the bedroom, took off the rest of his clothes and rejoined Meniu in bed.

"Do you always make love with your socks on?" she laughed.

"Only when my feet are cold."

She scrambled to the bottom of the bed to check the warmth of his feet.

"Your feet are warmer than mine. I want to know if you can make love without socks."

And so, in time, they made love again, something that surprised Donovan, as he had not had climaxes so close together in years.

4

Over the next year and a half, the affair between Donovan and Meniu evolved according to the patterns that have always shaped secret lovers' lives. At first, they met only in the safety of Meniu's apartment during the infrequent times her roommates were away. This satisfied them both while their relationship went through tentative, exploratory phases as each tried to become comfortable with the other. But as their enjoyment and pleasure grew, they became bolder, willing to risk more to be together.

Late afternoon visits in Donovan's office turned into early evening, doors-closed, lovemaking sessions, she sitting astride him on his chair, the two of them half-clothed, laughing at the sounds of the night cleaning crew approaching from down the hall. The risk of discovery excited both of them.

It was inevitable that he ask her to accompany him on overnight regional academic conferences so they could spend more time together, sleep together. She didn't hesitate to accept, saying she wanted the same thing. Through it all, Paula seemed oblivious to what was happening, though once she inquired why Meniu hadn't visited the house for some time. Donovan had replied that Meniu had met some new friends and left it at that.

Over the years, he had felt that Paula instinctively sensed

when he was having an affair but chose to remain silent about it. He thought of this characteristic as a form of denial, a defense mechanism that Paula and other wives of her generation employed to protect themselves from pain. Now that the studies showed more women were in the workplace having affairs of their own in greater numbers, Donovan wondered whether their husbands would practice the same kind of denial. In any event, he didn't have to worry about Paula. However unfair it may be, he knew she had always been faithful to him.

Even if Paula had confronted him with her suspicion, it would have been difficult to end the affair. Donovan believed you had to take what life offered you and, for the moment, Meniu was his to have. He was not naive. He knew the affair wouldn't last, and the younger woman would leave him for someone her own age. He was not Chaplin or Picasso, geniuses whose intellects transcended generation gaps. That was the way life was. Nothing lasted; some things ended too quickly. For the present, he allowed himself to be mesmerized by Meniu, by her soft slightly British-accented voice, her small, hard, brown body, and the warmth of her affection.

As a longtime academic, Donovan was used to analyzing the events of his life in considerable detail. Whenever he considered the reasons why Meniu was attracted to him, he kept coming up with the same two explanations. He had been a mentor to her from the first day she arrived at the University, helping her to adjust to the new culture as well as shepherding her through the academic bureaucracy she had to face. Also he felt he had served as a substitute father figure to this young Naga woman whose own father had been absent from so much of her life. Somehow the two roles combined to create a third role of lover. This he understood.

What was less clear to him was how his mistress had acquired her considerable sexual experience. When he finally learned the answer, it was a cultural lesson worthy of Margaret Mead.

Donovan and Meniu had taken a room at the Harbor Marriott in Boston while he attended the autumn meeting of the New England Sociological Association at Tufts University. She assured him she would be content sightseeing and shopping until they met for drinks in the hotel lounge at 5 o'clock. When he arrived, he was surprised to see she was wearing a brightly colored red and black shawl over the gray slacks and sweater she had on that morning. Meniu had given Paula a similar shawl, a gift from her own culture.

"You look pretty," he said, "tell me about the colors. Do they mean anything?"

"Yes," she said, "My tribe, the Konyaks, like all colors as long as they are gay and festive. The red and black signify hope for a plentiful crop of rice and taro. It is the harvest season in Nagaland. I was thinking of home."

Donovan ordered two glasses of Beringer Chardonnay and prepared to listen to Meniu talk out her sporadic spells of homesickness, as she had done many times before. She seemed to want Donovan to know the experiences that had made her who she was. Her memories of home never failed to make her emotional.

"When the full moon comes, we first have a daylong village feast before beginning the harvest. The men kill many pigs to cook, and everyone gets drunk on rice-beer. It is a very exciting time. We call it Ouniebu."

"It sounds like homecoming weekend at the University."

She laughed and paused, as if considering what to say next. "If it is not cloudy, the moonlight changes the color of the palm roofs to silver. It is beautiful. You would love it, Robert."

It had taken Meniu a long time to call him by his first name. Donovan was always moved when she did.

"The unmarried girls prepare millet bread to give to their lovers and then the boys sing to them for a long time before taking them for walks in the hills to play at love."

Donovan knew from his research that Naga teenagers began their sex lives early. Meniu's reminiscence did not surprise him, but he sensed that she wanted to tell him more.

"How do the girls meet their lovers?"

"They meet in the summer in the rice fields. They work in groups weeding so that the crop will be good. It is very hard work."

"Co-ed weeding, very innovative," Donovan commented with a laugh.

"It is an old Konyak custom. When there is a boring job to do, let the boys and girls do it together. Then it is no longer boring."

"Did you do this work?"

"Yes, though I wasn't supposed to. My parents were against it, but they were usually away in New Delhi in the summers when I was home from school."

"Why were they against your working in the fields?" Donovan asked. He assumed it was a question of status since he knew that, by tribal standards, Meniu's family was considered wealthy.

Meniu's voice hardened in a defiant tone. "Because there is another old Konyak custom about members of our clan only being able to marry someone from the same clan. It is a stupid custom."

She hesitated and the dark eyes that had flashed in anger lowered until she was no longer looking at Donovan. "They were afraid I might take a lover like everyone else."

"Did you?"

"Yes. His name was Henyong. He is a Konyak also but from a different clan." She took a sip of wine and raised her eyes to look directly at Donovan. "He was my only lover until you."

"May I ask how old you were when it began?"

"Fifteen," she said quietly, staring at him, trying to gauge his reaction.

So that was it, Donovan thought. He couldn't think of anything to say.

"It lasted four summers," she said. "Ouniebu is both a happy and sad time for me because it was always the time I would say good-bye to Henyong and go back to school."

Then sensing the mood had turned too solemn, she asked for another glass of wine.

"Don't look so serious, Robert. Let me tell you more about our weeding parties. I can teach you more sociology than you learned at your conference today."

"That wouldn't be difficult," Donovan answered.

"When the weeding is ended, the boys take the girls from their working parties to feasts in the field houses. The whole idea is for the boys to make their girls so drunk on rice-beer that the boys must carry the girl home to her parent's hut. And the parents don't care at all. They expect it because they did the same thing when they were young."

"Did you and Henyong do this?"

"Yes, though my parents didn't live in a hut, and they were rarely home. But that is how they found out about Henyong and me. One of the servants was angry with me and told my mother that Henyong brought me home drunk. My mother told my father and that was the end."

"Why was that the end?"

"Because my father is very powerful and has ways of getting others to do things that he wants done."

"Did you love Henyong?"

"I think so. I think I still do."

Donovan blanched inwardly at the thought of having to compete with the memory of a virile Naga youth.

"But I love you too, Robert, in a different way. Sometimes I don't know who I am being unfaithful to, Henyong when I make love to you, or you, when I think of Henyong."

"You must be very independent to have done what you did."

"If I am that way, it must come from being sent off to school so often on my own. It is my parents' fault. They have made me independent. After graduation, when I go home I'll tell them I will not obey that stupid old custom. I will only marry someone I love."

"Will that be Henyong?"

"I don't know. Our fathers warned both of us not to see each other a long time ago, but we have managed in spite of them."

"You are a remarkable young woman, Meniu."

Meniu sat back and sipped her wine. "Now you know all about me, Robert. I wanted to tell you before, but I didn't want you to think badly of me."

Donovan leaned forward to touch her glass with his. "I would never think anything but good of you. Let's drink a toast to Ouniebu."

The suggestion delighted Meniu. "We can have a feast of our own in the room. If we are lucky, we may be able to see the harvest moon above Boston harbor."

5

Nine months had passed since Meniu's revelation that night in Boston. Now the two of them were still together, ten thousand miles away, on an Indian Airlines jet headed east towards Nagaland. While Donovan was eager to begin his work, he could not rid himself of a lingering sense of foreboding that had been with him ever since the US State Department issued an advisory warning against unnecessary travel to India after the Gandhi assassination.

They had flown to Bombay from London on a British Airways 747, a long, tiring flight. Meniu laughed at Donovan's reaction when the flight attendants sprayed the cabins with disinfectant shortly before landing, but the implications were unsettling. So too was the sight of the Indian army soldier who guarded the passageway leading into the terminal. The soldier, a fiercely bearded Sikh dressed in military camouflage fatigues, cradled in his arms the largest automatic weapon Donovan had ever seen. He never took his eyes off Donovan.

"Security will be especially tight now because of the assassination," Meniu said.

It was somewhere at this point, after the first touching down on Indian soil, that their roles with each other began to reverse, she becoming the mentor, he the student. Meniu became very protective, warning him about pickpockets, the consequences of drinking anything but bottled water, and pleading with him not to give money to the beggar children who continually solicited them on the streets.

"The children don't keep the money," she explained. "Their parents, or masters take it for themselves."

In Bombay they stayed at the Taj Hotel taking separate but adjacent rooms. The hotel overlooked the Gateway of India, the portals to Bombay harbor which welcomed ship traffic from the Arabian Sea. After a long recuperative sleep, Meniu and Donovan were pleasantly surprised when two hundred and fifty prospective students came to the hotel in response to a newspaper ad inviting them to his lecture on "Understanding the American Educational System."

"Don't be fooled," Meniu cautioned, "most of them are here just to pass time and perhaps learn something new. Even those who are serious will have a difficult time obtaining an exit visa from your embassy."

They celebrated their success that night in the hotel bar where Donovan learned quickly that the "five-star" rating Meniu had assigned to the opulent Taj Hotel did not apply to the spicy curried chicken dish they ate and especially not to the wine selection. Instead they drank gin and tonic with lime, warm to the taste because of the lack of ice at the bar.

"It's just as well, the ice will make you sick," Meniu said.

"I feel like a British colonial out of some E.M. Foster book," Donovan said, as he sipped the drink slowly.

"What did he write?"

"One of his best-known novels was *A Passage to India*."

"I saw that movie a few years ago," she exclaimed, delighted at having recognized the title. "Something mysterious happened to one of the characters in a cave … do I have it right?"

"Yes, you have it exactly," Donovan said, "They were the Malabar Caves. The plot was about a relationship between an Indian man, a doctor I think, and a British woman. It had to do with the prejudice British colonials had towards Indians."

Meniu said nothing in reply. She finished her drink and stood extending her hand to Donovan. "Come with me, I'll show you The Gateway of India."

They walked out of the bar, through the crowded hotel lobby, and down the driveway which curved up from the waterfront. It was dusk and the outline of the famous archway loomed ominously against the darkening night sky. Shadowy figures clustered around the base of the stone monument called up to Donovan to join them.

"What do they want? I can't understand what they are saying," he said.

"They want you to come to them so they can sell you something, steal something from you, or worse."

The scene made Donovan feel uneasy. "Let's go back to my room," he said, "we can see all of this from the window and feel safer."

Back in his room, Meniu surprised him with a request.

"Close your eyes, sit on the bed, and wait for me. I won't be long." She retreated into her connecting room, which the front desk manager had been pleased to arrange for them.

Donovan waited, wondering what surprise Meniu had in mind. During the year and a half affair, their lovemaking had become more intense, more unselfish, something he thought of as a healthy eroticism. She had no interest in the Playboy philosophy, X-rated films, sado-masochism, sexual toys, or any of the other diversions that men and women in the West were experimenting with to keep their sexual fires lit. He had correctly sensed what she was comfortable with and tried not to push her beyond that point. There was no need. She satisfied him totally. He thought of her approach to lovemaking as completely natural, and the thought appealed to him greatly.

"You can open your eyes now," she said. "I want you to look at me."

She stood naked facing him, her brown skin glistening with freshly applied oil. Her short black hair swept back over her exquisitely round face reminded Donovan of one of the Siamese children in "The King and I."

"You look beautiful. Why have you put on the oil?"

"So that you can see how brown my skin is. Does that bother you?"

"Not at all. It makes you look more sensual."

"Have I ever told you that most Indians look down on Naga people; they think of us the way some Americans think of black people."

She turned slowly, letting him see all of her body.

"The British used the term 'black' to describe Indians even though it is inaccurate. You think Indians would have learned from their experience with the British. The irony would make Gandhi turn over in his grave ... I like touching your white skin."

"I'm glad. It's too late to change it."

She moved closer to the bed. "Take off your clothes," she said, "I don't want to stain them."

Donovan awoke early the following day so they could catch the morning flight to Madras. Meniu stirred beside him. He sat on the edge of the bed going through his daily flexing and stretching ritual. She rolled smoothly out of bed and went to pull open the window curtains. As Donovan turned towards the daylight, dark shapes flew by the window blotting out the morning light.

"What are they?" he asked.

"Haven't you ever heard of the buzzards of Bombay? They are excited by what is happening down below, in the back of the hotel. Come see for yourself."

Donovan took his camera to the window and focused on the scene four stories below where men and women searched desperately for food in the back of a broken-down garbage truck.

"That is a terrible sight. It makes me feel guilty," he said.

"They are hungry."

"These vultures are the ugliest birds I have ever seen."

"They can also be very bothersome. I heard a funny story once about the Parsees, a religious sect who do not bury their dead but leave the corpses outside. The buzzards come and pick the bodies clean. The story is that some rich Bombay merchants were having a party on the deck of their apartment. Just as dinner was being served, a buzzard flew over and dropped a leg bone of some dead Parsee right in the middle of the dinner table."

Donovan shook his head, his laughter at the story tempered by the scene below him on the street.

Madras, Calcutta, and Delhi did little to change Donovan's impressions of India. The assistant manager of the hotel in Madras warned him directly not to leave the hotel by himself. "There is still great anger among the people about the killing of Rajiv Gandhi. There are so many theories about who did it that anything can happen."

Donovan read the English-edition Indian papers each morning. He was surprised to see that wide credibility was apparently being given to the theory that the US Central

Intelligence Agency was somehow involved in the assassination. How preposterous, he thought, how ignorant of any of these people to believe such absurdities.

Another article from the same newspaper warned travelers about Indian taxi drivers who would drive with a companion or helper in their cab, usually a young teenage boy. At some point in the trip, the driver would ask the passenger if his helper could sit with them in the back seat, saying there was not enough room in the front. According to the article, if the passengers agreed, the youth would join them, take out a small knife, and ask for money. The threat of violence was more implied than directly stated, but many frightened passengers paid up rather than challenge the youth and the driver.

Unbelievably, the taxi driver at the Calcutta Airport had a helper with him who he insisted was his son. He asked if the boy, who Donovan judged to be about thirteen, could sit in the back seat. Before Donovan could respond, Meniu spoke sharply to the driver in Hindi. The anger in her voice was evident and there was little response from the driver.

"What was that all about?" Donovan asked.

"It's all right. He won't bother us anymore," she said.

Over six hundred people crowded into the Calcutta seminar forcing the panicked hotel staff to move the group into a larger room. Donovan was surprised by the number of doctors, lawyers, and scientists, who apparently could not make a satisfactory living in their own country. They came looking for a better opportunity in the United States. He also had the distinct impression that some of the crowd were just curiosity seekers, attracted by the air-conditioned hotel on a hot and humid June afternoon.

The next day Donovan and Meniu took a cab to 54A Circular Drive where Mother Teresa's Home for the Dying was located.

Before leaving Rhode Island, he had been asked by a group of parishioners from the catholic church on campus to deliver a gift of money to the saintly nun. The drive through the city that Kipling described as an "urban apocalypse" was one of unsettling extremes. The stately administration buildings left over from the British colonial period were set off by well-manicured fields where the British cavalry once trained and young men still played cricket. These sights contrasted sharply with the densely crowded sections of the city where, according to estimates, eighty thousand hand-pulled rickshaws were still in use. The sights and smells of Calcutta shocked Donovan.

When they arrived at Mother Teresa's, he and Meniu had to step carefully through the foot-deep garbage and refuse that filled the gutters of the street. Emaciated beggars hunched in the alleyway that led to the office of the Missionaries of Charity, their hands extended upward in supplication. They were not aggressive, and Donovan found it difficult to ignore their pleas. He looked at Meniu, seeking her approval to give them some rupees.

"You are better off making a donation to Mother Teresa," she said, "she will see to it that they are taken care of when they are ready to die."

Inside in a dark, plainly furnished room, they met Sister Frederick, whose pleasant but austere manner reminded Donovan of the nuns of his youth. She accepted the money with quiet thanks.

"If Mother Teresa were here, she would tell you to thank the people in Rhode Island for acting as God's hands to serve the poor and for being God's heart to love the poorest of the poor all the time."

Donovan was moved by the nun's words. "May I ask where Mother Teresa is?"

"She is in Romania ministering to the victims there. From Romania she will travel to Baghdad to open up another home. There is much to be done since the Gulf War."

Donovan visualized the image of the eighty-year-old nun traveling barefoot around the world, bringing relief to one disaster spot after another. "Sister, I know you are busy," he said, "but can you explain how the Missionaries of Charity have grown all over the world at a time when religious vocations are declining everywhere?"

"God works through weakness," she replied. As she stood to leave the room, Donovan thought he noticed the beginning of a smile forming on the nun's lips.

Meniu and Donovan sat in silence after Sister Frederick left. "Thank you for bringing me here," he said.

Delhi was the last stop on their educational lecture tour. After a harrowing drive from the airport to the hotel during which the taxi driver reached speeds which Donovan thought would have qualified for the pole position at the Indianapolis 500, he was badly in need of a drink. Meniu led him to the Emperor's Lounge where a classical string group played a soothing Brahms melody.

"Why didn't the driver slow down when you asked?"

"He probably couldn't hear me because he was honking his horn the entire trip, even when there was no one in front of him," Meniu replied.

They sat at the bar and ordered a bottle of Chablis which was warm but drinkable. Four Australians directly across from them talked loudly to the bartender. Donovan and Meniu listened as the Aussies explained they were a television crew just returned from Kashmir. They had gone there to cover the kidnapping of an Australian doctor by a separatist group. They interviewed the guerilla leader, played the interview on Australian television and the doctor was released unharmed.

They were a jubilant group celebrating their getting the story, the doctor's release, and their own safe exit from a dangerous part of India. Donovan asked the bartender to send the Aussies a congratulatory drink which set off rounds of toasts back and forth. It was the last enjoyable evening for Robert Donovan in Delhi.

The next day, Donovan's stomach finally succumbed to the unfamiliar onslaught of minced meats, unusual orange-colored sauces, fish dishes made in mustard oil, curried chicken, and other spicy foods. An inadvertent drink of tap water may have delivered the final blow, driving him to his room where he fought a pink-tinged Kaopectate battle with diarrhea. In his stable moments, he struggled through a final seminar, and accompanied Meniu on a short auto tour of the nation's capital city. Donovan's blurred impression of Delhi was that it was cleaner and more orderly than the other three cities they had visited. What he remembered most was Meniu's comment when she pointed out the government house where her parents lived during the years her father was in Lok Sabha.

"That house is where my parents stayed. It was their home for years, but not mine. I only went there a few times. They were too busy for me." Donovan said nothing in reply but reached across the back seat of the car they were in to gently squeeze her hand.

6

The capacity for revenge ran deep in the blood of the "Great Ang" of Mon. It was a basic cultural belief throughout the Naga Hills that when an outsider violated a member of your clan or tribe, punishment must be meted out. There was no other way. It wasn't as if there had to be personal animosity between individuals or groups. It was enough that a wrong had been committed. The law of nature demanded that balance be restored, and revenge evened the scales.

Years ago, before the British outlawed the practice, nearly all of the Naga tribes took the ultimate revenge against their enemies by cutting off their heads and keeping the captured head as a trophy, proof of their masculinity. But, Chingmei remembered, his father would lead warriors from the village on raids only after an elaborate ritualistic preparation during which he studied chicken bones and the gall of pigs for omens. Surprise was essential to these raids, and if the headhunters encountered signs of resistance or defense, the attack would be postponed until another time when surprise could be achieved. A bloody slaughter would follow.

Chingmei had learned all these lessons well as a youth. He used them often in the chaos that was Nagaland politics as well as in his years in the Lok Sabha. Though the time for headhunting was over and he no longer consulted omens, preparation and surprise were still essential for an act of revenge to be successful. He was confident of the plan he had arranged for Robert Donovan. Surprise should be on his side also, but one could never be too careful. He would size up this Donovan tonight at the hotel in Kohima over dinner. It was always best to study your enemy before any attack.

The flight from Calcutta appeared out of the monsoon clouds above the hills of Dimapur an hour behind schedule. Chingmei stood outside the arrival lounge with his driver, Kiwang, a trusted aide who had been with him throughout his political career. How the world and Nagaland had changed! What would his dead father have thought of his son who stood dressed in tan slacks and a white tropical shirt waiting while his enemy descended from the sky in a metal flying machine? His father, who in another time and place not so distant, had run naked into enemy villages using spears and machetes to satisfy his wrath ... would he have understood? Chingmei wanted to think so as, for all his savagery, his father had possessed a natural intelligence. He knew the world of the Naga Hills was changing, and when the Baptist missionaries encouraged him to continue his son's schooling, his father agreed and, in so doing, changed Chingmei's life forever. Ever since, his life had been a movement away from the primitive past into a world of wonders which he didn't fully comprehend, even now.

Meniu was first off the plane, followed by a tall, wiry man who looked as Chingmei imagined a professor would look. The man had a friendly face, but Chingmei instinctively was uncomfortable with his enemy's greater height. Meniu greeted her father with a hug and a kiss, then turned to the man at her side.

"Father, I want you to meet Professor Robert Donovan of the University of Rhode Island." Chingmei greeted Donovan with a serious formality that had been well rehearsed during his years in Delhi.

"Welcome to the Naga Hills, Professor Donovan. We are honored to have you as our guest. We shall do our best to help you in your work. Thank you for helping my daughter attain her degree."

"It is a great pleasure to meet you," Donovan replied. "You have already been a great help to me, and I want to express my appreciation for your obtaining the entry permit. I hope to be able to learn a lot about your culture."

An imperceptible flicker of annoyance crossed Chingmei's face at Donovan's comment. "Let us get your luggage and start for Kohima where we will stay at the hotel tonight. Meniu, did you explain that it is too late to drive to Mon this evening?"

"I did, father," Meniu replied. "Is mother in the car?"

"No, she did not come though she wanted to; I asked her to stay home to prepare a feast for our guest's arrival."

"I am disappointed; she usually comes to greet me."

Kohima was seventy-four kilometers from Dimapur, a trip which gave Donovan his first glimpse of the Naga Hills. They drove in a state-owned black Ambassador which Chingmei had arranged with the Nagaland State Transport services in Kohima.

"The highway we are driving on is one of our new state roads which eventually will connect the seven districts of Nagaland," Chingmei explained. "Unfortunately, the road to our village of Mon is not yet completed. Tomorrow morning, when we leave for Mon, we will switch to our Jeeps which do much better over the secondary roads."

"My father is preparing you for a long, bumpy, uncomfortable trip tomorrow," Meniu said to Donovan. "Mon is over three hundred fifty kilometers from Kohima; the drive takes most of the day. You will be very happy to arrive at our house and meet my mother." Chingmei Konyak nodded his agreement with his daughter's remark even though he knew Robert Donovan would never see the plantation in Mon.

Donovan smiled and looked out the window at this wild, primitive land. Meniu spoke to her father about family and business matters; occasionally Chingmei switched to a language which Donovan presumed to be a tribal dialect. It was as if he was reminding his beautiful daughter that she was home now where she belonged.

Donovan's preliminary reading had acquainted him with the basic facts about Nagaland. Nagaland was the second smallest state of India and was bordered on the east by Burma, now the military dictatorship of Mynamar. It was a hilly-mountainous terrain with peaks as high as ten thousand feet from which one could see spectacular views of the Himalayas, something Donovan wanted to do.

He knew that Dimapur was the site of a grouping of fifty or so enormous stone monuments sometimes referred to by anthropologists as an "orgy in stone." The monuments were all symbols of the male phallus or the female vagina, fertility symbols whose precise origins were unknown. Donovan thought better of mentioning his interest in seeing the monuments, and the car continued towards Kohima.

As they drove into the Naga Hills, Donovan looked for the settlements that had been built on the slopes, usually at higher elevations. This, he knew, was to afford protection from enemies.

It began to rain. The raindrops seemed unusually large to Donovan as they washed the dust off the windshield and exterior of the car. "It is the monsoon season," Chingmei said. "It will rain on and off this way until August, sometimes as much as an inch a day. It is the reason our forests are so thick and why we have so many different plants and flowers, everything from rhododendrons to bamboo." Donovan had read that seventy percent of the people were farmers who grew a variety of crops including rice, wheat, and sugar cane. "I understand you grow tea on your land," he said.

"It is a wonderful tea, what Americans would call world-class, I believe. I look forward to serving you some," Chingmei lied.

The rain slowed. They drove in silence, Donovan looking in curiosity at the natives who stood on the side of the road and watched the state car go by.

They arrived in Kohima, the capital city of Nagaland, at 5:30 pm and checked into a hotel that Donovan mentally rated as two-star. Chingmei told them that Kohima was a former British hill station and that it was the site of a famous battle in World War II during which time Naga tribesmen helped the allies defeat the Japanese. After washing and unpacking only the essentials as Chingmei instructed, they met back downstairs in the lobby. Chingmei led Meniu and Donovan into a small restaurant where a host of servers brought out plate after plate of food in a banquet that Donovan thought was more Chinese than Indian. He did not recognize all of the dishes but was comfortable with the selection of fish, meats, rice, and fruits. He took only one sip of the rice beer and instead asked for bottled water which was available.

When her father left the table to speak to the restaurant manager, Meniu kicked Donovan gently under the table. "How will you like sleeping by yourself tonight?" she asked.

"I don't think I have a choice, do I," he replied.

"I will come to you if I can."

"It's all right. I wouldn't feel comfortable with your father in the next room."

Chingmei returned to the table. "Tell me about your successful tour of India," he said. "Your mother is eager to hear about it."

They described the reception of the eager crowds of students and hangers-on who had attended their lectures. Chingmei smiled and nodded his approval.

"And father," Meniu said, "you should know how good Professor Donovan and his wife, Paula, were to me while I was at the University."

Chingmei did not look up from his plate. "I thank you for that," he said in a flat voice.

After a brief awkward silence, Chingmei turned to the purpose of Donovan's visit to Nagaland.

"Two weeks is too short a time to learn about the Naga culture, but we will arrange it so that you see as much as you can in the time that you have. Fortunately, both the State Library and the State Museum are here in Kohima. They both have rare articles and books which contain much of the history and tradition of the Nagas."

"I am eager to see them," Donovan said. "Will there be time?"

"I have arranged with the curator, Dr. Ahon, for both to be open early tomorrow morning. He will show you the collections and, should you find them helpful as I expect you will, we can arrange for you to spend more time there at the end of your trip."

"That would be wonderful."

"Coincidentally," Chingmei continued, "Dr. Ahon is traveling north himself tomorrow to the district of Wokha, where the Lotha Nagas live. It is about two hours drive. He has agreed to ride with you in the second jeep and answer all your queries about the Naga people. No one knows more about our culture than he does."

"That is generous of him," Donovan said.

"We will go ahead in the lead car. That will allow me to talk to Meniu about the bright future ahead of her as the mistress of our tea plantation in Mon. Meniu will join you for the second part of the trip." Chingmei's smile was tight-lipped.

"Promise you will stay close, Father," Meniu said.

"We will," Chingmei replied, "you do not have to be concerned."

The servers took away the banquet dishes and brought pots of tea which Donovan thought excellent.

"This is tea from Darjeeling, the place where I went to grade school," Meniu said to Donovan. "Don't you remember my telling you about the toy train that we took up the mountain? There are three train stops along the way. My schoolmates and I used to sing a song about the three train stops. We would get very excited as we sang and the train got closer to Darjeeling."

As Meniu talked, Donovan envisioned her sitting in a train dressed in a school uniform with other little girls, all of them identical. How time changed everything. Now the schoolgirl was his mistress, his lover. What would Chingmei think if he knew?

"I should explain Meniu's comment about tomorrow's drive so you don't worry needlessly," Chingmei said. "It is election time in Nagaland and there is always an increase in violence at such times. But that is of little concern to us, particularly since I am no longer a candidate."

"You were almost killed once," Meniu said.

"That is true; an angry opponent had his guards shoot bullets into my office when I was there. He was a bad loser."

"What we have to be on alert for at all times are the nationalist groups," Chingmei continued. "Americans would probably call them guerrilla fighters or terrorists. We have a number of these groups who are loosely coordinated and often in disagreement. They are tough and dangerous, even more so than the Mujahideen fighting in Kashmir." Chingmei paused to let his words register.

"What is your relationship with these groups?" Donovan asked.

"I used to know many of them well. Many of the older ones understood why I served in Lok Sabha. They know there are different ways to fight the same battle. If Mohandas Gandhi had not been assassinated, the Nagas would have been independent a long time ago, but this never happened."

"Then you are in sympathy with the independence movement?"

"I am, in principle. Unfortunately, these matters are never that simple. Now, there are power struggles within the movement, and some of the younger leaders consider myself and anyone else who served in the government to be suspect."

"Why is it that there is little if any news of this situation in the western press?" Donovan asked.

"That is because the Indian government classifies the Naga Hills as a 'disturbed area,' accessible only with government permission. The suffering here is known only by those who suffer and those who cause the suffering."

"We should talk of other things," Meniu said. "Professor Donovan will have difficulty sleeping, as it is."

7

Donovan awoke after an uneasy sleep to the steady beat of the rain against his window. For the first time since coming to India, he had slept alone. He washed and shaved in the sink inside his room using some scented soap he had taken from the Taj Hotel in Delhi. Without his morning shower, he still felt grimy from the previous day's travel. To bolster his spirits, he put on a clean blue sports shirt, gray poplin slacks, and splashed Brut after-shave lotion on his face.

He joined Meniu and her father downstairs in the restaurant for a buffet-style mixture of Indian and western breakfast foods. Most of the other customers were not Nagas. "The people you are looking at are part of the thousands of government bureaucrats who occupy our land," Chingmei offered.

Meniu was unusually quiet during the meal while Chingmei seemed impatient to eat so that he could bring Donovan to meet the curator of the Kohima museum as he had promised.

"My father is anxious to go home," Meniu said finally. "He has this idea that the tea leaves do not grow as well if he is not there."

"It is true that they do not," Chingmei replied, "it is also true that they will thrive even more now that you are home to stay."

Outside, the streets of Kohima stirred as a small convoy of olive-green military trucks left in formation for a destination in the hills. The rain had ended. Naga farmers splashed through puddles of water as they set up stalls for the morning market. Meniu stopped at a line of food stalls. "You won't find these delicacies at the Stop and Shop in Rhode Island," she laughed. "We have a saying – Nagas eat anything that crawls."

She walked the length of the stalls pointing to the chunks of meat which hung from hooks or were displayed on tables. "You can have bear, wild boar, monkeys, squirrels, or an especially tasty dish, bamboo rat. Or perhaps the professor prefers porcupine today. If none of these suits your taste, you might try caterpillars, or turtles, smoked frogs, or dried eels."

Donovan's laughter encouraged Meniu even more as Chingmei looked on quietly. Meniu came to the end of the stalls where a wooden cage held four small dogs. The dogs wore black muzzles to prevent them from barking. "Here," Meniu said, "we have what Americans call 'Man's best friend.' In Nagaland, we call dogs 'Man's best meal.'" Donovan blanched and looked to Chingmei for confirmation. Chingmei nodded agreement.

Meniu was just getting started. "Don't you remember the recipe in the book I gave you as a present?"

"The Naked Nagas? Of course I remember the book. It was wonderful, but I can't say I remember any recipe."

"How could you forget it?"

"Perhaps I deliberately blocked it out." Over the years he and Paula had three Golden Labradors. Each was like a substitute child to them, and he thought of his present Lab, Prince III, as Meniu continued her extended joke.

"It doesn't matter because I remember it. Would you like to hear it?"

"Not really."

"Fine, then I will tell you. First you give a young dog castor oil. When that does its work, give him as much rice as he will eat. Then you kill him, tie him up, and boil him along with the rice. That is how you prepare stuffed dog."

"Enough," Donovan pleaded, "I get it. I get it."

"Actually, only the Angamis eat...." Meniu was interrupted by her father.

"We must go meet Dr. Ahon now," he said. "He will be waiting for us at the monument in the center of the town."

Dr. Ahon was the Naga version of the stereotypical academic – thin, wiry, and soft-spoken. He wore thick wire-rimmed glasses and dressed casually in khaki pants and a loose, cream-colored shirt unbuttoned at the neck. Donovan had no trouble imagining the curator on an American campus.

Ahon greeted the group cordially and then addressed Donovan. "All visits to Nagaland should begin at this monument which stands as a reminder of the courage and bravery of the Angami Nagas in the great war against the Japanese."

Donovan had the impression Ahon had given this same speech before.

"Most Americans today have never heard of Nagaland," Ahon continued, "but just fifty years ago we fought side-by-side with the Americans and the British. Time has a way of clouding people's memories."

The monument stood at the entrance of a military cemetery which was considerably plainer than those Donovan had visited in France. Nonetheless, the rows of crude white crosses gave a solemn tone to the moment. Donovan stepped closer to the weathered memorial cross to read the inscription. The words moved him:

"Here around the tennis court of the Deputy Commissioner lie men who fought in the Battle of Kohima in which they and their comrades finally halted the invasion of India by the forces of Japan in April 1944."

Donovan walked down the first row of crosses trying to make out the names of Americans. He had been eight years old in 1944, born at a time when some of his earliest impressions had been those of wartime; air-raid wardens on bicycles, shades drawn in the night, newspaper collection drives, and food and gasoline ration stamps. Only the accident of birth prevented him from being one of those decayed bodies in a grave so far from home. Somewhere he had the sense that he had heard of the Battle of Kohima before, most likely in a newsreel which preceded a double-feature movie in a theater on a Saturday afternoon many years ago.

The group lingered silently at the monument until Chingmei urged them to leave. "We must go now. Our drivers are waiting, and Professor Donovan still has to see our museum."

Dr. Ahon hurried the group through the museum promising Donovan that, when he returned, there would be more time to study the artifacts and books in the museum. Donovan did pause to examine the life-size stone sculptures which stood outside the museum entrance. The figures depicted men and women from different tribes farming, fishing, hunting, and performing ceremonial war dances.

At exactly 9:30 am Chingmei led the curator and Donovan to the two jeeps. Chingmei held open the back door of the second vehicle. "Enjoy our beautiful land and learn all you can from each other while you have the chance," he said.

As Donovan followed the curator into the back seat, he heard Meniu speak to her father with concern in her voice. "Where are the guards?" she asked.

"Really, Meniu," Chingmei replied, "you are more of a worrier now that you have your university degree. Relax and enjoy the trip."

For the next hour and a half, the two jeeps drove north into the Naga hills on their way to Wokha. Dr. Ahon talked animatedly the entire trip.

"The most important thing you need to know about the Naga people is that they have struggled for their freedom against the Indian government ever since India gained its independence from Britain in 1947. The world knows of all the great revolutionary movements – from the French Revolution, to your own, and continuing up to Mandela's South Africa. But the world does not know about our fight in Nagaland. And nobody cares except us."

As Ahon talked his dark eyes liquefied with intensity. Donovan reconsidered his first impression of the curator. This is no academic, he thought, this is a zealot.

"Americans in particular need to know what is going on in Nagaland," Ahon continued. "Your people have a natural empathy for just revolutions, and the US government does not always see eye to eye with the Indian government."

Donovan nodded agreement, noting to himself that it was highly unlikely that the US would get involved in an internal Indian dispute that did not affect its own national interest.

As Ahon began to present a chronological history of the separatist movement, Donovan turned his attention to the heavily forested highlands into which they continued to climb. The farther they went, the rougher the roadbeds became. More work crews and their equipment appeared on the sides of the roads. It was a scene he had seen countless times before on American highways.

"Do all these men work for Chingmei?" he asked.

"In a manner of speaking. They work for the Ministry of Public Roads and Highways," Ahon replied, not put off by the interruption of his monologue.

Up ahead, the jeep carrying Meniu and Chingmei disappeared around a bend in the road just as a member of a road crew stepped into the path of the second jeep signaling with a red flag for them to stop. One man dressed in the green uniform of the road crews approached the jeep and began talking to the driver. The driver turned and said something directly to Dr. Ahon.

"He says there will be a short delay. We may as well get out and stretch." Nothing in Ahon's voice indicated that he considered the delay anything but a minor inconvenience.

Donovan stepped down from the door of the jeep welcoming the chance to loosen the stiffness in his back and legs. The tropical, humid air contrasted sharply with the air-conditioning of the jeep. It felt like rain was about to start again. He noticed two workmen walking towards him. He stood on his toes, and placed his hands above his head to begin a vertical stretch. Just as he reached the high point of his stretch, two pairs of strong, rough hands encircled him from behind and threw him to the ground. He started to shout out to Dr. Ahon, but the sound was stifled by a towel jammed into his face. The towel had an antiseptic smell to it, a smell that triggered some neural memory from a long-ago experience in a hospital.

The last thing Donovan saw were the faces of the men who pinned his arms and legs to the ground. Their expressions were fierce, reminding him of the faces on the carvings at the museum in Kohima.

PART TWO

8

When Philip Lynch first learned that Robert Donovan had disappeared into the Naga hills in northeast India, the victim of an apparent political kidnapping, he knew at once that his life would never be the same again. The phone call came from Paula Donovan, the woman Lynch had loved since they first dated almost forty years ago in high school.

When Philip answered the phone, all Paula could say was "Philip, it's me," before she broke down into an anguished cry that revealed the depth of the pain she was feeling.

Caught off guard, he didn't know what to say. Finally, he pleaded with her, "Paula, tell me what is wrong. Whatever it is, I will help you. Don't worry. I will help you." He repeated the statement over and over until Paula was able to speak.

"I have some terrible news," she said, "James Ferguson, a man from the State Department, called late this morning. Robert has been kidnapped in India. He said there is no certainty at this time, but the speculation is that the kidnappers are a guerrilla group who think of themselves as freedom fighters."

"My God, what would a guerrilla group possibly want with Robert? He is an academic, not a politician; does it have anything to do with the Gandhi assassination?"

"No, they don't seem to think so. Their theory, and Ferguson stressed that it is just a theory, is that the kidnappers want to draw international attention to their independence movement."

"Wasn't he traveling with one of his students? Was she kidnapped also?"

"No, she wasn't. Ferguson told me the report came from the student's father who is a politician of some kind in Nagaland. It was all corroborated by local military police. Robert was in a separate car that was somehow stopped and attacked by the kidnappers while the father and daughter drove ahead. By the time they realized that something was wrong and went back, Robert was gone into the jungle. The curator of a museum with whom he was driving and the driver were found tied up on the side of the road. They were unharmed. The vehicle they were driving in was stolen."

"Why would they only kidnap Robert?"

"Because he is American. Ferguson explained that other nationalist groups in India have kidnapped foreigners knowing the media will cover the story. They want a platform to use to deliver their message. Ferguson didn't want to create false hope, but he said that the pattern of these groups is to release the hostages after they have accomplished their purpose."

"Let's pray that this is the case," Philip replied, still stunned by the possible meaning of the conversation and the ambivalent emotions he was beginning to feel. "When did it happen?"

"It happened yesterday morning. India is nine and a half hours ahead of us."

"What did the man from the State Department suggest you do? Does he think you should go to India?"

"No, he was quite emphatic that it would serve no purpose for me to go there at this time. He said the first priority was to establish communication with the people who have Robert. Meniu's father is trying to help with that."

"Meniu is the student Robert was traveling with?"

Paula paused before replying. "I think she was more to Robert than one of his students ... but I don't want to talk about that now."

There was an awkward silence before Philip replied. "You won't be going there?"

"Not right away, not until Mr. Ferguson tells me that my going would help Robert in some way. Robert had to obtain a special permit to enter Nagaland and, not only would I have great difficulty getting one – the Indian government hates any bad publicity that might hurt tourism – but I wouldn't be able to do anything when I get there. Nagaland is quite a primitive place. The natives used to be headhunters."

"I remember Robert talking about that in Ireland last summer. That was the reason he went, wasn't it, to do field research?"

"It was one reason," Paula answered, "there may have been another."

"Have you called Robert's brother? Isn't he in Chicago?"

"Yes, there isn't much more we can do, but wait until some communication takes place. Ferguson assures me that every possible effort is being made, but Nagaland is not an easy place to get things done. Meniu's father is our best hope."

"How are you holding up?"

"I am as good as can be expected," Paula replied, her voice starting to quaver. "The people from the university have been great warding off the media and keeping me informed of whatever develops. The story was on the national news an hour ago. Robert got fifteen seconds of fame instead of fifteen minutes."

"He would laugh at that."

"Philip, what will I do if he is dead, if Ferguson is wrong and these savages have killed him?" Paula sobbed. "I know it sounds like a stupid cliché, but I feel so helpless."

"Put that thought out of your mind, Paula. You know how resilient Robert can be. Tell me what I can do to help you. Do you want me to come to Rhode Island?" As he asked the question, Philip tried unsuccessfully to control the tone of his voice, knowing that it gave away just how desperately he welcomed a reason to go to her ... any reason.

There was a momentary lull in the conversation, "Yes, would you come stay with me for a few days, Philip? Perhaps you can help me understand all of this better. Can you get away from the university?"

"That's not a problem. My primary duties this summer are trying to keep two doctoral candidates from going insane while they finish their dissertations."

"I hope you are empathetic," Paula said, "I remember how you and Robert both struggled yourselves."

"That seems like a long time ago. It's seven thirty now. I can come tonight if you want."

"No, you don't have to do that. Tomorrow will be fine. You need time to pack and tend to business. Why not plan on leaving early afternoon so that you miss the rush hour traffic at New Haven."

"That will get me there around five o'clock. I'll bring some wine, you can probably use it."

"Thank you, Philip. I can't tell you how badly I need to talk to a friend."

"I'll be there, Paula. Try to get a good night's sleep. Goodbye."

Philip sat motionless on the side of his bed trying to process the significance of what he had just learned. It was too much to do. There were too many possibilities, too many ramifications, too many future scenarios to contemplate. The only thing that was certain was that he had to get ready to drive to Rhode Island to be with Paula Donovan.

He stood up and looked at himself in the mirror above his chest of drawers. It had been a year since he had last seen Paula in Ireland. Had he changed so much since then? A few pounds extra around the waist perhaps, his full grayish-brown hair was in need of a haircut, otherwise he was pretty much the same, a five foot ten inch, one hundred eighty pound widower, whose angular face, deep-set green eyes, and classic nose had enabled him to deal with the world confidently for most of his fifty-four years.

But neither his looks, his intelligence, nor his confident personality had been enough to keep Paula by his side when they had dated years ago in high school. That was all in the past and, though he had never fully gotten over the hurt of losing her, he had managed the hurt and gone on with his life, a life in which he resigned himself to the reality that Paula had chosen Robert Donovan over him.

Then there had been the events that took place last summer in Ireland and the phone calls from Paula during the past months. And now – Robert in captivity in the jungle of northeast India – Philip had no idea where it would all lead, but he was already uncomfortable with the thoughts and feelings that forced themselves into his mind no matter how much he resisted them.

9

Philip lived in a four-bedroom red brick colonial house on Beach Avenue in the village of Larchmont, twenty miles north of New York City in Westchester County. His parents, second-generation Irish immigrants, had built the house in 1939 after his father was promoted to vice-president of a medium-sized New York bank. An only child, he inherited the house when his father died in 1968, followed a year later by his mother. His wife, Catherine, had thought it a perfect size home while their two daughters, Judy and Beth were growing up, but now that Catherine was gone and the girls shared an apartment together in the city, the house was much too big for him. He had considered selling it after Catherine's death from breast cancer in 1989, but the thought of moving to a smaller condominium was unacceptable. And so he had stayed, clinging to the most tangible piece of his roots, however impractical that might be.

He spent the morning after Paula's phone call preparing for his trip to Rhode Island. Paula had asked him "to stay for a few days," and so he packed enough casual clothes for a week along with a blue blazer, a short-sleeved white button-down shirt and two striped ties. As he usually did when he traveled, he called his neighbors, the Benedicts, asking them to bring in his mail and newspapers while he was away. He ate a light lunch and left Larchmont early afternoon. On the way to the thruway entrance in Mamaroneck, he stopped at a liquor store and carefully selected six bottles of California Chardonnays and Pinot noirs. Preparations completed, he headed north on Route 95 towards the ocean and Narragansett, Rhode Island.

Philip had spent most of the previous night unable to sleep, bothered by the conflicting emotions he felt immediately after his conversation with Paula. One part of him was deeply concerned for Robert, and what may have happened to him. He wished him no harm and only wanted him to be safe. At the same time, he was excited, almost physically aroused at the idea of spending so much time alone with Paula. He thought of the theory that people are essentially selfish beings motivated by self-interest in everything they do. He had always found that concept to be distasteful, somehow degrading to the human spirit, but, at the moment, it had taken on greater credibility.

Driving through Stamford on the Connecticut Turnpike, Philip remembered a story Robert had told him of a one-night encounter he had had in that city many years ago, shortly before he married Paula. He had met an attractive young woman auditor, who was in Stamford for a few days on business. They had drinks, dinner, and ended up in bed in her hotel room. It wasn't Robert's style to provide the physical details of the numerous affairs he had had over the years. If he let you know he had been with someone, he relied on your imagination to fill in the images of your choice.

Robert and his new friend were making small talk after lovemaking when suddenly the young woman said she wanted to tell him something about her past.

"Sure, go ahead," Robert replied, "I'd like to learn more about you."

"Well you may think this is a bit odd," the woman began, "but I was once a rickshaw driver in Calcutta in a previous life."

That was the story. It always got a big laugh whenever he told it. In many ways the story was typical of the way Robert was. There was always something at the end that left you feeling good, something light-hearted, just a little bit crazy. Women loved that quality in Robert while other young men, less successful in the pursuit of the opposite sex, envied it. Whatever the elements of personality that made up Robert Donovan's appeal, they were enough for Paula to break off a two-year dating relationship with Philip in senior year of high school. Philip had revisited the pain of that experience often over the years. Concerned about being hurt that way again, he had changed, become more cautious, more self-protective in his relationships with other young women.

Years later, he could remember clearly the exact moment he began to lose Paula to Robert. He was playing an after-school tennis match against the number one single's player from Archbishop Stepinac, Iona's major catholic high school rival. Paula had come to watch him play along with some girl friends. Acutely aware of her presence, Philip put on a show exaggerating his athleticism by tossing the tennis ball higher than usual on his serve, then arching his back to pound balls past his opponent. He won the first set easily 6-2.

He was changing sides of the court when he noticed Paula and her friends leaving to walk to the baseball field on the other side of the sports complex where Robert was the starting pitcher for the varsity. Distracted by her departure, Philip began overhitting his strokes and lost the next two sets and the match to his less talented opponent.

Later, Paula explained to him that one of her friends had a

crush on Robert and had talked the group into going to the baseball game. Somehow Philip knew this wasn't the whole truth. Though they continued to date, their relationship cooled perceptibly that summer until, just before senior year began, Paula told him it was over. She hoped they would still be friends. Though he ached inside, Philip accepted the rejection with a maturity unusual for a teenager. Shortly after, Paula invited Robert to a school dance and, with the exception of a few short-lived separations during their college years, they had been together ever since.

To his credit, Philip never blamed Robert for his breakup with Paula. The two boys had been buddies since they first met in the sixth grade at Iona Grammar School where Robert was already established as a promising student and athlete. Philip's earlier education had been entrusted to the Dominican nuns at St. Augustine's Academy in Larchmont until his parents decided the firmer hand of the brothers was needed to help shape his character. There had been a series of disciplinary incidents, the last of which occurred when an elderly nun objected vigorously to Philip's pounding his new baseball glove during a class on the truths contained in the Baltimore Catechism.

Philip's parents persuaded the brothers to accept their high-spirited son during the middle of the school year. Philip arrived uncertain of his new surroundings and intimidated by the reputation of the brothers as strict disciplinarians who did not hesitate to inflict physical punishment on misbehaving students. Robert befriended him right away, easing his transition into the new group. Years later, Philip still appreciated that gesture of friendship from one eleven-year old boy to another.

From that beginning, the two boys studied together, played sports together and, in the seventh grade, attended Mrs. Chalef's ballroom dancing class together. It was here in the parish hall on Friday nights that they experienced their first sexual stirrings. For each of them, the moment was different and singular; it might have been the strange feel of a brassiere strap on the back of an awkward partner or, better still, the softness of a twelve year old girl's budding breasts as she moved self-consciously into their arms for the first time. Paula Ryan was in that class, a spindly, shy brunette whose pretty face was marred by a mouthful of silver braces and pockets of adolescent acne. Robert and Philip barely noticed her as they pursued other girls whose faces were prettier or whose prepubescent figures were more shapely.

Three years later, it was as if Paula Ryan had been transformed by some sudden physiological miracle. The braces were gone, the shyness replaced by a graceful assuredness that comes when young women realize for the first time that others consider them beautiful. Paula attended Ursuline Academy, a private catholic girl's school in New Rochelle. She wore the chaste blue and white uniform the nuns required in their efforts to conceal the developing figures of the young women in their charge. Paula was bright, talented, and personable. She quickly became one of the most popular girls in her class.

At the same time, Philip and Robert struggled through adolescence under the vigilant eyes of the black-robed brothers for whom corporal punishment was a way of life. Philip remembered the brothers as a mixture of saintly scholars, dedicated plodders, and a few social misfits who used the religious order as a sanctuary from a world in which they were not able to cope. Philip remembered these odd men as the ones who seemed to enjoy beating wayward students with thick rubber straps, rulers, or blackboard pointers. Parents often sent their sons to the all-male prep school because of the strict discipline, and complaints about excessive punishment were rare.

As a group, the Irish Christian brothers from Iona were good men, generally free from the scandals that plagued the Catholic Church in recent years which, along with the church's attitudes on birth control, had driven so many of Philip's generation away from active participation in their church. Whatever their shortcomings, there was no question that the brothers accomplished their mission as almost all of the young graduates went on to colleges and universities, and, not surprisingly, most were catholic institutions.

Robert and Philip graduated from Iona Prep in 1954, on the same weekend Paula gave the valedictorian's address at the Ursuline Academy graduation. The Korean War had ended the summer before and though both boys had to register for the draft under the Selective Service System, they were free to continue their education on a college deferment. Fate had treated them kindly. Too young for World War II and Korea, they were married and had completed their military obligation by the time the Vietnam War heated up. As Philip grew older, he often reflected on how fortunate he had been, not having had to fight in combat. Yet there was another part of him that wondered how he would have borne up, how he would have survived the horror of war or whether he would have survived at all.

Philip passed through Bridgeport, a smokestack city that never failed to depress him. He couldn't remember anything between Stamford and Bridgeport, so deep had he been in his memories. That always frightened him, that he would be driving at sixty-five or seventy miles an hour on automatic pilot, not consciously aware of what he was doing. He brightened as he left the city limits, knowing it was a short half hour's drive to New Haven where he would turn east up along the coast towards Paula.

Robert was accepted at Boston College. Shortly after arriving on campus, he enrolled in the Marine Corps Platoon Leaders Class, a move motivated by his admiration for his older brother, Jack, who had left high school and enlisted in the Marines in 1942. Jack had fought against the Japanese on the Marshall Islands in the South Pacific where he had been wounded by machine gun fire. After spending a grueling six weeks of training at Quantico, Virginia in the summer of freshman year, Robert's aspirations to be a Marine pilot ended when he had to undergo a series of three operations in sophomore year, operations which initially were to correct hernias but evolved into more complicated procedures. This doctor described the surgeries as "general plumbing repair," but they were serious enough to change the direction of his life. His doctors also prohibited strenuous exercise for an indefinite period of time which forced Robert to drop from the varsity baseball team where he had enjoyed a promising beginning as a first-year pitcher. When his healing was slower than expected, he resigned from the Platoon Leaders Class since he was unable to meet the physical requirements of a second six-week summer session at Quantico.

What Philip remembered was how well Robert handled these setbacks. Instead of bemoaning his bad luck, Robert switched his energy and focus to academics. He chose to major in sociology at the beginning of his junior year and became involved in student government. Robert graduated magna cum laude and his only remaining obligation to the Marine Corps was six years of reserve service. This allowed him to continue his courtship of Paula while he studied for his Ph.D. in sociology from Fordham University in the Bronx. The two were married in June of 1963, a wedding which Philip did not attend. He gave the reason that he had to be at a summer study-abroad program in Bath, England as part of his Ph.D. program in British literature. The truth was that the program started the week after the wedding, but Philip used it as an excuse not to go. Instead, he sent a Waring blender as a gift and managed to avoid seeing the newlyweds for some time after.

Paula Ryan surprised the nuns at Ursuline by choosing to study psychology at Sarah Lawrence College in Bronxville. The small liberal arts college had a reputation for the leftist social and economic leanings of its faculty. The women of Sarah Lawrence were encouraged to learn through independent study and, in so doing, many were predispositioned to be supporters and activists of the social upheavals already stirring in the second half of the 1950's. Paula loved being involved in the stimulating atmosphere at Sarah Lawrence. She also enjoyed taking the train to Boston to visit Robert for football weekends or formal dances.

After graduation in 1958, Paula was hired by the New Rochelle school system to be a guidance counselor in its middle schools. She and Robert decided to postpone marriage until he finished his studies at Fordham. After two years of working in the school system, Paula returned to Sarah Lawrence in 1961 to work towards a masters degree, which she completed in a year and a half. It was during this period that something happened to cause Robert and Paula to stop dating. All Philip ever heard was the rumor that Paula became involved in the civil rights movement on campus and began dating a black graduate student who was active in the movement. Whatever the truth of the matter, the split lasted only three months. Robert and Paula got together again and decided to move up their wedding date a year earlier than originally planned. With her new degree, Paula went to work as a child psychologist in the Mount Vernon school system. She supported Robert for the next year while he labored to finish his dissertation as an underpaid graduate teaching assistant.

Philip decided to attend Holy Cross, his father's alma mater. He never seriously considered another college – so thoroughly had he been indoctrinated over the years by his father's bias concerning the superiority of a Jesuit education. He majored in English and played four years of varsity tennis, finishing his senior year as the number two singles player. During the summers, he earned expense money by giving lessons at Bonnie Briar Country Club. He decided not to join ROTC but, after graduation, opted for a two-year stint in the army infantry as an enlisted man. He had hoped to get away and see some of the world after basic training, but his military service took an unusual turn.

Trained as an infantry "grunt," his initial assignment was to nearby Fort Devens, Massachusetts. Here he spent more time hitting tennis balls than firing rifles. The commanding general of Fort Devens had a passion for tennis and, when he learned that Philip had not only played varsity tennis in college but also worked as a teaching professional, he immediately had him reassigned to base headquarters staff. His main duties were to teach tennis to the general, his wife, and their two boys, aged twelve and fourteen. He also had to be on call to play singles or doubles with the general and members of his staff. When not on the court, Philip learned how to type in the general's office, a skill which later proved invaluable in graduate school.

When his unconventional army career ended, he applied and was accepted into the English graduate program at the University of Minnesota in January 1961. His father and mother thought it a strange choice, but it made sense to Philip. The program had a good reputation, but it was also in the Midwest, a good distance away from the east coast where he had spent the bulk of his life up till then, and where Paula and Robert were happily planning their marriage.

Soon after arriving on campus, he met Catherine Gallagher, a fellow literature student from Xenia, Ohio. Catherine was decidedly Midwest conservative, and often kidded Philip about his New York ways. There was something steady and reliable about Catherine, something that told Philip he could be sure of her. At five foot nine, she was almost as tall as Philip, a trait which their daughters had inherited. Catherine had long dark hair and soft brown eyes that highlighted a face that was wholesome and honest, if not beautiful.

They dated until the spring of 1963, when Catherine finished her master's degree and decided to return home to Xenia to teach highschool. It was the same sad spring that Philip received the invitation to Paula and Robert's wedding. Disconsolate, he went off to England for a month and a half. When not in class or on field trips, he spent most of his time getting drunk on warm beer and feeling sorry for himself in a friendly pub in Bath called the "Crown N' Feathers."

The day before the wedding, armed with a pocket full of British coins and entirely intoxicated, he tried to place a long distance call to Paula. He didn't plan to say anything; he just wanted to hear her voice one more time. Fortunately the combination of the operator's cockney accent and the strange coins was too much for him to manage. He lost his coins without ever getting through. In total frustration, he returned to the pub where he passed out a short time later.

When he returned home later that summer, he flew to Ohio to propose marriage to Catherine on her front porch. Catherine, knowing nothing of his feelings for Paula, quickly accepted. They were married a year later in Xenia. Robert and Paula were not able to attend. Catherine resigned her teaching position to move back to Minneapolis to be with Philip as he finished his studies.

Philip passed through New Haven just before 3 o'clock, early enough to avoid the later afternoon traffic congestion. He had been driving fast and was ahead of schedule. He didn't want to get to Paula's too early. He would need a glass of wine to calm the nervous tension he had been feeling since the previous night. He tried concentrating on the driving, but it was of little help. His mind kept wanting to remember, drifting back to the events of years ago that had led up to this day, this moment.

After graduate school, the two couples drifted apart. Robert was hired as an instructor at the University of Rhode Island, and he and Paula moved to Narragansett. Philip stayed closer to home partly because both his parents' health was declining and because there were few jobs to be had for young unpublished English Ph.D.s. After teaching for two years as an adjunct faculty member, he was hired by Iona College in New Rochelle, teaching on the same campus where he had once attended grammar and highschool. For the next two decades, Philip's contact with Robert and Paula was limited to meetings at weddings and funerals of friends, the occasional holiday visit, and the exchange of telephone calls and cards.

All that changed with Catherine's death two years ago. It was at the funeral that the idea to travel to Ireland first came up, an effort by two old friends to help cheer Philip after the loss of his wife. But much more had happened in Ireland. Images of Paula in the bedroom of the small hotel in Kilkee appeared again to Philip as they had so often during the past year. When this happened, he was helpless. He could only give himself up to the memory and the pleasure it gave him.

The 4 o'clock traffic slowed Philip's progress in New London. He welcomed the change of pace. His reflections during the drive had unsettled him. Events were moving too quickly. He decided to stop at the scenic lookout in Mystic. It would give him a chance to gather himself, to settle his thoughts. And yes, he would take from his briefcase the letter Paula had written him a few weeks after they returned from Ireland and read it again, just as he had done countless times during the past year.

10

August 4, 1990.
Dear Philip,

    I once had a professor who taught that an effective first step in counseling was to have clients write down what was troubling them. She believed the act of writing helped identify the cause of a problem. I used the technique for years with my students, and it seemed to help. Think of this letter, then, as an exercise in self-therapy, an attempt on my part to bring clarity to the mix of emotions I have felt since we returned from Ireland.

    I have long thought of myself as a logical person. Whatever remains of that capacity to reason tells me I need to begin this self-examination by asking two basic questions. Why did we make love when Robert went to Cork, and what is the future of my marriage to Robert?

    As we discussed over breakfast in Kilkee (one of the nicest mornings of my life that I think about way too often), Robert and I have had problems for many years. I have known for some time he has had other lovers. This has permanently damaged our relationship. He and I have not dealt with this problem directly which is as much my fault as his. As I told you, it occurred to me to have an affair, to do the same to get even, but that never quite worked out.

It is important that I tell you these things because one possible answer to why I made love to you is that consciously or subconsciously, I was striking back at Robert. I hope this is not the total answer, but I know enough about why we humans do the things we do to conclude that this rather ignoble motive was at work somewhere.

My other answer as to why we made love is more positive. Philip, I made love to you because I could feel the affection you have for me, and I wanted to return it. Was I so grateful for your love because Robert has withheld his love from me? I believe you were sincere when you said the things you said to me. At first I thought it was the wine talking. Then I realized not only that you meant what you said, but that you had felt that way for years. I was astonished.

Is it so awful to want to be loved? Perhaps as a fifty-three year-old woman, I am more vulnerable in this regard than I once was, but at least I recognize my need. Robert hasn't said the things you said to me in years, and I wasn't aware how much I needed those words, your words. You have no idea how wonderful you made me feel. I know I am not as beautiful as you said (over and over), but I remember the saying about "beauty being in the eyes of the beholder" and, for one night and morning, you were my beholder.

Rereading the last paragraph makes me appear so selfish, someone taking affection and sex because she is so needy. If it were as simple as that, there would be no need for this letter which is already much longer than I intended. But it is not so simple, not simple at all.

What struck me most was how unselfish a lover you are. Do you understand when a woman is loved that way, so fully, both physically and emotionally, that she wants to reciprocate that love, *give it back in all its fullness. That is what I did, and that is what shocked and surprised me then. Please don't interpret "shocked and surprised" as meaning I am sorry for or regret what we did. My memory is that I was the one who initiated the lovemaking.*

No, there was no regret then and that is not what I am feeling now. What I am trying to sort out is the confusion I am experiencing about my feelings for you and Robert.

I know now how much it hurt you when I began dating Robert in highschool. It says a lot about the kind of person you are that you have continued to be a friend to both of us in spite of what happened.

Now, we are supposed to be adults, and I do not want to hurt you again. Equally important, I don't want to lose you again. Which brings me to the question of Robert and myself and the future.

Despite all that Robert has done, you know that he has many qualities that are good and loveable. I think I am right that you still count him as a friend. He and I have had many wonderful years together, and I can't just give up on him. I am going to try to make my marriage work one more time, do my best, and see what the future holds.

I don't think we should make plans to see each other at this time. It would be impossible for both of us. It is important to me that I separate my effort to save my marriage from my feelings for you.

I do promise to call you, to see how you are. I will probably need a glass of wine to give me courage, but I will call. I owe you that much. Do you think my writing this letter has clarified anything? Probably not. Psychology never had all the answers anyway. Sometimes I think art offers the most help. Music comes to mind. Do you remember these lyrics:

"Isn't it rich, Isn't it queer
Losing my timing this late in my career...?"

Stephen Sondheim, I think. There I go ending on a depressed note. I have found myself crying more lately, usually when I listen to music.

Know that I care about you very much and, Philip, please be patient with me.

With affection,
Paula

Philip folded Paula's letter and put it back in his briefcase. He got out of the car and walked to a bench that looked out over the old whaling port of Mystic that was now a thriving tourist destination. A light breeze off the water had begun to cool the earlier heat of the day.

One of the last things Paula had written in her letter was the request that he "please be patient." Well, he had certainly been patient though it had not been easy. In many ways, it had been the most difficult year of his life, a year in which he immersed himself in his work, spent much more time than usual entertaining his two daughters and their friends, and played so much tennis that the matches ran together in his mind until he wasn't sure if his game was getting better or worse.

In between all this activity, he thought of Paula, waited for her sporadic phone calls, and tried to recapture the sensual images of the time they spent together in Kilkee.

11

The mid-summer trip to Ireland had been Paula and Robert's idea and, even though Philip did not care enough for the woman he was seeing to invite her along, he welcomed the invitation. Robert's proposal to deliver a paper at an international sociological conference at Cambridge University had been accepted and, in order to facilitate a visit to the fabled birthplace of their grandparents, he had arranged to be a visiting lecturer for a day in the class of an academic colleague at the University of Cork.

The three of them talked about going to Ireland at Catherine's wake. Philip had been moved by the fact that Paula and Robert had taken the time to drive down to Larchmont from Rhode Island for the wake and the funeral. After the service, back at the house, he became emotional as he told the couple how much he appreciated their coming. Robert put a comforting arm around Philip's shoulder and suggested that "it would do Philip good to get away and what kind of Irishman would he be if he never got to set foot on the old sod."

Time passed and Philip's life gradually returned to normal. When Paula called to suggest the trip, it didn't bother him knowing that the invitation had in part been out of concern for his loneliness. Irish wakes had a way of bringing people back together again, even those who had been apart for a while.

They flew Aer Lingus out of Logan Airport on a hot Sunday evening in July. The overnight flight would put them in Heathrow Airport the next morning where they would catch a train to Cambridge. Philip could close his eyes and still see Paula standing in the long customs line inside the crowded international terminal. She wore a yellow blouse over tan slacks, both of which were just snug enough to accentuate the shapely curves of her figure, a point which did not go unnoticed by two male college students who winked their approval to each other when Paula bent over to tie tags on her luggage. She was well-tanned from time spent on Narragansett Beach and, when she turned to smile back at him, her green eyes shining with excitement, streaks of gray setting off her black hair, she was as beautiful to Philip as she had ever been.

Whatever awkwardness they felt was quickly dispelled as the red haired stewardess brought them drinks. They sat three across in the economy section of the Boeing 747, Paula squeezed between the two men with the taller Robert taking the aisle seat.

"Don't forget," Robert said, "the booze is free on international flights. Everyone must drink; it would be foolish to abstain, fiscally irresponsible."

They started with three bottles of Guinness ale but switched to small bottles of Chardonnay for the second round.

"I am so excited," Paula said, "I can't believe I am actually going to see the place where my mother lived when she was a little girl. She spoke about Ireland so often; I hope I won't be disappointed."

"Your family had the closest ties to Ireland of any of us," Philip said, "but I don't remember why."

"Robert has heard this all before," Paula said. "His family was very different. They were not interested in their Irish roots."

"That's because they wanted to get ahead in the world and flaunting your Irish heritage didn't help in that regard," Robert replied. He opened his briefcase and took out a set of notes on the talk he was to deliver in Cambridge and Cork. Paula turned to Philip.

"All I need is an audience of one," she said. As she smiled, Philip noticed the rosy glow the wine had brought to her cheeks. "My mother's parents emigrated to New York at the turn of the century. She and her sister, my Aunt Mary, were born in New York. My grandfather worked on the docks of the New York waterfront as a stevedore. He was killed in an accident when cargo from a freighter he was unloading broke loose and crushed him to death. He was twenty-eight when he died, and my mother was five years old."

"How awful," Philip said. Robert looked up from his work. "Your mother once said that there was the possibility that it wasn't an accident, that your grandfather may have been murdered."

"If he was, it was never proven. The waterfront was a tough place to work then."

"It still is."

"What happened to your grandmother? How did she get by?" Philip asked.

"She wasn't able to earn enough to take care of her two daughters so she took them back to her birthplace in County Clare. She left them with her family and returned to New York to find work."

Philip thought of his own two daughters and how they had been inseparable from their mother when they were children.

"How long did they stay in Ireland?

"My mother was always vague about that, but I think it was for five years. My grandmother went back and got them when she could afford it."

Robert stood up. "I think I'll stretch my legs in the galley for a bit, keep the circulation going." He started towards the rear of the plane.

"Stay away from the stewardess. She's not Maureen O'Hara," Paula called to him without smiling.

"I'm only interested in her brogue."

"I bet," Paula said.

Surprised at the tone of the exchange, Philip tried to return the conversation to things Irish.

"Your grandmother must have been quite a woman."

"She was very independent," Paula replied. "Tough might be a better word. She was also very beautiful."

"I'd say you have inherited her genes," Philip said.

Paula paused for a moment, surprised by his comment. "Thank you, Philip, that's a nice thing for you to say ... actually, I wish I had inherited more of her toughness, her independence."

They both were quiet until Paula turned to Philip as if to give him her complete attention. "Enough of my ancestry – tell me how you have been; how you're getting along. It must have been terrible for you after Catherine died."

"Things are alright now, though I miss her, her calmness, her steadiness." Paula gently squeezed his arm. "However," he continued, "at the moment I feel like Robert Cohn in 'The Sun Also Rises.' Do you remember: he was the third wheel?"

"That would make me Lady Brett Ashley, an unlikely comparison."

"Will you settle for Ava Gardner? She played Lady Brett in

the movie. Come to think of it, you always reminded me of her," Philip said with a smile.

"Aren't you sweet."

"Just truthful." Philip tried to change the tone of their conversation. "Did you see the movie? Except for the scenes of the bullfights and the running of the bulls, it was dreadful. The men who run in front of those bulls have to be crazy."

"Sometimes I think all men are. When was the last time you read the book?" Paula asked.

"It's been a while."

"If you recall, Lady Brett ended up with Robert Cohn, at least for a time." The tone of Paula's voice was playful.

Robert returned. "Kathleen tells me you'll have to come to the galley if you want another drink."

"I've had enough," Philip replied, "I'm going to try to get some sleep."

"You're smarter than the rest of us," Paula said, "I'll join Robert for one last drink to see that he behaves himself." She stood up and smiled down at him. "It's good to be with you again."

Philip closed his eyes thinking of the conversation he had just had with Paula and what it might mean.

Their itinerary called for a three-day stay in the historic university city of Cambridge. Robert would deliver his paper on the socio-economic implications of the European Economic Union on Wednesday, the last day of the conference. Thursday morning they would fly to Shannon Airport where they would pick up a rental car and drive west to the coastal village of Kilkee. Here they had made reservations for three nights in a seaside bed-and-breakfast. Robert would take the car early Friday morning and drive south to the University of Cork where he would stay overnight, returning to Kilkee Saturday afternoon.

Paula and Philip would spend Friday evening treating Paula's elderly cousins to dinner. They lived in the nearby village of Querrin, the same village where Paula's mother and aunt had lived as young girls.

The three, badly jetlagged on Monday, were further wearied by the train ride to Cambridge and the tiresome process of checking into the dormitory-style room where they unpacked their luggage. That evening they nodded through the welcoming speeches at the opening banquet of Robert's conference and retired early.

Things picked up for Philip after a much-needed sleep when he learned his main responsibility in Cambridge was to be a companion to Paula while Robert attended conference sessions. What good luck, he thought; he couldn't have planned it any better. He would be with Paula for two full days before meeting Robert at day's end for pub crawling and delicious stew dinners.

The time he and Paula spent together those two days had a wonderful innocence to it. Two old friends learned once again to enjoy each other's company in this medieval city which had been home to one of the great centers of learning in Europe since the beginning of the thirteenth century.

Properly awed by the ancient architecture that surrounded them, they took in all the tourist attractions. They walked the hallowed grounds of King's College, took an open-air bus tour of the city which dropped them at Fitzwilliam Museum, and attended Even Song in King's Chapel while Robert was at a late session.

It was great fun, enjoyable fun, but, at the same time, something else was at work, another force that was drawing them closer, taking them to a point that was far beyond innocent friendship.

The first time Philip felt this was Tuesday morning, a clear sunny, comfortable day. They strolled through King's College to the banks of the river where they hired a small boat and went "punting on the Cam." The ride amounted to a leisurely drift down the river under a series of old stone bridges that crossed the waterway. They sat at opposite ends of the square-ended punt which was steered by a young, brown-haired boatman dressed entirely in white. The boatman pushed a long pole against the river's shallow bottom to propel the punt. Paula had brought a camera and they took turns taking pictures of each other as well as the boatman.

It was an idyllic moment, and both Paula and Philip sensed it. Paula put the camera away as they glided quietly down river. Occasionally the boatman would comment on a particular building or landmark that they were passing. At one point, Philip looked at Paula at the other end of the punt. He was surprised to see she was looking not at the passing scenery but directly at him. Their eyes met, and she did not turn away. There was something different in her expression, something that had to do with him. She looked as if she was seeing him in a new light for the first time. As he stared back at her, Paula smiled and said, "Perfect, this is perfect."

The next morning was cloudy with a forecast of light rain. They enjoyed the museum in the morning, and then walked back through the city looking for a suitable luncheon place. They both spotted the red and black "Pizza Hut" sign at the same time. They looked at each other and began laughing.

"I'll buy if you promise not to tell anyone we ate here while we were in Cambridge," Philip said.

"You've got a deal," Paula replied, "how does pepperoni and cheese sound?"

The expected rain greeted them after lunch. They stood under a restaurant awning deciding what to do next. Neither was big on shopping the stores. Suddenly Philip spotted a storefront on the other side of the street which brought a broad smile to his face.

"Follow me," he said, reaching back to take Paula's hand as they crossed at the light at the intersection.

"Where are you taking me?"

"It's a surprise. Do you like horses?"

"Love them; it's an Irish thing."

"Good, you can help me pick them."

Philip spotted Ladbrooke's Betting Parlor, where patrons could wager on horse races that were simulcast from race tracks around England. Ladbrooke's was a modest enterprise centered in a small room which reminded Philip of a cafeteria complete with tile floors and long formica-covered tables where the bettors pondered their selections.

Paula was delighted at the unexpected surprise. "What a great place to stay dry," she said. That is what they did for the rest of the afternoon, betting modest amounts on horses they knew nothing about, spending considerable thought trying to figure out how much they were actually betting in American dollars with the British currency they had converted. They agreed to leave the betting parlor at 4:00 pm in order to meet Robert for drinks.

With about half hour to go, Paula spotted a horse on the betting sheets that the parlor provided.

"Look at this, Philip. 'Irish Currents.' With a name like that, we have to bet him."

"What are the odds?" he asked.

"Eight-to-one on this sheet. Is that good?"

"Depends on how you look at it." A glance at the television monitors showed him the odds on "Irish Currents" had gone up to ten-to-one.

"I do want to bet him, Philip!"

"Well if you feel that strongly about it, let's do it the right way."

He went to the betting window and returned with a handful of tickets which he spread out before her. "These are presents for you, the only stipulation being that, if Irish Currents wins, you buy dinner tonight. You will certainly be able to afford it."

As the horses approached the starting gate, he explained that he had bought win tickets and a number of "exotic" bets, all including Irish Currents, costing a total of forty American dollars. He was still explaining the complexities of the "exotic" bets to Paula when the horses left the starting gate. Irish Currents, a dapple gray colt, fell immediately into sixth position in the eight horse field where he loped along lackadaisically while the favorites engaged in a speed duel in front. Paula urged him on noisily, oblivious to the fact that he appeared hopelessly outclassed.

The race was a mile and a quarter and, at the half way mark, Irish Currents was ten lengths behind.

"It doesn't look too promising," Philip said.

"The race isn't over yet," Paula replied and, with that, the gray horse began to move. He passed one horse at a time until, at the top of the stretch, there were only two horses left to pass, the two favorites. As the track announcer explained after the race, the favorites burned each other out in a speed duel which allowed Irish Currents to pass them easily in the stretch, looking more like a champion thoroughbred rather than a horse who hadn't won a race in two years.

As it became apparent that Irish Currents was to be the winner, Paula threw her arms around Philip shouting with joy. Philip, who was able to calculate in his head approximately how much she had won, responded with equal enthusiasm. She gave him a series of short affectionate kisses on the lips and cheeks. "You're the best," she said, "the very best" and the way she said it suggested she meant it to apply beyond his ability to bet the horses.

"Wait until you see how much you've won," he said. "Don't forget it was you who picked the horse."

Paula took her winning tickets to the clerk where it took several minutes to process them all. She returned to the table with a stack of British currency which she placed before him. Together they counted the pile and made the mental conversion to US dollars. The combination of the high odds win ticket and the exotic combination payoffs totalled $1360 US.

The high of Irish Currents' improbable victory sustained Paula through the rest of the time in Cambridge as well as the flight to the west coast of Ireland. With the insistence of Philip and Robert, she paid for Wednesday's dinner as well as Thursday night when they dined in Kilrush, a neighboring town of Kilkee. She still had well over $1100 of her winnings left and best of all, she was for the first time in Ireland, the place she had dreamed about for years.

Robert left early Friday morning in the rental car to drive to the University of Cork. Paula and Philip walked out to the boardwalk after breakfast, feeling at once the cool breeze that blew in from the cold waters of the North Sea. The seawall followed the contour of the horseshoe-shaped harbor whose waters were calmed by a breakwater out some distance from the beaches. A string of small hotels and rooming houses, all appearing neglected and in a state of disrepair, ringed the boardwalk. It did not appear as if these businesses had many customers, and only a few people sat on the beach.

"Looks pretty bleak, doesn't it," Paula commented. "Now I understand why Mother was always sending money and clothes back to Ireland. The west coast is one of the poorest parts of the country."

"The European Economic Union may help. I read some Irish businesses are beginning to thrive around Galway."

Paula brightened at the prospect. "It would be nice if that happened. Most people here are still on the dole, including my cousins who we are having dinner with tonight."

"I guess that means I'm buying," he said, and they both laughed. She linked her arm in his and they walked in silence back to Ann Prendergast's Bed-and-Breakfast in the center of Kilkee. An excursion bus was waiting to take them up and down the coast to the quaint little village of Doolin and then to the majestic Cliffs of Moher which looked out over the Irish sea to the Aran islands.

Just after they took their seat on the bus, Paula turned to him and took his hand in hers. "I want you to know I appreciate your staying here to keep me company. Cork would have been much more interesting for you."

"Nonsense," he replied, "You forget I am on vacation from university life. Besides, I would much rather be here with you."

She nodded and turned her attention to the tour guide who began to explain the afternoon's itinerary.

That evening they ate at the Strand restaurant, the finest eating establishment in Kilkee. They were joined by Paula's second cousins, Davey and Madge McDonnell. Davey was overweight with a florid face and a shock of white hair that looked as if it could stand a good trimming. He was single, a sometimes cow farmer with no other means of support. His sister, Madge, was a thin woman whose severe facial features belied a cheerful disposition. Madge had separated from her husband because of his drinking and moved into her brother's modest cottage. She was unemployed. Both were lively conversationalists who were knowledgeable about world affairs and had a keen interest in United States politics. Philip guessed them both to be in their late sixties.

Paula sat across from Philip enjoying the relatives she had heard so much about but never seen. She smiled and gently kicked Philip under the table when he made two successive blunders in his efforts to make conversation.

"Do you come here often?" he asked Madge who sat by his side.

"I should say not," she replied with emphasis. As she looked at him as if he were some sort of odd creature, he remembered Paula saying Madge and Davey were on the dole, both unemployed unless you counted the four cows Davey kept in the rented field.

Undaunted, Philip plowed on, perusing the small wine list which listed six different French wines. "Would you like a cocktail or would you prefer white or red wine?"

Davey answered more quickly than his sister. "Neither," he said, "Madge and I are both teetotalers. We took Father Mathew's pledge of abstinence at confirmation and have never broken it."

Philip apologized for the mistake and ordered a bottle of Chablis for Paula and himself. So much for Irish stereotypes.

The four lingered over their coffee after dinner. Eating at the Strand was a big occasion for Davey and Madge and Paula was genuinely delighted to be with them. Finally Philip paid the bill, and they went outside into the chilly night air. Davey and Madge drove off in his battered, old red Datsun with Paula waving a tearful goodbye.

The breeze billowed Paula's skirt as she turned to say "thank you for dinner."

"Let's get out of the cold," Philip said, "There are plenty of pubs to choose from."

"I'd just as soon go back to our rooms. It will be warm there as well." She looked up at him, took his hand and led him down the street.

The rooming house was dark except for a single lamp in the parlor which had already been set up for the next morning's breakfast. Judging by the sounds of gunfire and galloping horses, Anne Prendergast was still awake watching an old Western on television.

Paula went ahead up the narrow staircase that led to their rooms which were across from each other on the second floor. There was just enough light for Philip to see the ankles and calves of her legs. Neither spoke until they reached their rooms which increased the tension that had been building since they left the restaurant.

She broke the silence first. "I'd ask you in for a nightcap, but I have nothing here to drink. Robert took the last bottle of wine with him." She put the key in the lock and looked back at him trying to gauge his reaction.

He already knew he would not be the one to act first. Whether he was protecting himself from rejection or whether the guilt of betraying Robert held him back wasn't important. "I've had enough to drink," he replied, "but I'm not ready to go to sleep."

"In that case, it doesn't matter that we're dry," Paula said, holding her door open indicating that he should enter first.

Robert and Paula's room was the same as his, a double bed, dresser, a small sofa and floor lamp, a closet, and a bathroom with a narrow stall shower. Plaster marks on the wall of the bathroom suggested the stall showers were recent additions for the comfort of the bed-and-breakfast patrons. With choices limited, Philip sat in the armchair as Paula switched on the light and locked the door. She took the black shawl from around her shoulders and hung it on a hook on the inside of the closet door. She came and stood over him.

"I want to kiss you and hold you." She spoke slowly as if she had thought about what she was going to say beforehand. "I want you to know that I want to make love tonight if that is what you want."

That was it, the moment when the line was crossed, the moment when he could have stopped it. He could have stood up, put his arms around her, kissed her on the cheek, said something about the drinks getting to them both, and left. She would have been momentarily hurt, her pride bruised, but she would have gotten over it before Robert returned the next afternoon. He could have done all that.

But he didn't. Instead he told her the truth, what he really was feeling. "Paula, I don't have to tell you how much I care for you because you already know. You've always known." He didn't use the word "love." It wasn't necessary. What he said was enough. It was just right.

He stretched out his arms inviting her into them. She hesitated, uncertain of how to sit on his lap. Did it cross her mind to straddle him with her legs wide open? If it did she must have thought it too bold for this first moment and settled sideways on his lap with both of her legs across the arm of the sofa. He took the back of her head in his right hand and drew her to him in a long kiss, a kiss that gradually ended a forty year separation as it built in its intensity.

They both savored each other's taste, Philip recalling the way Paula pressed against his lips from long-ago highschool necking sessions. He remembered how sensual her breasts had seemed to him then and the few times she had let him undo her brassiere and kiss their softness. That was as far as they had gone then, but that had been another very different time. Now, Paula's quickened breathing indicated how excited she was becoming. She broke away from the kiss, hurriedly unbuttoned her blouse, and guided his head down to the whiteness of her chest which rose in vivid contrast to her summer tan.

His own arousal was immediate. He knew Paula could feel the hardness of his erection as it rubbed against the side of her thighs. He pushed the strap of her white bra aside, covering her breast with his free hand. Her nipple had hardened and he began to manipulate it with his thumb and forefinger. Paula became more agitated as he touched her, twisting free from his grasp and sliding to the floor until she was on her knees.

She took her blouse off and tossed it behind her. She reached to unfasten her bra and let it drop to the floor. She knelt before him, bare-breasted, her eyes full of desire. It had been months since Philip had last had sex. He wondered how long it had been since Paula last made love to Robert.

She buried her face in his lap, nuzzling and kissing his groin through his pants. She did not unzip the pants, but put her arms around his waist so she could draw him even closer. He bent forward sliding his hands down her back until he was able to pull up her skirt uncovering her buttocks. She wore white panties. He gently pushed his hands inside the top of her panties until he was able to cup both of her plump cheeks in each hand. Paula moaned with pleasure as he stretched to touch her between her legs. Years ago, when he clumsily tried to touch her like this, she had become upset and stopped him. Now he felt her wetness, how ready she was for sex as she pushed against him.

"Can we go to the bed?" she asked, kneeling upright and taking hold of his arm to lead him there. He stood and laughed at himself, embarrassed at how awkward it was for him to walk. Paula rose and sat on the side of the bed where she removed her skirt. She wore only panties as she waited for him. Philip thought she looked even more desirable than he had imagined all the countless times he had fantasized about making love to her.

He started towards her and stopped.

"What is the matter, Philip?"

"I don't feel comfortable making love to you in the same bed Robert will be sleeping in tomorrow night," he replied.

She started to say something, but stopped as he undid the buckles of his belt and stepped out of his pants and shorts. Paula's eyes dropped to his erection and lingered there. "You're beautiful,' she said. He sat back down on the middle of the sofa and extended his arms to her.

She slowly removed her panties, continuing to stare at him as if mesmerized by the extent of his passion. She came to him, naked, carefully swinging her right leg around him followed by the other until she sat on him, gently guiding him inside her with her hand. She smiled and began to kiss his lips hungrily as she started to move on him. "I want you so much," she said, and kissed him again.

What he remembered most about that first lovemaking was how tightly they fit together and how out of control they both became, lost completely in the feel and touch of each other's body. Paula seemed frenzied as she pushed his shirt up to squeeze his chest with one hand and dig her nails into his back with the other. He lowered his head to her breasts alternately sucking and nibbling each nipple which stiffened in his mouth in response.

In retrospect, Philip was surprised at how long he was able to make love that first time without climaxing. Usually, wine reduced his ability to make love. This night, the first night, it seemed to prolong it.

Paula climaxed early and often. After each climax, she slowed her movement and rested her head on his neck while he continued to move beneath her. After a brief respite, she joined him again, increasing the pace of her thrusts until they were in rhythm with him again. The pattern repeated itself, the two of them oblivious to everything else around them, until he could restrain himself no longer. She joined him as his delayed climax surged and burst inside her, kissing him furiously until he wrenched his mouth apart to let out a strangled groan, a sound he did not recognize as having made before.

They clung together, empty and smelling of sweat and sex. Paula did not move off him until he had softened. She sat next to him on the sofa, took his face in her hands and kissed him lightly on his lips.

"If you only knew how much I needed you tonight," she said.

"What would I think if I knew?" he asked.

"I'm not sure what you would think."

"Well then, tell me how much you needed me and why you needed me, and I'll tell you what I think."

"Give me time, and I will."

Uncertain as to what to say next, Philip stood up. "I need to wash off," he said and went into the bathroom.

When he returned, Paula was lying on her side on the sofa,

naked except for the black shawl which she had wrapped around her shoulders. The nipple of her right breast peeked out from the fringe of the shawl, still firm from the excitement of the lovemaking.

He thought she looked beautiful and told her so. "I enjoy looking at you this way," he added.

"I'm glad I make you happy," she said.

"Are you alright?" he asked.

"I am fine, Philip," she said, "but I am tired." She paused. "Will you be able to sleep okay?"

"Yes, I will be fine." He took the comforter off the bed and placed it over her. He bent to kiss her lips, and Paula held the soft kiss for an extra moment before dropping her head back on the cushion of the sofa.

"Good night," he said.

"Can we have breakfast together in the morning?" she asked.

"That would be nice. Is 8 o'clock too early?"

"No, I'll meet you downstairs at eight."

"Great, sleep well."

"I will, and Philip?"

"Yes."

"I promise to tell you why tonight means so much to me."

He smiled at her and went back to his room, closing the door behind him.

12

Philip's first thought when he awoke the next morning was whether Paula would regret having made love to him the night before. How would he respond at breakfast to an outpouring of guilt and remorse if that was what Paula was feeling? He could blame it on the wine they had drunk, but Paula only had a few glasses over the course of the evening and had been sober. As for himself, he was overwhelmed by what happened and his desire to have it happen again. Everything else, his long friendship with Robert, his understanding of the risks of such an affair, even his own moral code, all were secondary to the realization that, though it had taken almost forty years, he had finally made love to Paula, and she had returned his love.

The breakfast room downstairs was crowded with guests eager to begin touring the Irish countryside. Paula sat at a corner table sipping tea and reading an Irish newspaper. She was dressed brightly in an emerald-green blouse and white slacks. Her eyes shone as she smiled to greet him. He sat down and when she reached across the table to cover his hand with hers, he knew his concern about morning-after remorse was unwarranted.

"You look incredibly well-rested," he said, "beautiful as always. You must have slept well."

She nodded agreement. "And you look handsome and athletic," she said, referring to the dark blue jogging pants and white polo shirt he was wearing.

"I'm starved," he replied.

They joined the short line for the breakfast buffet, helping themselves to generous portions of eggs, sausages, and thick Irish soda bread. As they ate, they talked about what time Robert was expected back from Cork, finally agreeing he would not get there until 3:00 pm at the earliest.

They ate quietly, Paula finishing first. She put her knife and fork on the table and leaned forward so as not to be heard by the other guests.

"I want to say some things to you, Philip."

"You promised to tell me why last night meant so much to you."

"You remembered ... that's nice of you to do that."

She hesitated as if she were thinking about what she had just said.

"There are some things we need to talk about, some things you need to know."

"Okay, I'm willing," he said, curious now as to what was coming next. For the first time, he noticed Paula appeared nervous as if she were struggling to find the words to say what she had to say.

"I'm not sure how to start, but let me try by saying I hope last night didn't shatter any illusions you may have had about me."

"I'm not sure what you mean."

"I'm talking about my being unfaithful to Robert. I certainly don't want you to think this is something I do regularly with other men."

"I have no reason to think that," he replied. It was a half-truth because the question had briefly crossed his mind.

Despite his assurance, Paula continued.

"Robert and I have been married for a long time, twenty-eight years. Most of that time, we have been happy together. He is part of my life, and it is difficult for me to imagine living without him."

He nodded sensing this was the time to listen.

"You know all that. What you probably don't know, at least I think you don't, is that Robert has been unfaithful to me for most of those years. For a long time, I ignored it, pretended it wasn't happening, but deep down, I knew something was going on. I just didn't want to admit it."

"Did you talk to him about it?" Philip asked, thinking as he spoke that what she had said about Robert being with other women didn't surprise him.

"Philip, I don't want you to have to listen to every detail of our marriage. Besides, it's not fair to Robert. He's not here to defend himself."

"What I meant is ... are you certain that he had affairs?"

"Yes, I am positive. I just don't enjoy recounting the details. It's too painful."

Paula's voice quavered and her eyes filled with tears.

"You don't have to do this," he said, "it's making you upset."

"No, I want to finish," she replied, taking a tissue from her purse to dry her eyes. "Until a few years ago, we had what I thought was a great sex life. Robert can be a good lover."

The statement made Philip feel uncomfortable, uneasy about how Paula compared him to Robert. He had lost this competition once before.

"What went wrong?" he asked.

"He stopped making love to me," Paula said, "Oh, we've had sex occasionally, but it hasn't been the same. We don't make love. I feel like he has just been fulfilling a perfunctory obligation he thinks he owes me."

Philip had difficulty imagining his ever losing interest in making love to Paula, but he said nothing.

"It is hard to explain to you what that has done to me, having Robert lose interest in me that way. It has done a job on my self-confidence."

"I know the feeling," he said and immediately regretted saying it.

Paula looked at him and nodded.

"Yes, I did the same thing to you in high school. I know it's too late, but I am sorry."

"It wasn't the same thing. It was very different. We were adolescents."

They were silent for a few moments.

"What have you done about all of this?" he asked.

"This isn't the first time we have been through this. When I was at Sarah Lawrence, I learned Robert was seeing someone else while he and I were planning to be married. I was angry when I found out, so I decided to get even."

"How did you do that?"

"I had a brief relationship with another graduate student. We were on the same committees together. It was too short to be called an affair. I acted like a child."

Philip winced inwardly at the thought of another man having been with Paula besides Robert.

"How did it end?"

"It ended when Robert and I made up. He promised he would be faithful, and we moved our marriage date up. That was it."

"I need to know something."

"Ask me."

"Was last night another attempt to get even with Robert?"

"Philip, you and I could make love every day for the next year, and I still wouldn't be even with Robert."

"That sounds like a great plan to me, but you still didn't answer my question."

"It's just hard to know the truthful answer to that question, but I'll do my best. To begin with, I already tried having an affair earlier this year with a man I've worked with for years. He is a nice guy but when the time came, I couldn't do it. Maybe I am too old to be satisfied with revenge. It wasn't enough."

"Why me then?"

"Because with you, everything feels different. Philip, you're a giver, not just a taker. And you care for me; at least I think you do."

"There's nothing new about that."

"I know ... last night you gave me back everything I thought I had lost ... I still haven't answered your question, have I?"

"You're getting there."

"Striking back at Robert was part of my motivation at first. I know that doesn't sound romantic, but it's true, and I want to be truthful with you. There's more, much more.

Paula stopped talking and took a drink of water before continuing.

"Now that we have been together, I see things differently, perhaps from another perspective. It's not that Robert's affairs don't matter any more. They do, but they don't hurt as much. What matters to me now is you and what happened last night. Philip, the reason last night meant so much to me is that you made me feel loved again, valued again. You are so good for me, and I need you so much."

"I don't know what to say."

"Don't say anything. We have four or five hours until Robert gets back, and I want to spend that time with you, by ourselves."

"I'm ready," he said.

"Philip," Paula said, "let's go to your room now."

Philip led the way up the rooming house stairs, eager to hold Paula again, this time in his own bed. Another couple passed in the hallway on their way to breakfast. They exchanged greetings. Did he imagine it or had his voice given away the excitement he was feeling?

They turned to each other in the room and embraced, holding each other tightly. He moved towards the bed but Paula stopped him.

"No, not yet," she said. "First, I have a surprise for you, a way of returning some of what you gave me last night. But you have to be patient and sit on the sofa for a bit."

"Should I close my eyes and count to ten?"

He sat on the sofa as she answered.

"No, just the opposite," Paula laughed as she crawled on to the bed. "Last night, just as you were leaving, you said you enjoyed looking at me."

"I remember; it was the understatement of the year."

"Well, if that's what you enjoy, that's what I'm going to give you. Keep your eyes open and forget about counting."

Paula began a slow strip-tease, unbuttoning her green blouse. Her face was flush with her own arousal.

"My God," he said as she took off her blouse revealing a transparent black bra which not only increased her ample cleavage but also showed her full breasts and pink nipples through the sheer fabric.

She fell back on the bed and began to take one leg at a time out of her white slacks. Paula had some difficulty unrolling the second pant leg which bunched around her ankle. In frustration, she raised both her legs to kick the slacks to the floor with her feet. She wore green thong panties which covered only a small patch between her legs.

"Do you like my surprise?"

"I love it, don't stop now."

"I like being an exhibitionist," she said, "but I haven't had an appreciative audience for years."

"If you want evidence of how appreciative I am, take a look,"

She looked at him. "Impressive," she said.

She rolled over on to her stomach, and put both hands inside her thong. That moment, with the cheeks of her behind jiggling as she touched herself, was too much for Philip to resist.

Unable to restrain himself, he moved to the bottom of the bed where he pushed his sweat pants and undershorts to the floor without stepping out of them. He took Paula's ankles and gently pulled her back to the edge of the bed.

Instinctively, she raised up on her knees so he was able to push the strap of the thong panties aside and enter her from behind. She kept her face down on the bed, supporting herself with her arms.

"I wish I could see us," she said.

He was consumed by the erotic pleasure of the moment, thrusting himself into her, holding the cheeks of her behind with both of his hands so that they were able to move in rhythm with one another until they climaxed together in a way that was both violent and tender at the same time.

Afterwards, they lay side by side on the bed, drained by the intensity of their lovemaking, both surprised but not displeased at the direction their sexual sharing had taken. Paula rolled over on her side and kissed his nose.

"You're wonderful," she said.

"D.H. Lawrence would be proud of both of us," Philip replied.

"There you go again with the literary allusions. Hemingway was easy, but you have to help me with Lawrence. You forget I was a psych major."

"Sex was a kind of religion to Lawrence; the more erotic the sex, the more potential it had on a spiritual level. He saw sex as a basic form of human communication."

Paula was quiet for a while. He put his arms around her and held her while she gathered her thoughts.

"I don't know much about Lawrence," Paula said, "but I do know I love the way you make me feel. I hope I make you feel the same way."

"If you only knew."

"Do you know something else, making love the way we just did requires mutual trust. Lovers usually take more time to get to that point."

"We've known each other for a long time," he said.

"I trust you, Philip, and I need you."

They clung together until Paula abruptly sat up, feigning anger.

"Wait a minute," she said, "I just got the Lawrence thing."

She raised the pillow as if to hit him. "Does this mean you are thinking of me as Lady Chatterly?"

"That's not what I intended, but if you want, I can be Lady Chatterly's lover."

"She was a hot number, am I right?"

"Hot! Horny is more like it. Her lover was a gamekeeper, a man of the soil. He made love to her in ways I can only describe as 'earthy.'"

Paula dropped the pillow and swung her leg over Philip so that she lay naked on top of him.

"If you remember what they did, I'll do my best to do justice to Lady Chatterly's role," she said, laughing as she covered him with kisses.

And so they made love for the third time in twelve hours, trusting more this time so that they were able to open themselves, devouring the other with their lips, tongues and mouths, taking yet giving, exploring every part of their bodies until it was as if each had discovered the other for the first time and was in wonder at what had been found.

They paid no attention to the passing of the hours until a knock on the door by the chamber maid reminded them that Robert was by now driving north from Cork. It was time to let their passions calm, to exchange last affections and say the things lovers say when it is time to part. Robert would be full of funny tales about the Irish academics at the University of Cork and Paula and Philip would laugh and say the right things, trying not to have each other's eyes meet in case the way they looked at each other would tell the world they were for the moment, wildly in love.

13

Philip left Mystic to rejoin the traffic on route 95. The Rhode Island border was just a few miles north and, from there, only three exits to route 138, a narrow, winding country road that led east to Paula. The memories of Ireland had distracted him. He found it odd that he was able to recall specific details of the time he spent alone with Paula, what they each said, how they touched one another, the scent of their bodies after lovemaking. However, the last part of the trip, after Robert returned from Cork, was just a blur in his mind. He had been nervous, feeling guilty, he and Paula playing the role of happy tourists as if nothing had happened between them.

But he knew better. If he needed proof, it was there in the packet of pictures Paula had sent him a few weeks after their return. Somehow, the inexpensive camera they were using captured the expression on her face as she sat at the other end of the punt on the River Cam looking back at him. She was framed in the middle of the arch of a bridge they had just passed through with the young boatman standing behind her intent on guiding the boat with his pole. Philip had looked at the picture many times over the past twelve months and reached his own conclusion. That moment, when he asked her to smile one of her prettiest smiles, was a moment of revelation for Paula, the exact instant when she decided that she wanted him, Philip, to be her lover.

The University of Rhode Island sign at exit three reminded him of Robert's current dangerous predicament. It was painful for Philip to even think of his friend in captivity. After Robert had taken the "URI" tenure track position, he and Paula had grown to love Rhode Island despite its sharp contrast with New York. Philip imagined how much Robert would give to be safe at home in his adopted state at this moment.

Philip thought back to an essay Robert published in an academic journal in the early eighties. In the essay, he argued that young people should choose a place to live which was compatible with their nature and personality rather than have corporations move them around as if they were dominoes. He quoted data claiming that the average American moved thirteen times during his lifetime, and contended that this excessive mobility was a major factor contributing to the breakdown of communities. The issue was topical enough to be quoted by some national media, but Robert never wrote again on the subject. Other scholars picked it up and developed it further. This was surprising because, as was the case with many research-oriented academics, Robert was always in search of the issue that he could become a recognized expert on, a subject that he could feel passionate enough about to devote his time to, a subject that could be his own. It wasn't an easy thing to do as Philip knew quite well.

Philip drove through rural western Rhode Island past a shopping center, housing developments, a place with the odd name of Usquepog, dairy farms, a burnt-out public golf course, into the historic colonial village of Kingston, the home of the University of Rhode Island.

As he approached the university campus, Philip saw groups of students gathered along the road holding up signs to get the attention of the passing motorists. Traffic slowed allowing him to read the messages, all of which called for Professor Donovan's release in a variety of different ways. Yellow ribbons hung everywhere, from poles, fences and out of the windows of administrative buildings as well as sorority and fraternity houses. Considering most students were home for summer break, Philip thought it an impressive outpouring of concern and affection for Robert.

An especially large group of students gathered at the corner of Upper College Road, the main entrance to the campus. Young men and women handed out leaflets to the passengers of automobiles that stopped at the traffic lights. A young woman dressed in a halter and shorts approached Philip's car. He rolled down his window.

"One of our faculty has been kidnapped in India," she said, "We are asking people to help by writing or calling their representatives in congress to get the state department to do more to get him released. I hope we can count on your help. I had him in class. He's a great guy."

"I know," Philip replied. He started to say more, that he knew their professor, but the young woman was already gone on to the next car. Philip watched her through his side-view mirror. Her long blond hair was tied in a ponytail with a yellow ribbon.

Something about the demonstration of student support at the university gates stunned Philip into a new awareness. He reminded himself that the reason he was in Rhode Island was to comfort Paula, to help her get through this troubling time, to do what a friend ought to do. The fact that they had made love a year ago and clearly had strong feelings for one another was secondary to Robert's predicament. He resolved to keep this his focus, difficult though it may be.

Fifteen minutes later, he pulled his Camry into Paula's driveway next to a van with university markings on its side. Another car, a black Ford sedan, was parked on the sidewalk in front of the house. Philip was not surprised that Paula had visitors, and in a way that he couldn't quite explain, he felt relieved that other people would be there to cushion his first meeting with Paula. He took his briefcase and one piece of luggage from the trunk, but decided to leave the box of wine in the car for the moment.

Paula and Robert lived in a dark gray split-level house which they had built in 1984 just before real estate values rose dramatically in the Ocean State. It was quite ordinary in appearance from the street in front of the house. Philip remembered Robert walking visitors down to the beach in the back to show them that the house was larger and more distinctive than it first appeared. There were five different levels, all with large picture windows that looked out over the brackish waters of the Narrow River, a tidal estuary that emptied into Narragansett Bay five miles to the south. Whenever Philip had been present, Robert always gave Paula credit for working closely with the builder on a design that took full advantage of the water views.

He rang the doorbell and waited. No one came, which momentarily alarmed him. Maybe something had happened to Robert, and the visitors were just now telling Paula. He rang again and after a moment a younger man, whom Philip thought to be about forty, opened the door. A golden Labrador retriever stood by his side, his tail wagging expectantly.

"Hi, sorry, we were on the deck talking with Mrs. Donovan.

I'm Bill Glasby from the president's office at the university. You must be Philip Lynch, a friend of Professor Donovan?"

Philip shook hands and acknowledged the greeting. "How is she? Is there any more information about Robert?"

"The state department has assigned one of their people to be available to Mrs. Donovan at all times in case there are any new developments. Her name is Jennifer Pitman; she is upstairs. She brings a report to Mrs. Donovan every day." Except for the white shirt and striped tie he wore, Glasby looked like one of Philip's graduate students, earnest and dedicated. "Why don't you leave your bag in the hall, and we'll join them on the deck."

Philip followed Glasby up a small flight of stairs which led into a large open area that was divided into a kitchen, dining room, and living room space. A screen door opened to the deck whose view of the river was only partially blocked by the large oak trees which grew down to the beach. An attractive black woman stood next to Paula, her posture suggesting to Philip that she had just arrived and not yet sat down.

Paula came to him immediately, greeting him with a light kiss on the cheek, her arm barely touching his shoulder.

"Thank you for coming,' she said and then made introductions all around. "Philip is an old and dear friend of Robert's and of mine. We grew up together in New York many years ago."

She was dressed in what appeared to be a man's white shirt (was it Robert's?) which she wore out over blue jeans. She wore no makeup and looked very fatigued. Even though he had not expected Paula to collapse in his arms, clinging to him while last summer's passion rekindled, he nevertheless felt a sense of mild disappointment which he quickly banished from his mind.

"Please sit down and have something cool to drink," Paula

said, gesturing towards the table on which she had set a pitcher of iced tea and glasses. "Jennifer was just giving me today's update on Robert's situation. I would like Philip to hear it as well." They sat while Bill Glasby did the honors pouring each a glass of ice tea.

Jennifer Pitman had a briefcase with her which she did not open. Instead she reached across the table to squeeze Paula's hand.

"First let me say that Paula has shown all of us how brave and courageous a person can be in a time of incredible stress." She withdrew her hand as Paula wiped her eyes with a tissue. "The second point I want to emphasize to you Paula, to the university community through you Mr. Glasby, and to all of Robert and Paula's friends such as you Mr. Lynch, is that every possible thing that ought to be done to accomplish Robert's safe release is being done. Be assured that this is a multi-pronged effort involving not only the state department and other US agencies, but their Indian counterparts as well.

"What is important to note, however, is that Nagaland is a most difficult area for us to operate effectively. The fact that Nagaland is one of India's 'protected' areas that is only accessible with special permission tells you all you need to know. It is my understanding that the reason Professor Donovan went there was because it is such a unique part of India." Paula nodded agreement but said nothing. "The same things that make Nagaland so unique are also what make it so dangerous." Jennifer Pitman paused to let her last statement be considered. "As you know, there is an underground nationalist movement in Nagaland consisting of a number of different factions who often are in conflict with each other as well as with the central government of India. We believe one of these groups is holding Professor

Donovan for their own purposes. We do not know which group but we think we know their motive.

"We believe the group that kidnapped Professor Donovan wants to use a prominent American academic to be a spokesperson for their cause. That opinion is shared by the Naga minister who was traveling with his daughter and Professor Donovan when the kidnapping took place.

"Our assessment is that armed intervention is not the way to free Professor Donovan. There are too many factors working against success with such an effort, not the least of which is that we don't know where he is being held. Also the jungle in that part of Nagaland is virtually impenetrable and finally, we don't know the danger that a rescue attempt might bring to Paula's husband."

"What is being done?" Glasby asked, "Is there any reassurance we can give to the university community? There aren't many students on campus in the summer, but those that are here are very concerned."

Philip supported Glasby's statement with a recounting of his experience driving by the university a little earlier.

The state department representative was prepared for the question. "Rather than police or military solutions, we believe our best hope lies in a negotiated solution. We want to give these underground guerillas what we think they want. We are trying to send them the message that, if Professor Donovan is willing to make a statement, written or recorded, that they think would be helpful to their cause, we will guarantee an international audience."

"How can you do that?" Philip asked.

"It is not as easy as you might think. To begin with, the Indian government is not eager to provide a forum to a group they believe to be outlaw insurrectionists. They are likely to block distribution of any message of Professor Donovan's by Indian media. But this doesn't prevent CNN or BBC from broadcasting his message internationally, and we expect the world press will continue to report the story as they are doing now."

"You mentioned you were trying to send a message," Paula said, "How are you going to do that if we don't know where Robert is or who is holding him?"

"That is the hard part since no group has claimed responsibility at this point. The Indian authorities tell us our best bet is the minister, the father of the student your husband was traveling with. Apparently he has access to channels of communication within the tribes that the Indian military do not have. He is something like a tribal elder or chief."

"Are they asking for a ransom or if not, is there anything we can offer to help them decide to release Robert?" Paula's concern was evident in her voice.

"Yes, there may be, and we are working hard on it. The idea is to get to a member of congress, who serves on the committee that approves foreign aid. If we can promise that the issue of the Indian government's treatment of Nagas will be raised in the sub-committee, the next time aid to India is debated, this could be the deciding factor. We are very close to making that happen."

"It sounds as if you feel some optimism at this point. Am I correct in thinking that?" Philip asked.

Jennifer Pitman took her time formulating her answer. "Yes, the consensus is we are guardedly optimistic. One major reason for that is that we know the Naga people have no personal enmity towards the United States. If anything, they are pro-US. A small number of them already live in the states. Also, we feel strongly that whoever has Professor Donovan must understand that harming him would do great damage to their cause."

Philip and Bill Glasby nodded agreement with Jennifer Pitman's reasoning.

"To sum up, we are hopeful that all this will have a satisfactory ending however difficult it may be at the moment. At the same time, we do not want to create expectations that are not yet warranted."

"Isn't there something I can do," Paula asked, "some message I can send Robert?"

"The best thing you can do is stay home and wait for us to communicate any developments to you. I promise you there will be no delay. If and when Professor Donovan is released, you can decide what to do at that time."

"Would I be expected to go to India when that happens?"

"Not necessarily. The Indian authorities will want your husband to return home as soon as they debrief him. The last thing they want is the world press shining a spotlight on the Nagaland problem. They are already uncomfortable with the publicity."

Paula sighed, acknowledging that the discussion was over. "Okay," she said, "I think I understand as best as anyone can understand this whole mess." She stood up and began to pick up the now empty glasses of ice tea. The others followed her into the kitchen area where they shook hands.

"Thank you, Jennifer, you have been a great help, Paula said, and Bill, the people at URI could not have been nicer, you especially."

Philip let Bill Glasby and Jennifer Pitman out the front door. He walked them to the driveway and, when they had left, opened up the trunk of his car to retrieve the box of wine he had purchased earlier in Mamaroneck.

Paula was sitting on a kitchen stool, looking forlorn when Philip came back up the stairs carrying the wine. The moment was awkward, neither one knowing what to say. Philip put the wine on the kitchen counter. "Shall I chill some of this," he asked.

"That would be great. There's a large bottle of Chardonnay already opened."

Paula busied herself getting down the wine glasses and laying out some crackers and cheese. This seemed to help her control her emotions which appeared to Philip to be on the brink of collapse. "Let me go upstairs and change. I must look a mess."

"You look fine," he lied. "You have been through a lot." Paula went upstairs leaving Philip to wonder if he should have come at all. He took his drink out on the deck trying to sort through the chaotic situation he was now part of where conflicting emotions coexisted with one another, leaving those involved in a condition of absolute uncertainty. No prior guidelines existed as to how an individual should behave in this situation. Or did they? Again, he reminded himself that the primary reason for his being here with Paula was to provide the support she clearly needed. His personal feelings for her would have to wait.

Down below, the river was peaceful with just two small sailboats moving on the light breeze. It was a balmy June night, one in which the sun would remain on the river for another two hours and, when it set below the cloudbanks, create a spectacular show of pink and purple colors whose reflections would shimmer on the currents of the river.

Paula carried her wine glass out onto the deck and joined Philip. She had put on lipstick and changed into a light blue sweater and slack combination. She stood beside him looking out at the river. "I never realized how beautiful a spot this is," Philip said.

"It's been a wonderful place to live all these years," Paula replied, "The views change with the seasons." She paused and once again, became teary-eyed. "Do you know what Robert's favorite sight on the river was?"

"No, tell me."

"It happened each Christmas day in the early afternoon for the past six or seven years. Without any notice or fanfare, a motorboat pulling a water-skier dressed like Santa Claus would come down the river. Santa would shout out greetings and wave to the people in the houses. Robert always wanted to find out who the skier was to tell him how great he thought the idea was."

"The kids who live on the river must love it."

"I'm sure. I wish Robert and I had been able to have children. It might have changed everything."

Philip thought it best to change the topic. "I was very impressed with Miss Pitman. Her explanation was impressive."

"She is very thorough. Most of what she said I told you last night on the phone. The only new point was the idea about having the problem in Nagaland raised in a congressional subcommittee."

"That could mean a lot to members of a nationalist movement, a big step in getting their message out."

"Let's pray that it works."

Paula stepped away from the rail of the deck to sit at the table where she helped herself to a cracker with cheese. Philip took the cue and sat at the opposite end of the table inwardly disappointed that, even with the two of them alone, the communication was still stilted, still reserved. He wanted to get up, go to Paula, give her a comforting, loving hug, and tell her things were going to be okay.

"There's something Jennifer Pitman doesn't know that I deliberately haven't told her," Paula said after a moment.

Philip became alert. "Is it something important, something you can share with me?" he asked.

"Yes, it's very important, but it would serve no purpose telling Miss Pitman.

"Can you explain?"

"Robert has been having an affair with a student for over a year, the same student he traveled to India with on university business, the same student whose father was traveling with them both when the kidnapping occurred."

"I can understand why you don't want to tell anyone. Why are you telling me?"

Paula took a long sip of her drink before replying. "Because what I just told you had a direct bearing on a decision I made the day Robert left for India. This is going to shock you, but I decided that day to divorce my husband; not separate, divorce."

Philip was jolted by Paula's statement. For a moment he wondered if the strain she was under was making her say things she didn't really mean. Then he thought what her statement might mean to their future together.

"I learned Robert and Meniu were having an affair months ago and, Philip, I am absolutely certain what was going on, not a doubt in my mind. At first, I couldn't believe it; even though Robert has had affairs before, I never thought it would be with a student."

"That surprises me also," Philip said quietly.

"During the last year, we had a number of talks about the state of our marriage. He denied seeing anyone else whenever I asked that question. I never told him I knew about Meniu; perhaps I felt guilty about you and me in Ireland. Deep down,

I was probably hoping he would just quit and come back to me."

"He had a chance to do that. When Rajiv Gandhi was assassinated, there were travel advisories warning about going to India. He could have used that excuse to stay home. His little co-ed would have gone home to Nagaland, and that would have been the end of it. He made a decision to go, and that's when I made my decision."

Paula started to cry and Philip instinctively went to her side, put his arm around her, and kissed her softly on the top of her head. She did not pull away but lay her head on his chest as she tried to compose herself.

"Let me fill your glass," Philip said, "Some wine might help you relax." He was still processing what he had just learned when he returned with the drinks. Something still nagged at him about the things Paula had said.

"Are you sure that you shouldn't tell Jennifer Pitman about Robert and his student?"

"Yes, I am sure. They already asked me those kinds of questions, but I told them nothing. It was too painful, too embarrassing." Philip said nothing further on the subject.

They sat together quietly sipping wine as the sun began to set. When the glasses were empty, Philip opened a new bottle and brought it out to the deck in an ice bucket. He sat down by her side.

The wine seemed to soothe Paula, at the same time making her more reflective. "Philip, do you think a person can love more than one person at the same time?" Paula turned towards him, her eyes dry but her voice full of emotion.

He answered quickly. "Yes," he said, returning her gaze, "I loved my wife all the years we were married, but I never lost the feeling I had for you. Only that feeling was dulled by your absence."

Paula dropped her eyes. "A year ago I thought I was in love with both you and Robert. Then I fell out of love with Robert. Everything was clear, and now this awful thing has happened to him. Now, I don't know what to feel."

"You should have told me what you were...."

"I tried to in that letter I wrote you and in the phone calls. Don't you understand? I didn't want our making love in Ireland to be the cause of the failure of my marriage. My marriage was already failing before Ireland. I had to separate the two. That is why I couldn't see you all this time."

He bent over to kiss her, but she stopped him. "Let's go inside. Our neighbors sometimes walk the beach at sunset. They wouldn't understand."

They went inside, but he did not kiss her right away. Instead he held her close and told her he would help her get through this awful thing, and that is what he and she should focus on and, when it was all over and Robert was safe, they could concentrate on the future of their own relationship. "I am going to prove to you that I can be a good friend, not just a good lover," he said.

Paula smiled up at him and nodded her head in agreement. "The neighbors have sent over enough casseroles to feed the entire block. My telephone has been rerouted to the university to ward off the media and the cranks. They let through all legitimate calls so we can stay home and wait for news."

They ate at the dining room table. Philip opened a bottle of Pinot noir to "wash down the hamburger casserole." The wine and her fatigue quickly caught up with Paula who returned to an earlier topic of conversation.

"I do wish we had children. God knows we tried. I think Robert's operations were the problem, but who knows. His students and my clients became our surrogate children – we shared anecdotes about them for years and then we stopped. We just weren't interested any more."

She switched topics without warning. "Do you ever think it is strange that we made love for the first time in Ireland?"

"No, I didn't think it was strange; I thought it was wonderful."

"Irish Currents was wonderful, what a wonderful horse. I love that horse," she said.

He laughed. "That was a grand horse," he said, trying his best to imitate the brogue of her relatives.

Philip let Paula talk. At one point, she stopped, suddenly aware that she was rambling. "It's okay, Philip, I need the catharsis. It will be good for me." He smiled to say he understood.

"What I really need now is to go to sleep. I haven't slept much since I got the news. We can do the dishes in the morning."

He followed her as she carried her dishes to the sink in the kitchen. "Do you mind sleeping downstairs?" she asked. "There is a bathroom across the hall with a shower and the view of the river in the morning is a great way to start the day."

"That's fine," he said, "You get a good long sleep."

"I'm glad you're here," Paula said and leaned up to give him a kiss goodnight.

Philip went downstairs, washed up and got into bed in his undershorts. Outside the moon cut a perfectly shaped path across the width of the river. A cool breeze blew in off the river as he quickly fell asleep.

He awoke in the middle of the night to the sound of footsteps coming down the stairs to his room. A moment later, Paula stood in the doorway and whispered his name. "Philip, are you awake?

I woke up and can't get back to sleep. I feel frightened as if something awful is going to happen. Can I get in with you?"

"Of course, whatever you want."

She wore a short white nightgown. "Please hold me," she said as she turned her back to him and drew his arms around her. "I just need you to hold me."

He held her as she wanted. They did not make love. Paula went back to sleep until the morning when she awoke, still in Philip's arms.

PART THREE

14

The sound of animals howling and screaming awoke Donovan. As he emerged slowly from his drugged sleep, his first thought was that he had heard those same shrieks before in the monkey houses of the zoo he had visited as a child in the Bronx. But this wasn't a zoo; for a few moments he had no idea where he was. Then a bomb-like clap of thunder accompanied by vivid flashes of lightning jolted him to his senses and let him see, if just for a moment, the dirt-floor hut which was his prison. At the same instant he felt the heavy vine ropes which loosely bound his hands and feet, keeping him immobile on some sort of canvas cot. A torrential beat of rain followed the thunder and lightning, pounding on a roof just a few feet above his head. For the moment he was alone and as best as he could understand in his confusion and fear, it was the dead of night. He lay still listening to the sounds of the storm as a feeling of terror enveloped him.

What seemed like hours passed during which time he slipped back into unconsciousness, only to be shaken awake by the unbelievable horror of his situation. It couldn't be real; it was just a bad dream from which he would awake and his world would be back to normal; he would be home with Paula. But lightning coming through the openings in the walls that served as windows repeatedly lit up his room, finally convincing him that this was his new reality.

There wasn't much to see. The walls seemed made of some bamboo composite, a simple wooden table and two chairs sat on the opposite side of the dirt floor. A heavy hemp netting covered the openings in the walls through which muggy, tropical air entered. An oil lamp and some dishes and utensils sat on the table. There was no sink or toilet. Donovan realized his clothes had been taken from him. He wore only his blue undershorts which he had wet during the night.

He was not yet ready to confront the events that had brought him here. Instead, he again lapsed back into a semi-conscious state which gradually became a nightmarish dream. In his dream, he saw himself tied, helpless in the hut, but at the same time, he hovered in the air outside the hut. Large, olive-green snakes slithered towards the door of the hut only to be attacked by bare-chested savages who cut their heads off with oversized hatchets and then proudly nailed the heads to the walls of the hut. Behind them the decapitated bodies of the snakes continued to writhe wildly, finally coming together in an orgy of death. The savages nailed the last snakehead to the hut and then approached the door of the hut brandishing their hatchets. Donovan awoke in a feverish sweat, screaming in terror.

The vivid dream and the awakening brought him to another level of awareness. He heard voices outside the hut calling excitedly to one another. The storm of the night before was over, morning light came through the netted windows, and suddenly he remembered everything, the visit to the museum, the two jeeps driving up into the Naga hills, the incessant talking of Dr. Ahon, the construction workers waving a flag to stop their jeep, and then being wrestled to the ground while some anesthetic was shoved into his face sending him into darkness. He had been kidnapped. Voices came closer to the hut. Donovan heard the latch of the door opening. His captors had arrived.

A short, middle-aged man with rugged oriental features entered followed by two taller young men carrying spears. The older man, clearly the leader, wore an unbuttoned khaki shirt over green military pants. The other two, whom Donovan thought to be soldier guards, wore cane belts with small aprons in front covering their genitals. Their bare chests had no markings, but their faces were painted with black circular patterns around the eyes and V-shaped triangles which began at their chins and reached up to their ears and noses. Underneath the designs, innocent, boyish faces peered out at Donovan with curiosity and excitement.

The older man spoke sharply to the guards, pointing towards Donovan. The two guards immediately leaned their spears against the walls of the hut and began to untie the vine ropes that bound Donovan. Donovan sat up, terrified.

"What am I doing here?" he asked. "Who are you?"

"Our names are unimportant. All you need to know, Professor Donovan, is that the three of us are soldiers in the Nagaland Liberation Army. You are our prisoner."

"You were taken from your vehicle on the way to Mon. Your traveling companions were left unharmed and are probably being interrogated as we speak about what happened to you. They, of course, have no idea where you are. You were taken because you are a prominent American who may be able to help our cause. That is all you need to know for now. When there is more to tell, you will be told."

"What do you intend to do with me?" Donovan asked, his mind trying to recall the conversation in Kohima with Chingmei and Meniu about guerrilla fighters kidnapping foreigners to call attention to their cause.

"That depends on the orders we get. As is the case with soldiers all over the world, we obey orders. That is our duty." The man hesitated and then added, "You can call me Captain Nllamo." His voice was soft, calm, and non-threatening. His English was impressive.

Donovan rubbed his wrists and ankles in an effort to get his circulation going. His body was stiff and sore, and he suddenly realized he had to relieve himself.

"I have to … uh, is there a toilet?"

Captain Nllamo smiled. "The bush is your toilet as it is for all the soldiers who serve in this camp. Come with me, Ato and Lowang will take you to the ditches that we use as latrines. They will also show you the area where you will be allowed to exercise twice daily. When you are not washing, defecating, urinating, or exercising, you will remain in this hut. The guards will bring you food three times a day. I will personally bring you reading material, articles, and books about the history of the Naga people, books that explain why we deserve to be free from the tyranny of India. Read them please. If the decision is made to release you, you can return to your country and tell our story to the world."

Donovan looked up at his captor from the cot, "What do you mean 'if' the decision is made to release me. Who makes that decision? On what basis will that decision be made?"

"As I said before," Nllamo replied, "we are soldiers who do not always know who makes certain decisions or why those decisions are made. We do what we are told. Even if we did know the answers to your questions, we would not tell you. Come, let's get you to the latrine."

Donovan rose to follow the guards out the door of the hut. When his legs buckled beneath him, the guards took hold of his arms to keep him from falling.

"I hope everything is clear," Captain Nllamo said. "Do not even think of trying to escape. There are miles of dense jungle that surround our camp. You would never survive. And, if you did, we would find you and then, unfortunately, we would have to kill you." He said the words evenly, a simple statement of fact.

The guards led Donovan out the door of the hut into a small clearing where a large group of men and women awaited him. The guards stopped to display their captive, to satisfy the curiosity of their comrades who pointed and talked excitedly about this American who was under their control. The oppressive tropical heat staggered Donovan as he looked around trying to assess his predicament. He noticed that the men in the crowd, many of them just teenagers, were dressed in the same attire as the guards while the bare-breasted young women wore brightly colored cloth saris. Donovan had seen this same scene in *National Geographic* magazine many times. Now he was part of the scene.

The captain seemed to know what he was feeling. "The afternoon rains will cool the air some; your hut will always be a few degrees cooler," he said, adding, "If you are wondering about the way our freedom warriors are dressed, they dress as all Nagas did before the missionaries put clothes on us, before the Indian government took away our liberty and destroyed our way of life. These young people fight not only for independence but for the Naga way of life. Don't worry, they are not angry at you, just curious."

It registered with Donovan that Nllamo sounded much like Dr. Ahon. His kidnappers were dedicated revolutionaries, and he was their pawn.

Nllamo motioned to the group to disperse, gesturing to the guards. The orders he gave were immediately obeyed.

"Do what you have to do in our outdoor latrine, wash off in the stream, and then the guards will return you to the hut where you will be fed. You can read and rest for the remainder of the day."

The guards led Donovan, still dressed in his soiled blue shorts, past a row of huts similar to his own, and down a path which had been carved out of the jungle canopy. The trees were wet from the earlier rains and drops of moisture fell from the foliage.

The guards were solicitous of Donovan during the three-minute walk to the open ditch. Even though his stomach discomfort was extreme, he hesitated, looking at the guards in helpless embarrassment. The young soldier called Ato decided to be helpful. He took some large leaves off a tree and proceeded to squat over the ditch making a straining noise as if he were having a bowel movement. He looked up at Donovan and spoke English for the first time. "Shit, shit," he said, "shit make you feel better." He then took the leaves and went through the motion of wiping his behind. Donovan nodded understanding and tore some leaves from the same tree. "Will you leave me alone?" Donovan asked. "Yes, yes, we go," Ato replied and the two guards walked no more than ten feet down the path, turned and watched laughing as Donovan squatted and defecated loosely into the rancorous ditch, the odor of which was softened by a lime-like substance that the guards shoveled into the ditch when he was done using the leaves to clean himself.

Donovan's physical relief moderated the humiliation and embarrassment he felt. "Wash now," Ato said motioning to Donovan to follow. The three men walked at a leisurely pace pushing aside the jungle growth which threatened to cover the path. How ludicrous we must look, Donovan thought, the two of them in their loincloths followed by me in my blue Hanes undershorts.

After what seemed to be a walk of five minutes, they came upon a stream which quickly spilled into a river whose banks were crowded with younger men and women fishing with nets and swimming in the deeper pools. The two guards waded into the brown water up to their waist. They beckoned to Donovan to follow them, motioning to tell him he should cleanse himself in the waters of the river.

Despite the color of the water, Donovan eagerly dipped down up to his chin and did his best to rub his body clean of the grime and sweat that had built up over the past few days. Surprisingly, the guards left him alone while they went to join the crowd that had by now turned their attention to the tall, white-skinned visitor. He dipped his head into the water without submerging his face. He scrubbed his scalp vigorously, certain that his hair was now home for a variety of jungle lice. When he was done, he gingerly stepped across the rocky bottom until he reached the bank. Here he sat down on a fallen log, fatigued from his ordeal and this most recent exertion. Immediately, he felt the hot tropical sun beginning to warm his pale skin.

Farther upriver, the young men and women, all of them naked except for small pieces of cloth that hung loosely from cane belts, spoke animatedly with the two guards, obviously curious about Donovan. Two of the young women, Donovan guessed them to be teenagers, broke off from the group giggling as they splashed through the river towards Donovan. The rest of the crowd followed at a distance. Though short in stature, both women had firm, well-proportioned bodies that had been honed by manual labor and a rice-based diet.

The lead girl hesitated as she approached Donovan, looking back over her shoulder at her companion and at the spectators who followed. Voices from the crowd encouraged her, and she moved closer until she hovered directly above him. He halfheartedly attempted a smile. She said something Donovan didn't understand and then bent down and began to rub her small breasts against Donovan's head. The crowd laughed its approval as the exhausted Donovan moved his head out of the range of her nipples. Not discouraged, the young temptress turned her back to the American, pulled up the cloth skirt she wore revealing her behind which she then rotated provocatively to the roar of her friends.

Her companion chose this moment to motion to Donovan to stand up. He did so unsuspectingly and, in a flash, the young girl pulled down his blue shorts leaving him naked, his hands covering his flaccid penis, while the crowd laughed hysterically. Donovan felt mortified, but he did not feel any physical threat. He remembered Meniu's talk of the young Nagas playing at sex during the feast of Ouniebu. That was what was happening here. The crowd was playing at sex, and he was their toy.

He bent over to pull his shorts back up. As he did, the second girl gently spanked his bare buttocks, provoking another crowd reaction which was stilled immediately by the shouted commands of Captain Nllamo who appeared at the bend of the river. The two guards quickly dispersed the crowd yelling at the two girls who only moments ago had provoked so much merriment.

As the crowd splashed its way downstream, Nllamo took charge.

"I apologize to you, Professor Donovan, for the behavior of our soldiers. Many of them are still very young and don't fully realize how serious their work here is. They meant no harm."

Donovan shook his head to acknowledge that he understood.

"Come, we will take you back to the hut where we have some food for you. You must be hungry."

Again Donovan nodded agreement. The trip to the latrine and the washing in the stream had returned him to a level of normalcy. He realized he hadn't eaten in a while. How long had it been? Twenty-four hours? Only a short time ago he had been safe with Meniu and her father. But even then he had felt uneasy, as if some looming threat was present. His instincts had been right. His worst fears had come true.

Nllamo led the way up the path that led away from the river up past the ditch that smelled of Donovan's recent visit, to the small clearing outside his hut.

"I think it best that you eat first, rest a bit, and later this afternoon you can have your first exercise session. Also, I want to show you the book that I have brought you to read."

The captain opened the door to the hut and beckoned Donovan to enter. The dark coolness of the hut felt refreshing. Two young women followed carrying small bowls of rice, meats, and vegetables which they placed on the table along with utensils and a glass of milk. They waited expectantly to see if their prisoner would eat the food they had prepared. They needn't have worried as Donovan sat and immediately began devouring his meal. It was the first food since the breakfast he had eaten with Meniu and her father that previous morning in Kohima.

What would they be thinking? What would Paula do when she learned? How would she learn? What could they do to get him released?

As he finished the last of his food, Donovan noticed a large envelope next to the oil lamp on the table. The serving girls picked up the empty bowls, bowed slightly, and left the hut. Nllamo moved the envelope over in front of Donovan.

"While you are here, for however long that may be, we want you to learn the history of the Naga people and how they have been oppressed by the Indian government."

"I came to Nagaland to study Naga culture, but not in these circumstances," Donovan replied.

"I apologize for that. It is unfortunate. The world can be very complicated, very difficult to understand sometimes. You can be assured that you will be treated with respect until we receive orders telling us what to do with you."

"Thank you for that," Donovan suddenly felt a deep fatigue.

Nllamo watched his prisoner closely. "Now you should rest again. When you awake, you can exercise a bit in the late afternoon when it is a bit cooler. Then, perhaps, you will be up to reading about the Naga people."

15

Donovan's sleep lasted past mid-afternoon as Nllamo predicted. He woke to the soft sound of monsoon rain on the roof. Unlike the night before, there was no accompanying storm, no other sounds except the calls of jungle birds or the muted murmurs of people in the clearing outside the hut. The moment was peaceful, his basic needs had been taken care of, and for the most part, his captors had shown no personal animosity towards him. He needed to think about his situation, to formulate a course of action.

What was clear was that he was the kidnapped hostage of a Naga guerilla revolutionary group being held at one of their jungle bases. His capture would be an international story by now. Chingmei would have reported it immediately, the international press would pick it up, and interest in his predicament would last for a few days unless there were further developments. The American Embassy in Delhi would become involved, as well as the State Department, but their efforts would inevitably lead back through India's political bureaucracy, to people such as Chingmei who might be able to contact the revolutionary groups. It was a circle with Chingmei very much in the middle. Donovan thought briefly about Meniu and what her reaction would have been when the kidnapping was discovered.

He thought more of Paula and home. Paula would have been shocked by the news and fearful for his safety, particularly since he had shared so much with her of the headhunting background of the Naga tribes. The university staff would be there to help her get through it, and friends and colleagues on the faculty would come also, even though a few of them would secretly be thinking that his own foolish risk-taking had brought it on himself. Some of them might be on vacation with their families, doing the simple, normal things that people take for granted until they are taken away from them. That is all he wanted now, for life to return to normal and to be home safe with Paula.

Despite Captain Nllamo's matter-of-fact statement that he would be killed if he tried to escape, logic told him he was more useful to the Naga cause alive than dead. The political reality was that very little of the Naga struggle was known outside the borders of India. All that the people in western countries seemed to care about was whether India and Pakistan would end up in nuclear war over Kashmir or whether India or China had the greater population problem. What the Naga freedom fighters needed was a way to get their story to the world in the same way that had been done in the second half of the twentieth century by scores of revolutionaries from South Africa to Palestine.

Donovan assumed that vigorous efforts were underway to secure his release. Meniu would have been frantic urging her father to do what he could. What Donovan needed was to provide a reason for his captors to want to release him. He had an idea, an obvious idea that might win his freedom but, first, he had some reading to do.

He got up from his cot and went to the table where Nllamo

had left the soiled manila envelope, which he opened. Inside were a book and two typed pages. The book was titled *Nagaland File: A Question of Human Rights*. It looked as if it had been passed among many readers as did the separate pages, the first of which was titled "Summary of Political Facts." It was a chronological listing of significant political events in the history of Nagaland. Donovan estimated he could finish reading the material by morning. This should please his captor and give him a basis to suggest the idea that might win him freedom. He stretched out on the cot, propped up the thin pillow for his head, and began to read the history of the subjugation of the Naga people.

16

"Read the summary sheets first," Captain Nllamo had told him, "it will give you an overview of what has happened."

"Yeah sure," Donovan said to himself, "this is exactly what happened to POWs in Korea and Vietnam, ideological indoctrination." Nevertheless, he did what Nllamo suggested. Even though he knew what he was about to read would be propaganda in one sense or another, he felt favorably predisposed towards the material.

The information sheets stated that the desire for Naga independence went back over sixty years to 1929 when all of India was under British rule. The British had classified the Naga Hills as an "excluded" area undoubtedly due to what they considered to be the primitive cultures of the hill tribes. The tribes were under the direct control of the governor of the state of Assam to the south. At that time, a group of Naga representatives gave a memorandum to a British commission arguing for independence on the basis that they were "quite different from those of the plains" and had "no social affinities with the Hindus or Muslims."

The first formal political movement for independence began in 1946 calling itself the Naga National Council. Zapu Phizo, the first president of the Council negotiated an agreement with the Governor of Assam stating that the Naga Hills would remain an autonomous part of India until 1956 at which time the Nagas would be free to decide their own political future. A national flag was designed with a red, yellow, and green rainbow against a blue background. Even Mahatma Gandhi, the most influential political leader in India, supported Naga independence. One month before the British left India in 1947, he said to a delegation of Nagas, "The Nagas have every right to be independent. We did not want to live under the domination of British India, but I want you to feel India is yours."

He had assured them, "If you do not wish to join the union of India, nobody will force you to do that."

Despite the backing of Gandhi, the Indian government revoked its earlier agreement with Zapu Phizo and the Naga National Council a month after it gained its independence from Great Britain. Gandhi was assassinated the following year.

As Donovan continued reading, he recalled newspaper photos of the great Indian pacifist taken when he was fasting to bring about the end of violence between Hindus and Muslims. Those pictures of Gandhi's gaunt body certainly captured world attention. That is what the Naga cause needed, to somehow get world attention focused on their situation. How ironic, he thought, that one of history's most successful battles for independence would result in the oppressed becoming the oppressor shortly after they came to power.

"That's not what Gandhi had in mind," Donovan said aloud.

If what Donovan was reading was historically accurate, the Indian government's political oppression quickly turned into violent suppression in the 1950's when the Naga National Council organized Gandhian-style civil disobedience, the same tactics that helped India win its independence from Great Britain.

The Indian military imprisoned Naga leaders, abolished tribal councils, and declared the Naga Hills a "disturbed area." Donovan smiled ruefully, recognizing the old semantical game that George Orwell had identified years before in which despots use language as a tool of political power. The Indian government first called Nagaland an "excluded" area, next "disturbed," now the word was "protected."

The Indian army assumed the task of crushing the Naga resistance. Predictably, the Nagas reacted by forming a guerrilla army of fifteen thousand fighters and declaring its own federal government. The Indian army responded by sending hundred thousand troops into the hills, and a long period of intense conflict lasted until 1964.

Donovan scanned the rest of the chronological outline with growing interest. He wondered what the American veterans of World War II who fought side-by-side with Naga soldiers against the Japanese at Kohima would think of the plight of their former allies. But then, how could they care about something they knew nothing about? Apparently, Pakistan cared enough to provide the freedom fighters with aid and sanctuaries during the 1960's. There was even a reference citing Naga contacts with the People's Republic of China, but nothing about American interest. How fickle the world was, Donovan thought. Some of those same American veterans no doubt were driving Toyotas and doing other business with the prosperous Japanese, the same Japanese who committed unspeakable atrocities against American Marines on the cruel islands of Saipan, Tarawa, and Iwo Jima fewer than fifty years ago.

The summary notes provided little detail of the ongoing violence except to imply that it was extreme enough to warrant a formal ceasefire in 1964. Peace talks with the Indian government, including direct talks with Indira Gandhi, followed but were unsuccessful. The ceasefire ended in 1972 when the government officially outlawed the Naga National Council, the Federal Government of Nagaland, and the Naga army.

Naga representatives signed an agreement called the Shillong Accord in November 1975. The purpose of the agreement was to end the violent conflict. Weapons were to be turned in at designated "peace camps," and more talks were planned to finally settle the Naga problem. The Shillong Accord became the event which fractionalized the Naga nationalistic movement, which had been unified up to that time. Because Zapu Phizo did not openly defy the Shillong Accord, two of his more powerful leaders broke away, forming the National Socialist Council of Nagaland.

At this point, the notes ended with an admission that there had been further splits among the revolutionary groups, creating at least four separate "underground" groups fighting each other as well as the Indian army. The Indian troops now served in Nagaland under the Armed Forces Special Powers Act which gave them extra-judicial powers. Apparently, the once-unified independence movement was now weakened by the "cult of the gun" and charges that some political ministers paid the "underground" movements for protection.

Donovan knew that factionalism was common among revolutionary groups. The American Civil Rights Movement, the Palestinian Liberation Movement, the anti-apartheid movement in South Africa, all had been fragmented. Why should the Nagas be any different given their history of tribalism? The unfortunate fact about the violence was that it could overshadow what appeared to be a legitimate struggle for independence.

Donovan briefly considered beginning to read the book left

on the table. But he found he was once again tired and in need of sleep. He turned off the oil lamp and returned to his cot. He could hear the sound of light rain starting up again as he drifted towards sleep thinking about the material he had just read.

17

The next morning Donovan was sweaty and tense, the product of hellish nightmares he tried to blot from his mind. He sat on the edge of his cot and half-heartedly went through his morning stretching. He toweled his body dry and began to think about the day ahead, his third in captivity.

His meal of rice and beans was already set out on the table. He imagined what this food would do to a digestive system only recently recovered from the ravages of "Delhi belly." He longed for his usual breakfast of orange juice, raisin bran cereal with bananas, a piece of toasted wheat bread, milk, and a slice of cantaloupe or honeydew melon.

More than anything, he missed Paula standing in the kitchen, dressed in a robins-egg blue bathrobe which only partly hid the contours of her still lovely body, a body which he had not loved enough since he began his affair with Meniu. She would be holding a cup of coffee, looking early-morning sleepy, but beautiful nevertheless. It could be he was getting what he deserved. As trite as it may sound, perhaps he was being punished for being such a bastard to Paula ... but by whom? God? Fate?

Donovan willed himself back to the present. He ate hurriedly, eager to finish the previous night's reading. The idea he had the night before was to offer to write a statement in support of the Naga cause. According to the Australian TV crew he met in the hotel bar in Delhi, that was how the Aussie doctor gained his release in Kashmir. He had already begun shaping the statement in his mind. First, he needed to go to the latrine. He opened the door and, as expected, found Ato and Lowang waiting to accompany him. The morning was hot and muggy, a condition that would be only slightly relieved by the afternoon showers.

Back in his hut, he began reading the book, "Nagaland File" which Nllamo had left him. The book presented a more detailed explanation of the events he had already read about. Included were letters from Naga leaders to Indian presidents, the texts of different agreements, manifestos of the various Naga underground groups, and reports on the many violations of civil rights in Nagaland over a thirty-year period. The book was a collaborative effort between a Naga scholar, Iuingham Luithiu, and an Indian woman activist, Nandita Haksar. The two met while both were graduate students at Jawaharlal Nehru University in Delhi in the 1970's. In their preface, the co-authors wrote, "It was our common concern for democratic rights that brought us together." This added to the credibility of the book, Donovan thought.

Donovan found himself moved by what he read and by the lyrics of a Naga anthem which introduced chapter one:

> *God bless my Nagaland*
> *Land that I love*
> *Stand beside her and guide her*
> *Through the night, with the light from above;*
> *From the mountains, through the valleys,*
> *To the meadows where I roam*
> *God bless my Nagaland*
> *My home, sweet home.*

Unabashed plagiarism, but wonderful nevertheless. Where had the first Nagas heard "God Bless America" and decided to take the words for their own? Was it during World War II at the Battle of Kohima, from American GI's who they fought with against the Japanese? Or, more absurdly, from a traveling Naga who somehow made it to a Flyers hockey game at the Philadelphia Forum and heard Kate Smith belt out the song, bringing the crowd to its feet each time she sang. Donovan smiled at the thought.

His reverie was interrupted by the guard, Lowang.

"Captain Nllamo says time for you to exercise." Lowang held the door to the hut open.

The designated exercise area was the clearing outside his hut which served as the central meeting place for the camp, a kind of all-purpose square. The guard pointed to the open space and made a circling gesture with his hand, which Donovan understood only in the most general way.

He still wore just his blue shorts. His earlier exposure to the sun had begun to turn his pale skin pink and the soles of his feet felt rough and bruised from walking barefoot for the past few days. For the first time, he realized someone had taken his shoes, no doubt to discourage an escape attempt. As if on cue, Lowang said, "Stay here, don't go." "Fat chance," Donovan thought, "just exactly where does he think I might go? Rangoon, in time for gin and tonics on the veranda of some grand hotel? Doesn't he know I don't have the slightest fucking idea where I am?" Besides, a small group of spectators had gathered to watch the latest performance starring their own American captive.

He began to walk the perimeter of the clearing, shaking out his arms and doing shoulder shrugs as he went along. This brought a reaction from some of the teenage boys who laughed and poked each other with each of Donovan's strange movements. Noticing their antics, he decided to give them a show. He stopped, did five leg squats in place, then stood and windmilled his arms above his head.

Two young female spectators joined him in the clearing, doing their best to imitate this last movement. Donovan could not help but admire the way their young breasts became taut and pointed as they rotated their arms above their heads. Paula and his university colleagues will never believe this scene actually ever happened, he thought, assuming he would ever have the chance to describe it to them.

He stood on his toes to begin a vertical stretch. His two imitators did the same, provocatively reaching for the sky, quite aware, it seemed, that Donovan enjoyed looking at their shapely, naked bodies. Halfway into his fifth stretch, he was jolted by the memory that this was what he was doing when he was kidnapped on the road to Mon.

He stopped exercising and walked towards his hut. "I want to go inside," he said to Lowang, who squatted languidly in front of the door. The time had come to act. As he left, the two young girls continued their stretching, stopping only when it was clear the tall American was no longer watching them.

Donovan skimmed through the last part of *Nagaland File*, eager to begin writing out the proposal he would give to Captain Nllamo when he saw him next. He was shocked by a 1978 report from the Naga People's Movement For Human Rights detailing the "types and forms of repression used by the military and paramilitary of India on the Nagas...." These included: "1) executions in public, 2) mass raping, 3) deforming sex organs, 4) mutilating limbs and body, 5) electric shocks, 6) puncturing eyes, 7) hanging people upside down, 8) putting people in smoke-filled rooms, 9) burning down of villages, granaries, and crops, 10) concentration camps, 11) forced starvation and labor."

If these charges were true, even if only some of these atrocities had happened, where had the international outrage been, the cries for justice, the demands for intervention? Was this another holocaust that the world turned its eyes away from, pretending these outrages never happened? As an educated American, Donovan had never heard of the Naga's struggle for freedom until he met Meniu and, until this moment, he never knew the extent of the crimes allegedly committed by the Indian army. He continued reading.

One especially gruesome report was given by an old lady from Kohima, the town where Donovan had stayed overnight with Chingmei and Meniu. According to the lady, whose name was Dzuvia, "a girl from the Lotha area was first raped and then hung upside down, after which sticks were thrust into her private parts. Her hands and legs were severed and her trunk was again molested. All this was done in front of the villagers who had been rounded up by the Indian Army. This act of bestiality was equaled by another in which a pregnant woman was shot in the legs after which a rope was tied round her neck and she was dragged around. In this process, the foetus came out, which they put in her mouth."

Donovan was appalled and disgusted by what he read. He realized the Indian government would have a different story to tell, but the book had a ring of truth to it.

Donovan set the book aside and took up the pen and paper he had requested the day before. It was clear to him what he had to do. He would write a statement calling attention to the struggle of the Nagas and to the history of abuse detailed in *Nagaland File*. He would show it to Captain Nllamo and offer to make a public declaration of support for the Naga cause in exchange for his freedom. If Nllamo wanted, he would make a video recording that could be sent to the media. Further, he would agree that, when he returned to his faculty position at the University of Rhode Island, he would devote his research and writing to telling the Naga story to the world. Even in his desperate situation, it occurred to him that no other American scholar had tread this ground before him. A whole new world of possibility and purpose opened up before him as he began to write.

The words came easily as they always did when he felt conviction and commitment to his subject. He stopped only to reference the notes and the book Nllamo had left him. He continued working even when the guard brought his lunch to him, leaving the meal untouched. Afterwards, he couldn't remember which guard it had been. He finished a first draft by mid-afternoon, made some minor edits, and then rewrote a more legible copy on a fresh piece of paper. He read it aloud to himself, testing different intonations to see how they sounded. He would be prepared in case he had to make his statement in front of a camera. As best as he could remember, that is what the kidnapped Aussie doctor had done.

Finished, he picked up the paper and opened the door to the hut. Ato squatted in his usual position, his eyes half-shut. He looked up at Donovan, smiled, and then rose slowly to his feet.

"What does Mr. Donovan want?" he asked.

"I want to see Captain Nllamo. Tell him I have something to give him."

"He is not here. He is gone away."

"What?" Donovan replied, "when will he be back?"

"I don't know, he didn't tell. Maybe many days or maybe

tomorrow." There was clearly nothing unusual to the guard about his superior having left the camp.

Donovan was flustered by the unexpected news. "But what am I supposed to do? I need to talk to him."

The smile on the young Naga's face turned to a more neutral expression. "You are to be in hut," he replied. "You are to stay in hut."

"Is there some way to contact him? I want to tell him I have written something for him to read."

"No, you talk when the captain returns. Now, you go back in hut." Ato opened the door to the hut and gestured to Donovan to enter. "I will bring you food."

Donovan did what he was told, sat at his table, and only picked at the meal that was brought to him. It was the same as all the previous meals he had had and all the meals he would have at the camp. How many more would there be before Nllamo returned from wherever he was? What did Nllamo's absence do to his theory that he was just like the Aussie doctor in Kashmir?

Confused, he lay down on his cot, stared at the ceiling of his hut, and tried to think through his predicament. The positive energy of the afternoon was gone. In its place, a feeling of depression took hold, a feeling that he no longer had control of his own fate. The evening shadows darkened the hut that was his prison as night came to the jungle camp.

18

Donovan had taken to sleeping naked on his cot. Every morning he would put his shorts on and ask the guard to take him to the latrine. During each visit to that reeking ditch, he would close his eyes and squeeze his nostrils shut just to get through what had become the most unpleasant part of each day. The three bathrooms in his house and, yes, even the unisex toilet in the faculty lounge at the University had become tabernacles in his mind, shrines at which he would ever after pay homage should he again have that opportunity.

His morning ritual took him from the latrine to the river for his once-a-day washing. This day, his fourth in captivity, luck was with him. There was no group of young Nagas there to draw him into their good-natured play. Two older women washed clothes against the rocks in the river. They looked up when he walked into the water, but then returned to their work.

He submerged himself up to his chest in the cooling waters of the river and removed his shorts. Without soap, the best he could do to clean his shorts was to rub the garment against itself and then put it back on. When he emerged from the river, the shorts dried quickly in the hot morning sun.

How strange we human beings are, he thought, the way we

establish routines, patterns of doing things that put a sense of order into the most unusual of circumstances. As he stood by the river pondering this thought and the long day ahead of him, the guard, Ato, appeared trotting down the path. He was in a hurry to deliver his message. "Professor," he called, "the captain has returned. He wants to see you right away."

The news delighted Donovan who immediately started back up the path to the clearing in pursuit of Ato who was hurrying to meet his leader. Nllamo stood at the entrance to Donovan's hut dressed in the same khaki and green that was his uniform.

"I understand you have written something that you want me to hear."

"Yes I have prepared a statement as we discussed."

Donovan noticed the captain was holding a cloth sack, and that two other men were with him. One held a video camera, the other a piece of equipment that appeared to be a tripod.

"Are you willing to allow us to make a video tape of you delivering this statement?"

"Yes, yes, of course. That is the idea; what I hoped you would ask."

"Fine, then let's go inside your hut and get it done." The men walked into the darkened hut where Donovan's breakfast had been set out on the wooden table as it was every morning. Nllamo looked around checking to see if there was anything unsuitable. He removed the food from the table and then addressed Donovan directly.

"I am sure you know without my telling you that this statement that you have written is a voluntary act on your part. We are not forcing you to do this." Nllamo stared at him, trying to assess his reaction.

"I understand that. You will see that I make that point right at the beginning." Donovan held out the papers. "Here, read it for yourself."

"No, that won't be necessary. We are going to ask you to sit at the table and deliver your statement. My assistants, as you can see, are prepared to videotape you."

"In my shorts?"

"No, Professor Donovan, how foolish do you think we are?" Nllamo tossed the canvas sack on the table. "Your pants and shirt are inside. They have been cleaned. Try to arrange your hair as you best like it. Go put your clothes on. The quicker we do this, the better."

"Do you have my shoes?"

"You don't need your shoes to make this tape."

Donovan dressed quickly, excited by what was happening, the moment he had planned and hoped for, the opportunity that might win his freedom. "Is there enough light in here to film?" he asked.

"We will leave the door open and do our best. Netsoho is a skilled cameraman. There's a reason we do not go outside. There are too many clues that such pictures might give to the Indian army as to where our camp is. Here, sit down and review your text while we check the lighting and camera angles." The film crew of two busied themselves adjusting their equipment and pushing back the door of the hut to just the right point. That done, a broad shaft of morning sunlight poured through the opening, illuminating the exact place at the table where Donovan sat. Nllamo stepped off to the side and took an odd stance, prompting Donovan to try to make a small joke. "All you need is a director's chair," he said.

The captain's lips curled into what Donovan thought was the beginning of a smile. "No, I am not the director," he replied, "that is Netsoho's job. I am, however, the first tape editor. Please notice I said the first editor, not the final editor."

Donovan looked perplexed but said nothing.

"Let me explain before we begin. It might help if at any point in your statement, I feel you have said something that will hurt the Naga cause, I will stop you. I will tell you what you said that is not acceptable. You then may decide to retake what you have said or you may choose to leave it as it is."

"Okay. That's fair."

"In other words, whatever we end up with on the tape is entirely up to you. Whether we choose to send the tape to the international media is entirely up to us."

Donovan did not need Nllamo to draw pictures explaining the connection between his statement being usable for the media and his own chance of being released.

"So someone else needs to approve what I say besides you," he asked.

"Exactly. My superiors will have the final say about the tape."

"Where are they? Are they here in the camp?"

"No."

"How long will it take to learn their decision?"

"All I can promise you is that I will deliver your taped statement with my own recommendation as fast as possible. The rest is out of my hands." Captain Nllamo turned both palms upward to emphasize his point.

"We should begin," Nllamo said, "before the morning sun moves in the sky and we lose the light."

Robert Donovan gathered himself. Captain Nllamo had just raised the stakes and it was time to be at his best.

Netsoho, the camera man, signaled with his hand to Donovan. "You can start anytime now," Nllamo explained.

Donovan took a deep breath and began. "My name is Robert Donovan. I am an American academic from the University of Rhode Island. At the moment, I am being detained by a group called the Nagaland Liberation Army somewhere in northeast India. The first thing I wish to do is to assure my wife, Paula, as well as my friends, colleagues, and students that I am in good health and that they should not worry about my wellbeing. Since I was brought here, my basic needs have been taken care of, and I have been treated with respect.

"The second point I wish to stress is that I have not been threatened or coerced in any way to say what I am about to say. My statements represent my current understanding of the situation in Nagaland based on the research I did before coming to India and what I have learned since coming here. Do I hope that this message will help secure my early release? Yes. Absolutely. Above all, I wish to be home safe with my wife whom I love very much. But this does not change the fact that my words come from my heart and are not someone else's words that I am being forced to say."

Captain Nllamo interrupted, signaling Netsoho to stop taping. Donovan wondered what he had done wrong. "That is very good, so far. But I have a suggestion to make."

"Please, go right ahead."

"Try to be, uh, how do you say that ... more concise. Remember how television works. Time is valuable."

"I understand." Donovan glanced at his notes, mentally condensing what he had written.

Nllamo gestured to his two assistants. "Okay," he said, "continue."

Donovan was encouraged by the exchange. The captain seemed pleased. Once again, he began to speak.

"Two points appear to be indisputable. The first is that the Indian government has not kept its word and granted the people of Nagaland the independence they desire. This promise was first made by the great Mahatma Gandhi in 1947 and reiterated by Nehru in 1952. The terrible irony, of course, is that, for years, India had been subjugated by the British government. Unfortunately, once the oppressed were given power, they became, in the case of Nagaland, the oppressor. From a sociological perspective, the Indian government is no different than the British were when their misguided ethnocentrism resulted in their belief that it was "the white man's burden" to control the darker races. If he were alive today, Mahatma Gandhi would be appalled at what has happened.

"The second point I wish to make is that since the early 1950's, the Indian Army has carried on a program of brutal repression characterized by atrocities and indiscriminate killing of tens of thousands of innocent Naga civilians. Evidence of this attempted genocide can be obtained from the Naga Vigil Human Rights Group or found in the book *Nagaland File: A Question of Human Rights*.

"Supporters of the Indian government's actions will argue that elections were held in 1963 and the Nagas accepted the Indian constitution at that time. However, the Naga people know that those elections were fraudulent, forced upon them by an occupying army of two hundred thousand troops."

Donovan looked at Captain Nllamo, who nodded his head in approval at what he was hearing.

"The question," Donovan continued, "is why there has not been world outrage over these violations of basic human rights, why these people have not been given their sovereignty as has been the case with so many other peoples around the world in the last half of the twentieth century.

"The reasons why little attention has been paid to the predicament of the Naga people are much too complex for me to understand fully, but I can guess at a few. For one, India has helped keep the Naga secret by making Nagaland a "protected" territory and limiting access to it except with a specially granted government entry permit.

"Another reason is that, unlike Kashmir, Nagaland is not the focal point of dispute between nations. There is no threat of nuclear war as there is between Pakistan and India. In fact, the neighboring country of Mynamar has collaborated with India in subjugating the Nagas. The rest of the world doesn't know or care about Nagaland.

"At the very minimum, the United Nations should investigate this question of Nagaland's independence. As with all things political, the issue is most complicated. There is more than one national resistance group, and they are often in conflict with one another. Violence has bred violence. But, with effort, these problems can be resolved and the Naga people given the freedom that Gandhi promised them almost fifty years ago.

"It is my intention, when I get home to the United States, to do my utmost to inform Americans of the Naga struggle. I will remind them that in World War II, brave Naga warriors fought side-by-side with American soldiers to defeat the Japanese at the battle of Kohima. When we needed their help, the Nagas were there. Now the people of Nagaland need our help. I think groups such as the American Legion and the Veterans of Foreign Wars may be interested in lobbying on behalf of their former allies."

Donovan looked up to see Captain Nllamo motioning him to conclude. He was done anyways. He looked back at the camera and said his last words, "I hope to be home soon. Love to all." His voice quavered a little as he finished.

Relieved that the ordeal was over, Donovan looked for feedback. "How did I do?"

"You did fine. You were very convincing, very credible."

"If I was convincing as you say, it is probably because I believe what I just said."

"You spoke as if you were a Naga."

"Thank you."

"You probably took too long, but we both know television shows only what it wants to show. Your words were far more than I expected."

"Does this mean the first editor approves?"

"Very much so. My report will say so quite strongly. Now I must take your tape to my superiors for their final approval."

Captain Nllamo stepped forward, bowed, and then shook Donovan's hand. He turned to leave and remembered something he had forgotten. "Professor Donovan, please take off your pants and shirt and give them back to the guards who will hold them for you until you need them again. I will return as soon as I can."

Donovan did as he was told. Alone again, wearing only his blue shorts, he began to feel more hopeful about his future. He had done well and, judging by the captain's reaction, it seemed likely that his recorded statement would be favorably received by Nllamo's superiors whoever they might be. Now, he told himself, he had to be patient. Waiting was the hard part.

PART FOUR

19

Henyong Konyak learned the rules of the Great Ang clan at age fifteen when he brought a slightly intoxicated Meniu back to her home after a night of courtship and drinking during the feast of Ouniebu. He knew, of course, as did all the members of the Konyak tribe, that Chingmei was the Great Ang of Mon, a powerful village chief who, with the help of the tribal council, governed the village, settling any disagreements or disputes over land and other matters.

What he did not know was that the Great Ang clan was an exclusive community closed to outsiders. Even though Henyong was born into the Konyak tribe, he was one of the Ben people, a commoner, and not an eligible candidate to marry a daughter of the Great Ang. Henyong had been told of the old custom that daughters of the royal clan once had to wear lead rings in their ears as a warning to unsuitable males that the girls were off-limits, but he did not make the connection. Surely this old-fashioned tradition no longer applied. Meniu wore no such lead rings, and didn't hesitate to respond when he began flirting with her shortly after they first met at the harvest. He learned of his mistake from his own father a few days after the celebration.

During a family meal Henyong noticed that his father,

Shankok, had an unusually stern expression on his face and did not talk much. This was out of character for his father who was normally jovial and outspoken. When the meal was over, Shankok motioned to his son. "Come, take a walk with me. I need to talk to you."

"Have I done something wrong?" Henyong asked, worried by his father's behavior.

"You have," Shankok replied, "but I don't think you are aware of it."

They walked out of their house onto a path that led out of the village. "One of the tribal council members came to me today with a warning from the Great Ang himself," Shankok said.

"Chingmei, Meniu's father?"

"Of course, do we have another village chief?"

"No, but I thought...."

"It doesn't matter what you thought," his father said, "what matters is that you listen to what I am about to tell you."

"Of course, father, you know I will, but I don't know what I have done wrong.

"You were seen spending time and flirting with Meniu during the harvest celebration. It is said that you brought her home to her father's house and left her there, after she had been drinking."

"That is true. She is a pretty girl, and we enjoy each other."

"I hope you have not enjoyed her too much. It would be a bad thing for our family." Shankok hesitated, seeing as he had expected, that his son did not understand the mistake he had made. "You must not spend time alone with Meniu again. You are not to flirt or do anything else with Meniu. It is forbidden. As a daughter of a Great Ang, she may only marry a boy from her own clan. I do not have to tell you that ours is not such a clan."

The reality of what his father was saying hit Henyong, and he understood all of it immediately. His first concern was for his family, particularly his father, who worked on Chingmei's tea plantation. Meniu was a nice girlfriend to have, but he had only just met her. He felt sorry for her that her life had to be so restricted by a stupid, ancient custom that no longer made sense. He knew what he must do.

"You need not worry any longer, father. Go tell the council member that nothing happened. I made an innocent mistake that won't be repeated. I will not spend any more time with Meniu."

Henyong thought, as did his father, that that would be the end of it, but it wasn't. As it turned out, the feeling he and Meniu both had for one another grew stronger each time they saw each other. That mutual attraction and the fact that both young people were strong-willed and independent made it inevitable that they would find ways to see each other despite the warnings.

Meniu received a similar lecture from her father explaining the old custom and his expectations of Meniu as far as marriage was concerned. Since she was returning to private school in Hyderabad once the Ouniebu celebration was over, she did not protest her father's edict, but when she came home again for the winter holidays, she found herself wanting to see the boy, Henyong, again.

It was Meniu who initiated their next meeting. She knew that Henyong, along with the other young males of the village, spent time with their friends in the morung, the dormitory-style meeting place for unmarried males. She sent a message to him saying that she had something important to tell him, and that she must do it in person. When his reply came back agreeing to meet her, she knew she had judged him correctly.

They met on a chilly, bright day in January at a pre-arranged spot outside of town on the banks of the Dikhu River. Meniu had chosen the spot so that they would not be seen by people from the village. When she arrived, she saw that Henyong was already there, standing silently by a large oak tree, looking out over the dark waters of the river. He was wrapped in a shawl and looked taller and more handsome than she remembered from the fall. He turned as she approached and, when he smiled at her in welcome, she felt a warmth throughout her body that surprised her.

The two teenagers stood awkwardly for a moment, neither knowing quite what to do next. Meniu broke the silence first.

"It was nice of you to come," she said, "I hope you don't think I was too bold to send you that message."

Henyong reached out and grasped both of her hands. "At first, I wasn't sure what to do. It was my father who told me I was not to see you, and he works for your father. I did not want to risk his losing the good job that he has."

"What changed your mind?"

"You said that you had something important to tell me. I was curious."

"Is that the only reason you came?" Meniu asked.

"No, uh, there are two other reasons. The first is that we are two young people who should not be bound by the rules of the past which are out of date."

"And the other reason."

Henyong smiled again. "I wanted to be your friend," he said.

"Then that is the important message I have for you, that we will be friends. And if our friendship is strong, we can meet here from time to time so as not to upset our fathers."

The two were quiet for a moment considering the meaning of what they had just said. Henyong broke the silence.

"I like your message and agree with it. Now that is settled, we can enjoy ourselves."

"I brought the makings of a small picnic," Henyong said. He dropped his back-pack on the ground and took from it a tin of chilies and a jug of rice-beer. He had a small blanket which he spread out so they could sit and enjoy their food.

"I must be careful not to drink too much so that you do not have to carry me home."

"Don't worry, I will keep you sober," he said. "How much time do you have?"

"I can stay for a few hours," Meniu replied, "My father is away in Delhi, and my mother doesn't worry about me."

They sat together on the blanket sipping the rice-beer to keep warm and nibbling on the chilies. They talked about the same things all teenagers talk about, their plans for the future. Henyong had only traveled as far as Kohima and was very interested in learning about the strange-sounding places Meniu had been to while at private schools or traveling with her parents.

For her part, Meniu met an entirely different boy than she remembered from the harvest celebration. Instead of the flirting and showing off that was part of the festive mood, she found a thoughtful young man who took his time answering her questions. He spoke with a soft voice that made him appear older than he was. She told him of her plans to attend college in the United States after high school, and was privately disappointed to hear him say he had no plans for college since his father expected him to find a job and contribute to the support of the family.

When it was time to go, they both knew each other better and knew also that they had begun a friendship whose depth they had just started to tap.

"I will contact you the same way when I come home again in April," Meniu said.

"We will meet at the same place ... and drink more rice-beer."

"But not too much or else you will have to carry me home." They laughed together.

"Then we would be in trouble."

"Your face is flushed," Meniu said, pointing to him.

"So is yours," he said, catching her outstretched hand and pulling her to him on the blanket.

She did not resist, rolling over to be beside him on the blanket. He bent down to kiss her, softly at first and then with more pressure. She pulled her shawl off her shoulders and unbuttoned her blouse so that he could touch her all the ways he had touched her three months earlier at the harvest festival.

When he had done that, and she could feel him hard against her thigh, he pulled back from her and, without saying a word, asked the question with his eyes. She understood what he asked and nodded her answer, pulling him into her, and though he tried to be gentle and she felt the discomfort, the intensity of their youthful passion drove them forward and, soon, they were one, gentleness and pain joined in their pleasure.

This first meeting of Meniu and Henyong established a pattern for future secret rendezvous that continued throughout Meniu's years away as she finished highschool and then her university degree. Since they could not see each other in public in the village of Mon, they continued to meet by the Dikhu River and then, just to change their routine, moved to an even more remote glade in the forest. They met on school vacations when Meniu was home and only then when she was able to leave home without arousing suspicion. Both looked forward to their infrequent meetings as there were always fresh things to talk about, new things they had learned.

Henyong's adolescent body grew more muscular as he developed into an attractive dark-eyed, dark-haired young man. Meniu enjoyed admiring his body and looks, but she took special delight in the way Henyong thought and expressed his ideas.

"Isn't there some way you can go on to college?" she asked him. "Your grades are good enough."

The answer was always the same. "This is not my time," he would say, "My family needs me. Perhaps later when things change."

What Henyong said was true, in part, but there was something else that was driving him to stay in Nagaland, a cause for which he was willing to postpone his own individual goals. He had learned of the history of the Naga tribes' struggle for independence from India, and, as an idealistic, impressionable youth, he was an easy target to be recruited into the movement.

There were a number of separate guerilla groups, each with its own agenda and strategies for resisting Indian rule. Henyong learned of one of them in junior year of high school from Photon, a school acquaintance, who was already active in the movement. The group called itself the Nagaland Liberation Army. A few of his friends had left their homes and gone to live in the guerilla camps where they studied the history of the Indian betrayal and trained in guerilla warfare. While there, they adopted the dress and some of the customs of the Naga tribes as they were before the Indian army occupied the Naga hills.

It would have hurt Henyong's father too much if he left home, so Henyong decided not to live in the guerilla camps. Besides, there was another way that he could help the movement and still contribute to the support of his family. Photon encouraged him to try to obtain a job with one of the many administrative agencies of the Indian government. Once employed, he was to work hard to establish himself as reliable and trustworthy. After a period of time, depending on the agency he worked at, he might be in a position to obtain information that was useful to the guerilla movement. According to Photon, there were many such young Nagas working for the Indian government who were providing information to the underground freedom fighters. They passed on news and data regarding troop movements, the schedules of supply convoys, construction projects, policies and procedures, as well as major personnel changes.

As his high school graduation approached and Henyong developed a stronger conviction about the justice of Naga independence, the idea of becoming an informant for the freedom fighters took on greater appeal to him. He especially liked the irony that those he would be spying on would be paying him as he did it. He did not tell his family what he was doing, nor did he tell Meniu, as he worried about how she might feel about him with her father being so influential a person. Instead he began his search for employment.

It took him almost six months following graduation before he went to work for a supply unit of the Indian army. The Quartermaster Corps' role was to supply the military and administrative personnel in the northeastern section of the Naga hills with everything they needed to carry out their mission. Army engineers built a large warehouse facility at the outskirts of Mon to store the food, weapons, vehicles, machine parts, uniforms, ammunition, and basic administrative supplies to sustain the occupation of Nagaland. Henyong went to work in the warehouse unloading and stocking incoming supplies and then loading them on to the green army trucks which traveled in armed convoys throughout the territory.

Those supply convoys were the favorite targets of the guerillas. A successful ambush not only struck a blow against the occupying forces, but provided badly needed provisions and equipment. Knowing this, the army assigned a platoon of soldiers to each convoy. Alert for a guerilla attack, the soldiers rode in the back of trucks at the front and rear of the convoys, their automatic weapons and machine guns aimed into the jungle forest on either side of the road.

Henyong found the repetitive manual labor boring. He did not mind the physical work, but there was nothing to challenge his mind. Meniu had gone away to college in the United States, and he would not see her again until the spring. He tried to keep his spirits up by telling himself he was helping the underground movement but, in fact, he was not yet in a position to learn anything of value. He would meet his contact from the camps to tell him about the types of goods and equipment that had arrived at the supply depot recently. Photon acted as if the information was old news and of limited value. When Photon questioned him about future convoy schedules, Henyong had little to tell him.

It was during this period that Henyong began to doubt himself and, for the first time in his life, he periodically felt depressed. Meniu, the love of his young life, was thousands of miles away studying at an American university, and he could neither talk to her by telephone nor exchange letters. Many of his male friends from the morung now spent most of their time choosing their wives and planning families of their own. He was working at a meaningless job with no future, and his romantic dream of helping the underground movement seemed empty.

The treatment he received at his work made his situation even worse. The soldiers who supervised the young Nagas who did the manual labor in the warehouse were poorly educated young men from the rural areas of India. Listening to their conversations, Henyong concluded that most of them had ended up in the army because there was no other work in the villages where they lived. As a group they seemed ignorant and loutish. What bothered him most was that it was clear that the soldiers harbored a deep prejudice against the natives of the Naga hills. While there was no actual violence or physical mistreatment, the soldiers delighted in making fun of the workers and engaging in practical jokes intended to embarrass and humiliate them.

One soldier in particular, a corporal named Singh, seemed fixated on tormenting Henyong. Singh was a short, overweight man whom Henyong judged to be thirty years old. His receding hairline, hawk nose, and blackened teeth made him a decidedly unmilitary-like figure. His favorite joke was to use the microphone at the front desk of the cavernous warehouse to announce: "Would worker Hungdong please report to the desk on the double." Henyong, not recognizing the name the first time it was called, paid no attention to the summons. When Singh repeated the call for "worker Hungdong" over and over, Henyong heard loud laughter in the background. Finally a fellow worker came to tell him the announcement was for him. He hurried up through the rows of stacked supplies to the desk where Corporal Singh was sitting surrounded by three other Indian soldiers. Unaware that he was the butt of a joke, Henyong was apologetic.

"I did not understand you were calling me, Corporal."

"That is alright," Singh said in a pleasant tone, "perhaps I mispronounced your name. Tell me how to say it so that I may get it right next time."

"My name is pronounced Henyong, Corporal."

Corporal Singh could barely contain himself. "I thought that is what I said. Isn't that so, gentlemen?" Singh turned to the soldiers at his side who covered their mouths with their hands as they nodded agreement. "Let me try it again."

Corporal Singh flicked the switch on the microphone in front of him and slowly repeated his announcement, accentuating each word. "Will worker Hungdong please report to the desk on the double." With that, Corporal Singh and the men at his side burst into howls of laughter, doubling over and slapping their knees in glee. Henyong stood there totally flustered, and then he got the joke. He was being made a fool, and the Indian soldiers enjoyed it. Without smiling, he turned and went back to his work while, behind him, the men roared in laughter at his expense.

Corporal Singh repeated the same joke so often that first year that it eventually became stale and even Singh's lackeys stopped laughing. Singh seemed to have an odd attraction to Henyong that drove him to further harass the young Naga. One day in the spring, a few weeks before Meniu's expected return from the United States, Singh struck again.

When Henyong reported to work at 8 o'clock each morning, he had to sign a timecard on a board next to the corporal's desk. As he was signing in, one of the Indian soldiers spoke to him using his correct name.

"You, Henyong," he ordered, "drive that dolly of tyres back to the truck section and see that the tyres are properly stacked according to size."

Henyong nodded agreement. He was accustomed to driving the electric motorized carts that pulled dollies loaded with equipment behind them. As he walked to the dolly, he noticed the truck tyres were stacked unusually high, three rows of six tyres standing on end when normally only two rows were stacked. He thought nothing of it as the restraining chains that held the tyres on the dolly were secured. He sat in the cart and stepped on the pedal that propelled the cart towards the truck section at the rear of the warehouse. As he started up, he saw Corporal Singh and a group of his men watching him. He did not see the man who had given him the order sneak to the back of the dolly and undo the restraining chains that kept the tyres in place.

The inevitable happened as the third tier of medium-sized truck tyres were jostled free and careened off the dolly dragging the lower rows of tyres with them. The tyres landed on end, picking up speed as they hit the warehouse floor. They rolled in every direction knocking over everything in their path. The industrial shelving laden with equipment and materials collapsed from the impact of the tyres strewing the floor with their contents. Henyong, oblivious to the chaos happening behind him, drove forward until a tremendous crashing noise shocked him into awareness. He braked and jumped out of the cart just in time to see the last tyres take out their final targets.

He stood in the aisle devastated by the wreckage he had created. Then he heard the screams of laughter coming from the soldiers around Singh's desk. Anger welled up within him, anger that made him want to rush to the front of the warehouse and beat them all senseless. Then he heard Corporal Singh's voice calling him on the warehouse microphone.

"Worker Hung-Dong, get up here on the double and clean up this bloody mess you have caused." The microphone remained on and wild laughter echoed throughout the warehouse.

The incident with the dolly in the warehouse had an unanticipated effect on Henyong. At first, it took all that he could muster just to manage his rage. The fact that his father's failing health, attacks of emphysema brought about by excessive smoking, was preventing him from working full-time on Chingmei's tea plantation was a mitigating factor. Henyong's family needed the money he brought home. And so he, along with his fellow laborers, put up with the ongoing abuse from Corporal Singh and his men.

The thought that Meniu's return from the United States was drawing even closer helped him fight off depression. They would talk about their future together. He wanted to learn how she felt about the question of Nagaland's independence from India. They had not talked much about it, and he did not know her thoughts. What he did know was that his own conviction about a free and independent Nagaland had been hardened by the incident with the dolly. Corporal Singh's treatment of Henyong and the other Naga workers was unacceptable and should not be tolerated. The only reason he and his friends put up with it was that they had become dependent on the money. India must leave Nagaland and take their army and all the Corporal Singhs with them.

That was how Henyong now began to think. Unwittingly, Corporal Singh had transformed an uncertain believer into a committed convert.

It was the middle of May when Singh's treatment of Henyong began to change. Singh sent one of his men to the area of the warehouse where Henyong was busy unloading and stacking medical supplies. The soldier told Henyong that Corporal Singh wanted to see him. Henyong immediately steeled himself for another joke at his own expense.

He was surprised to find Singh by himself at his desk. Usually there would be a group of underlings just waiting to roar at their leader's latest stunt. What kind of joke could it be, Henyong thought, if there were no jackals around to howl and make the head jackal feel big.

"Sit down, Henyong," Singh said, "I want to talk with you." Henyong did as he was told, still on guard.

"I hope you are not still angry with me for the little joke we played on you with the tyres."

"That is over. I have forgotten about it," Henyong lied.

"Fine, that is good," Singh smiled, as a thin stream of red betel juice dribbled from one corner of his mouth. He looked as if he were bleeding.

"Those little pranks help relieve the monotony of the work," Singh continued. "Don't you agree the work can be monotonous?"

"Sometimes."

"Well, as the person in charge of this unit, I have to do certain things to be sure my men don't get bored. You do understand?"

Henyong nodded, uncertain where this conversation was going.

"Well, today is one of those days when I have a little treat for them. I am taking them to visit the women in the shack outside the base," Singh raised his eyebrows lewdly. "What do you think? That should take care of the monotony."

"I guess so," Henyong replied. He knew that all over Nagaland temporary camps serving as whorehouses had been set up to satisfy the sexual needs of the Indian army. Whores from Calcutta and Delhi came to the camps where, unfortunately, they were joined by Naga women down on their luck.

"The reason I am telling you all this is that I want you to be in charge of the desk while we are gone. It will only be a few hours, and there are no shipments coming in or going out this afternoon. We will be leaving right after lunch. What do you think? Consider it as a kind of promotion."

Henyong couldn't believe what the corporal had just told

him. His enthusiasm was apparent in his voice. "I will do my best, corporal."

"We are leaving directly after lunch. All you have to do is answer the phone and take messages. If anyone asks where I am, tell them I am out on a detail and will be back by 4 o'clock."

Henyong nodded.

"Fine, now get back to work and report back here at 1 o'clock."

"Yes, corporal. Thank you for giving me this new responsibility."

Corporal Singh and his men left for the whorehouse on schedule. Before they left, Singh made an announcement that Henyong would be in charge until they returned. This set off some good-natured teasing from Henyong's fellow workers who called him "Corporal Henyong" as they passed by the desk. The joking over, they returned to their work leaving Henyong alone.

While there was nothing of interest on the desk itself, it did not take Henyong long to find what he wanted. He opened the top right drawer and found that Corporal Singh had foolishly left a dispatcher's master schedule clipped to a manila folder containing other documents. Henyong felt a rush of adrenaline as he recognized the importance of the information. Listed on the report were the dates of shipments that would be leaving the warehouse through the month of June. The schedule also listed the general contents of the shipments as well as the destinations to which they were being sent. The papers inside the manila folder provided specific details for each shipment. Henyong tore a page from Corporal Singh's notepad and began to copy the information from the master sheet. He knew instinctively his notes would be of great interest to Photon and the underground movement. As he quickly jotted down the details of future shipments, he realized that, with this act, he was now an active member of the resistance.

Meniu returned home a week later and immediately sent a message to Henyong suggesting they meet at the river. Nine months had passed since they had last seen each other. Awkward at first after their long absence, the young lovers talked away their nervousness until they felt confident they still felt the same way about each other as they had when Meniu went away last August.

Meniu wore black shorts with a blue and white University of Rhode Island shirt that got Henyong's attention.

"Is your new school paying you to advertise for them?" he asked.

Meniu laughed and for the next ten minutes she talked non-stop about her experiences. Henyong learned about the dormitory she lived in ("it sounds like our morung"), her studious roommate from New Jersey, the quaint little village of Kingston where the university was located, the bars the students drank at and the beautiful beaches in Narragansett and South Kingstown. ("I went swimming in the Atlantic Ocean in early October; can you believe it!") She told him how well she had done in her classes and about her professors, a few of whom she thought to be strange and eccentric. ("This math instructor actually stands on the window sills when he lectures!")

"One of them, a Professor Donovan and his wife, Paula, invited me to their house during the holidays. They were very nice to me."

Henyong listened to the enthusiasm in Meniu's voice. As she spoke Henyong had ambivalent feelings. He was happy for Meniu whom he cared so much about, but another part of him was envious of all the life experiences he was missing.

Sensing that perhaps she was talking too much about herself, Meniu changed the focus of her conversation. "And Henyong, I have begun working for the international admissions office. By the time you are ready to go off to college, I will know how to help you get a student visa and how even to help you get financial aid."

"That won't be for a while," he replied, "my father is not well, and the pay I bring home from my job at the army supply center helps at home."

"How do you like your job?" she asked.

"There isn't much to like. It's just a job. Nothing as interesting as what you are doing."

"There must be something, some funny things that happened to you."

"Not really," Henyong's eyes dropped as he decided not to tell Meniu about the jokes Corporal Singh had played on him. "There is one new thing I want to tell you, but I want to ask a question first."

"What is it?" Meniu noticed the serious tone of Henyong's voice.

"What is your opinion of the underground movement? What do you think of Nagaland being its own nation, no longer part of India?"

Momentarily stunned, Meniu knew enough about how some young Nagas were joining the underground movement to guess why Henyong was asking the question. As he looked at her, waiting for her answer, she chose her words carefully.

"I think my opinion has been formed by what my father has said over the years about the underground. Now that you have asked, I don't believe I know enough about it to actually have my own opinion."

"What is your father's opinion?"

"My father has been part of the government as you know.

He has worked hard to help improve the lives of the people who live in the Naga hills."

"That doesn't answer my question. How does he feel about Nagaland being an independent country?"

"In his heart, my father believes in the idea of a free Nagaland, but he doesn't believe the tribes would be able to come together to rule ourselves successfully. He doesn't feel the time is right."

"Why does he think that way?"

"He says the movement itself is divided, that there is always fighting and killing among the different groups."

"That is true. I will have to think about your father's opinion.'

"Henyong, tell me why you ask me these questions. Have you joined the underground? Tell me if you have. You know I won't repeat it."

For some time, Henyong had been bothered that he had no one to talk to about his involvement with the "freedom fighters" as he preferred to call the underground movement. Photon was available only sporadically and then just for short periods of time.

Once he began to talk, it spilled out of him. He told her about his strong belief that India had broken the promises that Gandhi had made; he told her of Corporal Singh's prejudice and mistreatment of himself and the other workers; he told her that his role was to pass on information that would help the movement.

"Tell me you won't be involved in any violence."

"You don't have to worry about that."

As he continued, Meniu was struck by the realization that her handsome young boyfriend was growing up into a young man with a mind of his own and a sense of purpose. Though her grasp of the underground movement was limited, Henyong's involvement in it seemed somehow daring and romantic. Her father was wrong about a lot of things.

She reached to touch Henyong's face when he stopped talking. "Be careful," she said, "I need you to be here when I come home."

Henyong was relieved and exhilarated by the support he felt from Meniu. Of course, he had not told her about the information he had passed on to Photon about the schedules of the truck convoys that would be leaving the warehouse in June. That could wait until later.

"Are you ready for a swim?"

"The waters will be cold."

Henyong jumped to his feet, took off his pants and shirt and plunged into the river. "I will keep you warm," he cried.

Meniu left her clothes on and approached the water gingerly. Henyong reached out to her. When the water rose to her waist, she pulled the university shirt over her head and tossed it back on shore. Meniu slid into his waiting arms and the two lovers swirled in the waters of the Dikhu River.

20

During her four years at the University of Rhode Island, Meniu's feelings for Henyong deepened. Whenever she thought of her future, Henyong was a part of it. Perhaps as a way to help her get through the yearlong absences, she began to romanticize their relationship. Not only was their love secret and forbidden, an idea that she found often in the literature she read as part of her classes, but her lover was an agent for an underground nationalist movement trying to liberate her people.

Back home at the end of her sophomore year, she came upon an old Naga legend in a book in her father's library. She felt the tale described their love perfectly and was eager to share it with Henyong. "Listen," she read to him as they picnicked at their meeting place by the river. "Two rivers, the Teesta and the Rangeet are lovers who had to flee the mountains to hide their forbidden love. One came down in a straight line, led by a partridge; the other zigzagged, led by a cobra, and they were united at Pashoke. What do you think? Does that sound like us?"

"I want to be the one led by the partridge," Henyong said, "I don't like snakes."

"You are silly," Meniu said, "the cobra will protect you along the way."

"Who do I need to be protected from?"

"From our fathers, of course," Meniu burst into laughter and the two lovers rolled into each other's arms.

Before she became involved with Robert Donovan, most of Meniu's social activities at the university centered around the international students' club. Here she enjoyed meeting other young people from around the world and took comfort that they too were new to the American culture. She made many friends, but she did not have any romances until her friendship with the professor became more intimate.

When that happened, it never occurred to her to tell Henyong what she had done. It was true that she had strong feelings for Robert Donovan, but those were different from her affection for Henyong. Donovan was kind and gentle, and he helped her cope with her loneliness and being away from Henyong. She needed him to hold her as he did. He was wonderful to be with, someone she loved for being her lover during this difficult phase of her life. But Robert Donovan, older and married, had never been a threat to Henyong. Henyong, she realized, was the first love of her life, and even though their fathers were against their being together, he would be the last love of her life.

For his part, Henyong showed little interest in any of the many young Naga women who flirted with him to let him know they were available. He and Meniu worked out a schedule of once-a-month phone calls during her second year. Henyong looked forward to the calls but, at their conclusion, he always felt frustrated and envious that Meniu's busy and exciting life was so much more interesting than his own. To deal with the frustration, he devoted his energy to his work at the army supply depot and his other role as an informant for the Naga Liberation

Army. He lived at home and helped support the family while his father struggled with his illness.

For the first two years, Henyong took satisfaction from his dual roles. Shortly after he passed on the schedules from Corporal Singh's desk, Photon told him the information had been put to good use.

"What exactly does that mean?" Henyong asked. "What happened?"

"Just what I said," Photon replied, "The movement has benefited from what you did. That is all I can tell you. Besides it is better for you this way. The less you know, the less you can tell if you were to be questioned."

"But I don't really feel that I am a real part of what is happening."

"I assure you that you are playing an important role. My superiors are pleased with your work."

"But who are they?"

"That is something else you don't need to know for reasons I –"

"I understand that, but don't I ever get to meet anyone in the underground besides you?"

"Not unless you want to come live in the camps and, frankly, you are more valuable to us where you are now."

Henyong appeared skeptical, a skepticism which Photon addressed. "Think of all the great spies you have read about. All of them worked alone without any recognition. The only time they received any publicity is when they were caught or switched to the other side. Isn't that so?"

Henyong was far from an expert on the great spies of the world, but the movies he had seen or the little he had read on the subject confirmed what Photon had just said. It was okay to work in anonymity, especially if your lover considered what you were doing to be romantically heroic. Besides, his family appreciated his help.

It wasn't as if the chance to obtain information valuable to the movement occurred every day. Most days he just labored at the warehouse. Corporal Singh did not feel the need to relieve the boredom for his men by taking them to the whorehouse more than three times a year. When the group left, Singh still had Henyong watch the desk, but Henyong did not always find the valuable dispatcher schedules as he did the first time. Still, Henyong watched and listened and passed on whatever he could to Photon.

Then Henyong began to learn what had happened as a result of the intelligence he was providing. The government-controlled press and media reported periodic "skirmishes" between army troops and the underground, but gave very few specifics as to casualties or the reason for the clashes. From time to time, he would overhear Singh ranting to his men about "another blasted shipment lost" or having to "reship those medical supplies as they did not get through."

At first, Henyong felt good about such news, but one day, in his third year at the warehouse, what he was doing became far more serious. That morning found Singh bemoaning the death of two soldiers who had been in basic training with him. "Killed by those fucking, sneaky savages," he said, "They were as good as they get." He looked around wildly, his dark eyes venomous with rage. "I'll promise you this," he said to his men, "those bloody fucking black savages will pay for this or I don't know this man's army."

From that moment on, Corporal Singh's and his men's treatment of the Naga workers changed. The environment in the warehouse became tense with hostility. Trips to the whorehouse ceased, and Henyong no longer sat at the desk in Singh's absence.

Corporal Singh turned out to be right about the Indian army's capacity for revenge. Henyong was visiting with his friends at the morung a week after Singh's news about the death of his army comrades. The group lounged on the porch helping mend some communal fishing nets when a middle-aged man whom they recognized as being from the village of Tamlu approached them in a high state of excitement. "The soldiers have taken away our men," he shouted, barely coherent, "They shot them, killed them all, and brought their bodies back to the village square."

Henyong and his friends quieted the newcomer, bringing him water to drink. "Why did they do such a thing?" they asked him.

The man swallowed his water and then looked directly at Henyong, or so it seemed to Henyong. "They say men from Tamlu ambushed the supply convoy and killed their soldiers. We did not do that. No man from Tamlu did that. It was the underground, the army knows that. You had better be on guard. The soldiers are very angry and may come here next."

Despite the warning, the army did not come to Mon, but it was this incident that caused Henyong to reconsider what he was doing. It wasn't so much that he was bothered by the deaths of the Indian soldiers during the ambush of the supply convoys. The army had committed horrible atrocities against the Naga people over the past thirty years and deserved what they got. It was the army's reprisals against innocent Nagas that disturbed Henyong greatly. In a way, the information he provided led to the ambushes which resulted in the reprisals. Though he might not be directly responsible for those deaths, he was the first link in the chain of events that ended with the men from Tamlu being shot.

Shaken by these events and disheartened by the negative mood at the warehouse, Henyong decided to change the direction of his life. Fortunately, his father's health had improved some so that he was able to return to full-time work. He had a higher paying position as an office worker at the lumber company. Though he didn't talk much about it, he seemed happy to no longer be working for Chingmei Konyak. His father had even begun encouraging Henyong to strike out on his own and, if that meant pursuing more education, that would be alright too.

By the time Meniu was finishing her senior year, Henyong had made up his mind. He would leave his job at the warehouse and begin a college education, most probably in Calcutta where there were a few business schools likely to admit him. There were so many things to discuss with Meniu that it was impossible to do them justice on the telephone. (How could he ask her to be his wife on the telephone?) Instead he told her that his life was changing, and he had new and exciting things to talk to her about, but they could wait until she returned home.

He was mildly disappointed to learn she would be returning home later than usual this year because she had work to do with the university admissions department in Bombay, Madras, Calcutta, and Delhi. He hoped the American professor who was coming to Nagaland with Meniu to do research would not get in the way of their reunion. These were just small inconveniences, Henyong thought. More importantly, Meniu had sounded eager to learn about his plans. As for the small delay in her returning, it was okay. They would spend the rest of their lives together.

Meniu was expected home on June 8th. The spring had been an especially rainy one, but when Henyong awoke that morning, the sun shone brightly, a sign he interpreted as a celestial celebration of Meniu's new university degree and their love together. He was proud of her accomplishment and, now that he had decided to continue his own studies, he felt less daunted that she had more formal education than he.

He had given Corporal Singh notice that he was leaving three weeks earlier, wanting to have his days free when Meniu returned. Singh stared silently at him for an uncomfortably long time the day Henyong quit. Though he had hoped to stay on and be paid for at least another two weeks, Singh ended that idea abruptly. "If you don't want to work here anymore," Singh said curtly, "we don't want you hanging around. You're finished as of right now. You can pick up your last pay on Friday. Now, get out of here."

Henyong could barely contain his eagerness as he waited in the village to hear Meniu was home and wanted to be with him. He spent most of his time at the morung, making sure everyone knew he was there and where he could be found. He kept his eye out for Photon, his link to the underground. He needed to tell him that he had left the warehouse and would no longer be a source of information. The long day passed and, as dusk settled over the village, Henyong resigned himself to the fact that Meniu had been delayed. He went home to his family who, sensing his mood, left him alone.

The next morning, the rising sun was blotted out by heavy monsoon cloud cover. Henyong decided not to wake his sleeping parents and left for the village without eating. The shops were just opening, and he was the first customer at the counter of the small café that was his favorite. He exchanged the usual pleasantries with the owner and his wife, ate hurriedly, and left for the morung.

The streets of the village were still quiet in the early morning. The air was heavy with humidity, and Henyong began to sweat, which made him feel even more anxious than he already was. He did not want to go through another day without word from Meniu. The waiting made him feel helpless. He wished there was a way to contact her, to talk to her, to hear her voice.

As he turned up the path to the morung, he was surprised to see six young men talking animatedly on the porch. Henyong knew them all. Two of them were living in the dormitory temporarily which explained their presence, but it was quite early for the others to be there. Something must have happened. His heartbeat quickened. He had a sudden premonition that whatever it was the young men were talking about, it had something to do with Meniu. One of the men spotted him and came running down the steps of the porch to meet him. Henyong braced himself for the bad news.

The young man, whose name was Achin, blurted out the details of what he knew. Henyong heard only the key points, the ones he most needed to hear.

"We were coming to find you. Word has come that the underground has kidnapped an American university professor who was on his way here with the Great Ang and Meniu. Meniu and her father were not hurt. They are still in Kohima while the army investigates the kidnapping. But Meniu is okay. You don't have to worry."

Henyong tried to make sense of what he was hearing. While he and Meniu had succeeded in hiding their relationship from their families, the same was not true with his friends whom he had known all of his life. Achin knew that Henyong's main concern would be Meniu's safety.

Henyong joined the group on the porch of the morung trying

to sort out the facts from the distorted versions that were already taking shape. It was unclear which underground group had taken the American and, of course, no one knew yet why or where he had been taken. Henyong hoped it was not the Nagaland Liberation Army, the group for whom he had worked as an informant. As best as he could understand, kidnapping the American who had been so kind to Meniu had nothing to do with fighting for an independent Nagaland. The more he thought about it, the more furious he became. There was one person who might know which group did this stupid thing, and he knew how to find him. He thanked his friends for their concern and left to contact Photon.

He and Photon had set up a system for Henyong to use when he needed to arrange a meeting. It was simple, yet safe. Henyong would go to the café where he had breakfast and leave a message with the owner that he had a catch of fish to sell to Photon. The message would somehow reach Photon who would send his reply back to the café. Photon was a fish broker who collected catches from villages in this section of the hills and trucked them to Kohima for resale in the market place. The job earned him money and was ideal for his work with the underground.

Another long day passed without any word from Meniu. Rumors swept through the village about what had happened. Soldiers in jeeps and trucks drove through the streets displaying their weapons menacingly. The effect was unnerving to everyone. Finally, in the late afternoon, Henyong returned to the café for the fourth time. A message from Photon said he would meet him at the morung at 7 o'clock that evening to discuss the price of the fish catch.

By the time Henyong arrived at the morung, he was highly

agitated and the questions of the assembled crowd only further irritated him. "How is Meniu, Henyong? Has the American been killed? Will our chief be coming home? How did he allow this to happen? Will the soldiers take revenge on our village?" Because Nagaland was a "protected" territory, the Indian government controlled the flow of news through all of the official media into the Naga Hills. Both television and radio had mentioned the kidnapping of Robert Donovan, but no other details were given. The Naga people learned to depend on their own grapevine for news.

Photon had joined the Naga Liberation Army when he was in high school, soon after both of his parents were killed when a bus overturned and crashed into a ravine. An average teenager in every way, Photon found his purpose and identity in the underground movement. Unfortunately, his emotional maturity did not keep pace with his new role. He became overly officious, showing little respect to others who did not have his idealism and single-mindedness. There was talk in the village that he mistreated his girlfriend who shared his bungalow.

Now as he saw Henyong approaching in the early evening light, he pointed his finger to indicate they needed to move behind the building for privacy. Out of earshot, the two young men faced each other, Photon on guard, aware that Henyong would be upset by the events of the past two days.

"Good to see you again, Henyong," Photon said, trying his best to be disarming. "It has been a while since you gave me anything we could use. Surprise me and tell me you have something for us."

"I have nothing for you. That is not why I asked to meet with you."

"You have nothing for me. What are you wasting my time

for? I have important things to do." The expression on Photon's face reminded Henyong of Corporal Singh.

"I am wasting your time, because I want to know who kidnapped the American professor. Was it our group?"

"You know I can't tell you that."

"Do you know who did it?" Henyong's voice rose as his anger escalated.

"Of course I know. Who do you think you are talking to, some nobody?"

"If you know, you are going to tell me before you leave." Though Henyong and Photon were the same height, Henyong was more muscular and knew he would be stronger than this person he had never really liked and now was beginning to actively dislike.

"Get out of my way," Photon said, "You have wasted enough of my time."

He moved to brush past Henyong and return to the morung, but he never made it past the second step. With a roar of pent-up fury, Henyong lunged at Photon, tackled him around the waist and threw him to the ground. He was on top of Photon in a moment, his hands applying pressure to the throat. "Tell me who did the kidnapping or I will choke the life out of you, you phony fucker." Stunned by the attack, Photon looked up at the wild-eyed madman on top of him and decided he meant to do what he said.

Henyong partially relaxed his grip on Photon's throat. "Are you ready to tell me or do I have to choke you some more?"

Photon gasped for air, his face red from the loss of breath. "Don't hurt me again," he said, "I will tell you."

"It was our group, the Naga Liberation Army," Photon whispered, his voice hoarse from trauma.

Henyong bent over Photon and pounded his fists on the ground. "But why? What does this have to do with independence and revolution?"

"I can't answer that, but I know who can."

"Then tell me."

"You won't believe me if I do."

"Why not? Why won't I believe you."

"Because the Great Ang, Meniu's father arranged the whole thing."

"I don't believe you. How do you know that?"

"Because I am the communications link between the camps and the tribes. That is my job. How else would I know that Chingmei has not yet told us what he wants done to the American?"

Henyong released his grip on Photon. "Why would he do that? Why would he have the American professor who was so nice to Meniu kidnapped and held captive?"

"I don't know that. When you figure it out, let me know. Now, you have what you want; get off me and let me go."

Henyong did as he was asked and, as Photon stumbled back to the morung, he sat in the grass sweating and dazed.

"I have quit my job at the warehouse," he called to the retreating Photon.

"Good, we don't want you anymore."

21

The events surrounding the kidnapping of Robert Donovan profoundly altered the direction of Meniu Konyak's life. So deeply was she traumatized by what happened that, for years later, much of what took place was blurred in her memory. Confused and shaken, she made choices and decisions she would live with for the rest of her life.

The nightmare that haunted her dreams for years began on the drive to Mon, with their driver turning to her father to tell him, "I can no longer see the other vehicle behind us," and her father calmly replying, "They probably had to stop to relieve themselves by the side of the road. Turn around and go back to them." Puzzled more than alarmed, Meniu looked out the back window as their driver began to turn the jeep. There was no traffic to be seen as they had just come over a small hill which led down to a flat stretch of road that crossed a valley covered on each side by dense evergreen forests.

They drove back up the incline and headed towards the area where the highway work crew had been. It was at the point when it became clear that the other vehicle was nowhere to be seen and the work crew not in sight that the mildly unsettling situation suddenly became a full scale emergency. Meniu felt paralyzed as her father's voice took on a new urgency. "There must have been an accident. Faster, drive faster, someone may be injured."

The driver stepped on the accelerator as ordered and then, just as quickly, he jammed his foot hard on the brakes, bringing the car to a skidding halt. "Look! There on the side of the road." As her father and the driver jumped from the truck to run across the road, Meniu was overcome by a sense of growing anguish. Just off the road at the edge of the tree line, Dr. Ahon and the driver of the second vehicle lay bound, gagged, and blindfolded in the grass. The wriggling movement they both made at the sound of her father's approach reassured her they were alive. To Meniu's absolute horror, Robert Donovan was nowhere to be seen.

After that, it was chaos – Ahon blurting out the details of what happened as her father untied the two men and loosened the rough cloths that covered their eyes and mouths. "They threw Professor Donovan to the ground. He appeared to be unconscious immediately. When we tried to help, the work crew overcame us. There was nothing we could do. They took the jeep." Ahon did all the talking while the driver sat in the grass rubbing the circulation back into his wrists.

"The people who did this do not work for the Department of Highways," Chingmei said, "They must be members of the underground wanting to use the American for their own purpose." From that moment on, Chingmei's explanation of Robert Donovan's disappearance would be the one that prevailed and was accepted by both Indian and American authorities as well as the international media who covered the story.

At the mention of Robert Donovan's name, Meniu became

hysterical. She refused to accept what she saw before her, the pain of this new reality being too much for her to bear.

"No, no, this could not have happened," she screamed, "tell me this did not happen." Her father put his arms around her as she sobbed against his chest. "Why did they do this? What will they do to Robert?" Chingmei flinched at his daughter's familiar use of the American professor's first name but said nothing.

As he held his daughter, Chingmei took control of the situation. "We must return to Kohima immediately to report this to the authorities," he said. "They will send out patrols to search for Professor Donovan."

At first, Meniu did not want to leave, thinking that, by doing so, she would be abandoning Robert Donovan. Her father tried to guide her to the truck, firmly grasping her shoulder as she resisted. She pulled away, her anger now directed at Chingmei. "Where were our bodyguards? We always have them. Why did they not come with us?"

"I did not think it was necessary. It is my mistake," he replied. "What's done is done. The best thing we can do to help your professor is to return to Kohima as soon as possible." Meniu knew her father was right and allowed him to steer her to the jeep.

Heartsick, Meniu cried quietly in the back seat as her father continued to question Dr. Ahon and the driver. At her father's urging, the driver disregarded the posted speed limits, pushing the vehicle to its limits.

Even though her father had said "the best thing we can do to help your professor is to return to Kohima," Meniu knew better than that. She was well aware of the power her father had in his part of the Naga Hills. She knew that his influence extended in some way even to the underground groups. She was unsure how this connection worked, but conversations overheard over the years had clearly made that impression on her. Surely her father could do something to bring Robert Donovan back safely. But then again, if that was the case, why had they taken him in the first place?

What she remembered most about the ride back to Kohima was her father's response when she asked for his help. "Can't you do something, father, isn't there something we can offer the underground to release Professor Donovan?"

"We don't even know yet who the people are who did this. We think it was the underground because we are accustomed to their doing such things. But we don't know for certain. My guess is that whoever did this will contact the authorities to tell them their demands. Then we will know better what can be done."

"But will he be safe? Will they hurt him?"

Chingmei turned to look at his daughter huddled in the back seat next to Dr. Ahon and the other driver. "Things happen for a reason, Meniu. I cannot tell you what will happen to Professor Donovan. There may be some things we don't know yet that will have a bearing on all this. Sometimes in life, things happen that we can't control, but I believe there is a reason they happen."

Chingmei turned his attention back to the front seat. The tone of his voice suggested he had just said the last word on the situation, at least for the moment. Meniu tried to make sense of his words, but their meaning eluded her.

Chingmei tried to phone ahead to the military police station in Kohima from one of the transportation department stations along the road but, when there was trouble completing the call, he insisted on resuming the drive. By the time they arrived in Kohima, it was early afternoon, more than two hours after the kidnapping took place. The news they brought created an immediate uproar of activity.

Chingmei was very much in command as they approached the reception desk inside the old cinder-block building that served as the army's headquarters in Kohima. He had his business card announcing his position as Minister of Public Roads and Highways at the ready in case he wasn't recognized, but it wasn't necessary. As soon as he said, "I want to report a serious crime that took place on the road to Mon earlier today; it involves the disappearance of an important American visitor. I think you might want to call the officer in charge immediately" – he set in motion a small-scale military operation that would last long after Robert Donovan was found.

The commanding officer of the Kohima station was Captain Ghosh, a thin, imperious-looking man with angular features and a tightly clipped mustache. Once he grasped the basic details of what had happened, he barked a series of commands to the soldier at the reception desk. The best Meniu could make out was that military units should assemble immediately on the street outside and await further orders. They should report equipped for patrol duty of indeterminate length in the Naga Hills.

Ghosh then brought Chingmei into a small room adjacent to the waiting area and closed the door. He ordered all the others to sit and wait.

Five minutes passed and Ghosh reemerged. He pointed to Dr. Ahon and the two drivers. "Please go into my office. I will join you in a moment."

Thinking she was being left alone, Meniu once again broke down in tears and began to sob loudly. Captain Ghosh came to her side and gently patted her on the head.

"Your father has asked that you be given some medicine that will help you relax. Our nurse, Mrs. Dutta will take you over to the hotel and get you a room so you can rest. Your father will join you later after we have further discussions. Mrs. Dutta will stay with you until then."

"But what will happen to Professor Donovan?" she asked.

"We will do our best to bring him back safely. As far as we know now, there is no reason for anyone to harm him." Meniu nodded. Captain Ghosh was kind and reassuring.

"I may want to talk to you tomorrow after you have a night of sleep." Captain Ghosh removed his hand from her head. "I have to get back to the others. Mrs. Dutta will be with you shortly."

"Thank you," Meniu said and once again began to weep.

Mrs. Dutta, an army nurse assigned to the Kohima station, was a matronly-looking woman in her forties whose unflappable demeanor suggested she was accustomed to dealing with crises of many kinds. She brought Meniu two pills with water. After Meniu swallowed the pills, the nurse walked her out of the station and down the street to the hotel where she, her father, and Robert Donovan had stayed the previous night.

"You will feel better if you have something to eat," the nurse said once inside the hotel. "They have a nice restaurant here."

"I don't want to go in there," Meniu said, "we ate there last night and this morning with Professor Donovan."

"I am sorry. I didn't know that. I will have them send soup and sandwiches to the room."

They took the lift to the second floor. Nurse Dutta opened the door to the room and busied herself turning on the lights and pulling down the shade.

As Meniu sat down on the edge of the bed, a wave of fatigue

swept over her. "I feel very tired," she said. She looked around at the sparsely furnished room and wondered whether this had been Robert Donovan's room, this bed the one in which he had slept.

"The pills I gave you were a strong sedative. You need to sleep after all you have been through. I will leave you now. Call down to the desk if you need me."

Meniu lay back on the bed without taking off her clothes. She remembered little after that except her father looking in on her later that evening. She remained half asleep as he covered her with a light blanket. She awoke in the early morning to see the sun rise out her window. She washed and then ate some of the cold soup and sandwich that had been left on the night table as she waited for news from her father.

Chingmei knocked on her door at 9 o'clock, asking if she was dressed and ready for breakfast. She joined him in the downstairs restaurant which was crowded with an unusual number of men, many of whom appeared to be Americans.

Chingmei anticipated her question. "They are from the American embassy in Delhi, come to join in the search for your Professor Donovan."

"Why do you keep calling him 'my' Professor Donovan?" Meniu said in an irritated voice. "He doesn't belong to me."

Her father ignored her question. "You are still upset. It is understandable. Tell me how you feel."

"I feel groggy from the pills the nurse gave me and hungry. I didn't eat much. But I want to know what is going on. Tell me what has happened. Has anything been learned?"

Chingmei reached across the table to hold his daughter's hands which were trembling. "I am satisfied that all that can be done is being done. Captain Ghosh has handled things efficiently. He sent a number of patrol units up into the hills almost immediately. They took Dr. Ahon and the two drivers with them so they could show them exactly where this all took place."

"What about you. Why didn't you have to go also?"

"Captain Ghosh questioned me at some length, but I was not an eye witness to what happened. Besides, he was concerned about you being so upset. He thought it best I stay here with you."

"He has been very nice."

"Yes, he has." Chingmei reached into his pocket to take out the bottle of pills which Meniu recognized from the day before. "The nurse says you should take one of these every twelve hours for the next few days. But first you need to eat."

Meniu took the bottle of pills from her father. As she put the bottle in her pocket, she thought suddenly of Paula Donovan, the woman who had been so nice to her and whose husband was her lover. "Has Robert's wife been told?" she asked.

"Yes, she was notified yesterday, I am sure, by the American State Department. There are established protocols for these types of emergencies."

"I feel so bad for her," Meniu said.

Her father started to say something in reply but stopped himself. Meniu look at him oddly. "What is it? Is there something you are not telling me?"

"No, there is nothing else. Only that we must remain here in Kohima today. Captain Ghosh wants me to talk to the army intelligence officers from Delhi this morning as well as to the people from the American embassy. They are particularly interested in what group I think did the kidnapping and whether such a group will acknowledge that they have Professor Donovan."

"What will you tell them?"

"I will tell them what I told the captain, that I have no idea who has taken him or why. The best chance I have of learning something is if I return to my district of Mon and contact some sources. I can do nothing to help while I am in Kohima."

"What do they say to that?"

"They agree. If all goes well, we will be going home in the morning."

"Captain Ghosh said he may want to talk with me."

"He has changed his mind. I told him all about Professor Donovan's background. There is nothing you can add that would be of help. Our driver confirmed everything that we saw from our car."

Meniu was glad she would not have to go back to the station. The pills would help her get through what promised to be a long day waiting for some word about Robert Donovan.

The waiter brought a breakfast of rice and meats to the table. Meniu and her father ate quietly. Meniu thought about Paula Donovan and the pain she must be experiencing. She began to cry once more; her tears were tears of remorse.

The next morning Meniu and her father left again for Mon, this time with a military escort provided by Captain Ghosh. Nothing had changed; there had been no further news about Robert Donovan. Just before they departed from Kohima, Captain Ghosh came out to the car to inquire about Meniu's condition and to say goodbye.

"Do you think there is anything you can add to what your father has already told me about Professor Donovan or why this might have happened?" he asked Meniu.

"No, I don't think so."

There wasn't anything further to say. The fact of their affair had no bearing on what had happened. It was a private matter.

At her father's urging, she took one of the pills she had been given. It helped her sleep during the long drive which was prolonged by the traffic snarl-ups at the military checkpoints as the Indian army searched for the missing American.

They arrived at the great house in the late afternoon where Sipra had been waiting for them for three days. Sipra held her husband in a long, quiet embrace and then turned her attention to comforting her daughter who collapsed sobbing in her mother's arms.

"I am so sorry this happened," Sipra said, "but we will pray your professor will be released."

"Why didn't you come to meet me as you always do?" Meniu asked.

Sipra patted Meniu's back. "Your father wanted me to stay home and prepare things nicely for your guest. That doesn't matter now. What matters is that you are home safe and your father and the authorities will do what they can. Mendzing will take your bags to your room. The first thing you need to do is take a bath and put on clean clothes. That will make you feel better. Then come down and have a nice home-cooked meal." Meniu kissed her mother's cheek and followed the servant up the stairs. Mendzing turned on the lights in her room and placed her bags beside the bed. The expression of concern on the servant's face indicated she knew what had happened.

"I know you are upset, Miss, but this message came today from one of your girl friends in the village. I thought it might cheer you." She handed Meniu an envelope that looked like an invitation. The name in the upper left hand corner indicated it was from Shikna, a childhood friend from the village.

"Thank you. I think I will take a bath now." Mendzing bowed and left her alone.

Meniu took off her clothes, put on a robe, and turned the hot water on in her bathtub. While she waited for the tub to fill, she went back into her room and picked the letter off the dresser where she had laid it. She had little interest in its contents and decided it could wait until the morning. For now, she wanted only to sink in the warm water of her bath and try to recover from the ordeal of the past few days.

22

Meniu awoke early in the morning only partially rested after a long pill-induced sleep. The night before she had eaten with Sipra who was supportive and caring. Sipra had not dwelled on the possible tragic consequences of what had happened but, instead, focused on positive scenarios. She encouraged her daughter to eat and get some rest, all the usual things that Meniu now found so soothing. Oddly, Chingmei did not join them at dinner.

Meniu dressed in light tan slacks and a white blouse. Her face in the mirror looked tired and drawn, showing the stress she had been through. What she wished for with her entire being was news that Robert Donovan had not been harmed and would be released. How he must be regretting ever coming to Nagaland with her, that is, if he were still alive.

Almost as an afterthought, as a distraction from her recurring dark thoughts, she picked up and opened the letter she had set down the prior night. She was startled and pleased to see Henyong's name on the inside and not Shikna's. For the first time in days, she smiled, noting her lover's inventive way of getting a message to her. He must be as impatient to see her as she was to see him, but, with all that had happened, he had been far from her mind. However, as soon as she read the urgent first line, it became apparent that this was more than a surreptitious love note.

Dear Meniu,

I must see you immediately. I have important information about the American professor.

Please trust me and do not tell anyone about this note until we talk.

I will wait for you at the morung every day from early morning until late evening. Come to me as soon as you can or send a message where we can meet.

I have missed you greatly. Sorry about the name on the envelope, but I wanted this note to get to you.

Love,

Henyong

She reread the letter to be certain it said what she thought. How could it be that Henyong knew anything about Robert Donovan when the Indian army, American embassy people, and her father claimed to know nothing. It made no sense. Whatever it was, she knew Henyong would never lie to her about such a thing. He must have information.

She must go to him right away and, to do that, she must first convince her parents she was feeling well enough to leave the house. Mindful of Henyong's warning not to share the contents of his note with anyone, she made up a reason to go into the village early. She remembered her roommate at the university called that kind of untruth a "little white lie." That made it more acceptable as she did not like lying to her mother. She put Henyong's note in the pocket of her slacks and went downstairs.

"There you are," Sipra greeted her, "I hope you slept better than I did. After the past few days, I am exhausted. How did you do?" Mother and daughter embraced before sitting down to eat the breakfast that was laid out for them.

"I had a good sleep. The pills helped, and I don't feel as groggy as I did the other mornings." Actually, the news in Henyong's note had jolted her wide-awake.

"And, uh, how is your emotional state this morning? Did you think at all about what I said last night, about being hopeful even though it is difficult?"

"Yes, I did, you are right. The underground has no reason to harm Professor Donovan. It would do nothing to help their cause. I think today is the day we will learn something positive."

"Oh, I hope so, for everyone's sake. Last night, when I couldn't sleep, I thought about his poor wife and how upset she must be."

"Yes, I have thought of that also ... where is father?"

"He was up earlier. Our old friend Abhi Chandra is coming today on some important business."

"Has he tried to reach his contacts in the underground?"

Sipra shook her head. "Your father doesn't tell me everything he does though we talk about many things. You can be sure he is doing everything possible that can be done."

Meniu tried not to let Sipra see how impatient she was to leave. "Mother, you should try to take a nap this morning. You need rest badly."

"Yes, I plan to do so, but I am afraid I will sleep all day."

"Go ahead; you have done all that you can do."

"Will you spend the day resting?"

"No, I need to exercise and to see some friends. Perhaps company will help until some news comes. I may also stop at grandmother's if I have time."

"She wants to see you. That would be nice. Take her some tea leaves from the kitchen."

Meniu stood up and kissed her mother again. "I will be back later this afternoon." Sipra stayed in her chair and squeezed Meniu's hand, happy that her daughter seemed more composed this morning.

When Meniu left the great house after breakfast leaving her mother behind to nap, she had no way of knowing that many years would pass before she would see her home again. It was only a half a mile walk to the center of the village. Already the air was warm and humid. Meniu knew most of the families in the village and returned the greetings of the other early risers. Fortunately she did not run into Shikna or any other girl friends who would have wanted her to stop and visit for a while.

It was easy to find Henyong. He was where he said he would be, pacing by himself on the grounds of the morung. Because it was still early, no one else was outside although Meniu could see movement inside the hall. His back was to her, and she thought he was now taller than her father with the physique of a warrior.

"Henyong," she called softly, not wanting to have others hear her. He turned at the sound of her voice and ran towards her. They stopped short of an embrace, mindful that word of their actions might somehow get back to their fathers.

"I need to be alone with you," Henyong said, "I missed you so much. Thank God you are safe."

"Let's go to the river. I want to be with you too, but you must first tell me what you know about Professor Donovan."

Now that Meniu was with him, he was hesitant to tell her what he knew. He had been confident his note would bring her to him, but he was afraid what he had to say would turn her against him.

"I will tell you as soon as we get to the river. We need to be alone." He didn't say it but he worried Meniu would not be able to control her emotions. "While we are walking, tell me exactly what happened to you. It is important that I know."

"Alright," Meniu agreed reluctantly. She told him the whole story up to the point where Captain Ghosh had permitted her father and herself to leave Kohima. Henyong listened without interrupting. By the time Meniu was done, they had arrived at their usual meeting place where a soft morning mist covered the river like a thin bank of clouds.

"Kiss me first," Henyong insisted, "I need your kiss." Meniu raised her lips to his and, despite all that had happened, she knew that when she was in Henyong's arms, she was back where she belonged.

The kiss lingered until Henyong could no longer put off the moment he dreaded. He led Meniu to the trunk of a fallen oak tree where they often sat.

Meniu looked at him, her eyes apprehensive of what she might hear.

"Tell me what you know."

"I will, but first you must prepare yourself for a shock."

"He's not dead," Meniu sobbed, "please tell me they have not killed him."

"No, it's nothing like that. I don't know what the professor's condition is."

"Then what is it," Meniu half screamed, "I can't bear waiting any longer."

"I will tell you," Henyong said and took both of her hands in his. "But first, I want you to know that I love you and would never do anything to hurt you."

"I know that. Tell me; I can take it."

For a moment there was silence, broken only by the sounds of the river gently lapping the shore and the intermittent calls of birds in the trees above them.

"Your father arranged the kidnapping of the American professor. He is responsible for his disappearance."

Meniu's entire body became rigid and she pulled away from Henyong. She looked at him as if he were a total stranger.

"I don't believe that," she snapped, trying to keep calm.

"It is true."

"How do you know that?"

"I learned this from someone involved with the same underground group I was giving information to when I worked at the warehouse. There is no reason for him to say this if it were not true."

"How does he know this?"

"Because he is a courier; he delivers the messages to and from the camps. He is trusted to do this."

"Then why did he tell you?"

"He had no choice. We were fighting, and I threatened to kill him ... I was trying to help."

"My father has no reason to do such a thing. Why would he do this?"

"Perhaps there is a reason you are not aware of."

Henyong's words hung in the air and then it came to her, slowly, as if a great impenetrable barrier gradually swung open, revealing something she had never expected. Still she did not want to see the truth.

"Are you sure of this?" she asked.

Henyong did not have absolute proof that Chingmei was somehow responsible for the kidnapping. Still, he knew it was true in some respect since Photon had no other reason to say what he said. Also, as Minister of Public Roads and Highways, Chingmei would have known where and how to stage the kidnapping with a phony work crew. Chingmei Konyak's power was widely known and respected in the Naga Hills.

"Yes, I am as sure as I can be even though I cannot show you proof. What I don't understand is why he would do such a thing. Does he have a political motive?"

Meniu thought now she understood what had happened. Her father must have learned of her affair with Robert Donovan. That was the only explanation. How he had found out was another question. Long ago she had learned her father had ways of getting things done that others didn't. There was no point in explaining this to Henyong now. There would be time for that later.

"He may have a political motive; I am not sure." She got up from the log and walked to the river's edge where the last of the morning mist was just dissipating. "From the moment we got off the plane in Dimapur, he acted strangely. Now I know why."

"What did he do?" Henyong did not go to Meniu's side as he sensed she needed this moment to work through her thoughts.

"My mother didn't come with him to meet me at the plane as she always does. My father said she wanted to stay at home to get the house ready. I don't believe that.

"And you should have seen how weird he acted in the restaurant at the hotel. He seemed so … uh … uncomfortable talking to Professor Donovan. He even went on at great length about underground groups kidnapping foreigners. I didn't think it was appropriate."

Meniu turned back to Henyong. "Of course," she said, "I understand why Professor Donovan rode in the second car with Dr. Ahon. It was all a pre-arranged setup."

"I wonder if the others were in on it?" Henyong asked.

"Maybe so, maybe not; it doesn't matter. It would have worked either way." She paused and began to cry. "I will never forgive him for doing this."

Henyong came to her and put his arms around her. He let her cry a bit more and then said what he had been planning to say all along. "If your father did in fact arrange to have the Professor kidnapped, he should also be able to arrange to have him released unharmed."

"He has already been harmed psychologically. He must be terrified."

"Your father is the key to all of this. The underground would never have kidnapped the American unless he wanted it done. My guess is they will not harm him unless he tells them to do so."

The significance of Henyong's words hit Meniu all at once, and it became clear to her what she must do. The most important thing that mattered was that Robert Donovan be freed. She knew how to try to bring that about but to do that, she had to get away from Mon and her parents immediately. The thought of leaving home devastated her but she had to do it. She began to form a plan in her mind.

"Henyong, you are right. I must get my father to do what he can to release Professor Donovan. It won't be easy because my father can be very difficult. The first thing I must do is leave Mon right away, now."

"Leave, why must you leave?" Henyong asked, the thought of her leaving him so painful he could hardly bear it. Meniu explained why she had to go and the rest of the plan she was formulating in her mind. When she was finished, Henyong not only understood but agreed with her.

"I will go with you," he said.

"No, you don't have to do that," Meniu replied, though the idea of having Henyong to help her through this ordeal was appealing.

"I know I don't have to do it. I want to come with you. I love you. We are adults now and can manage our own lives." As he spoke, Meniu thought how strong he had become, and how she wanted to be with him. "What about your job and your family?"

"I haven't been able to tell you. My job ended two weeks ago. My father is feeling better and has a new job. He and I have talked about my going to college in September, perhaps in Calcutta."

"That is good news. I'm happy for your father."

"It will take me a while to catch up with you."

"It doesn't matter. I love you anyway." Meniu leaned up and kissed him.

"There is another reason it might be good to get away for a while."

"What is it."

"I am pretty sure the person who told me about your father will regret doing so. He is perfectly capable of making something else up about me so that I end up on a list of the underground's enemies. I am not afraid of him, but I don't think I want the underground after me."

"Would he do such a thing?"

"Yes, he is a spiteful, small person with an inflated idea of his own importance."

"Then that settles it," Meniu said, "you are as important to me as Professor Donovan. Come with me and if fate is on our side, it will keep both of you safe."

Meniu and Henyong headed back towards the village, refining

the logistics of their plan as they walked. They split up at the edge of the market area avoiding the morung in case someone had seen them earlier. It was just a little after 9 o'clock in the morning.

Meniu went first to her grandmother's bungalow where she had a warm visit with the old woman who still did not understand all the wonders that the modern world had brought to the village. One of those wonders was the telephone which Chingmei had installed for his mother, Shuidzing. Shuidzing's way of adjusting was unique. She would answer the telephone if it rang, but she had not yet reached the point where she would initiate an outgoing call. Meniu used her grandmother's phone to call home. A servant answered and told her that Sipra was napping. Meniu left a message that she was at her grandmother's but was spending the rest of the day meeting a group of her friends and would not be home until early evening.

Meniu left her grandmother's and went directly to the small bank in the village square. Her father had started a savings account in her name after her freshman year by depositing eighteen thousand rupees. He would add the same amount following each year she completed successfully, so, by the time she graduated, she would have the savings plus interest as her graduation present. She was glad to see her father had already made the deposit for her senior year. She withdrew all but five hundred rupees, taking twenty thousand rupees in currency, the rest in a bank check. From the bank, she went to the bus depot and purchased two one-way tickets on the 11:00 am bus to the Dimapur airport. Then she sat on a bench in the depot and waited for Henyong.

When they split up, Henyong went directly to his home. He was excited at Meniu's reaction to the news he had brought her and the plans they had made. He was about to leave his family and his village with the woman he loved. After almost four years of drudgery in the warehouse and only seeing Meniu for a short time each year, he was ready for this. Besides, the more he thought about Photon, the more he concluded it would be safer for him to leave the Naga Hills.

His mother was the only person at home when he arrived. He went to his room and packed a change of clothes and toilet articles in the only small bag he had. He took the small amount of money he had accumulated from his job which he had been saving to buy Meniu a special graduation present. When he told his mother he was going to Calcutta to visit colleges, she seemed surprised. "When did you decide to do this?" she asked.

"Just this morning," he replied. She nodded; her son had seemed unhappy lately and, at least, he appeared interested and motivated this morning. She gave him a few extra rupees and told him to have a safe trip.

The morning bus to Dimapur was crowded with businessmen and women from other states who greatly outnumbered the few Naga passengers. Meniu and Henyong found a seat in the back and settled in for the four hundred twenty-five kilometer trip to Dimapur. It began to rain as the bus pulled away from the depot. They both felt a certain sadness at leaving their village, knowing it might be some time before they would return. Being together made the moment more bearable for each of them. After a while, Meniu fell asleep on Henyong's shoulder. He closed his eyes, but he was too nervous at all that was happening, to sleep.

The bus stopped at the army checkpoints where soldiers came on board to take a perfunctory look at the passengers. Meniu awoke at these stops and, when the bus started again, she dozed. She did, however, stay awake to show Henyong the exact spot where the work crew had taken Robert Donovan. She shuddered as she pointed to the place off the road where Dr. Ahon and the driver had been left bound and gagged. Henyong put his arm around her and drew her closer to him.

The bus stopped in Kohima where Meniu pointed out the army headquarters where Captain Ghosh had questioned her father. It was 6 o'clock in the evening and the bus left again in a half hour for Dimapur. Meniu and Henyong used the restrooms in the bus terminal and then Meniu located a phone booth that was not being used. Her mother would be expecting her to arrive home shortly. She used her phone card to minimize the chance of the call being traced.

It took a minute or so for the connection to be completed. As she waited, her resolve weakened, but she told herself this was the only way she knew to help Robert Donovan. It had to be done. The phone was ringing at her house. To her dismay, it was her father's voice, not her mother's, she heard on the line.

"Hello," Chingmei said.

Meniu said nothing, so disconcerted was she by her father's authoritative voice.

"Hello, who is this?" Chingmei's voice sounded impatient.

"This is Meniu. Can I speak with Mother?"

"Meniu, where are you? Are you coming home for dinner?"

"I am with friends. I need to talk to mother."

"Of course. This connection is not good. You sound as if you are far away ... I'll get your mother."

Sipra came to the phone. "Meniu, I am sorry. I was in the kitchen. When will you be home? There is a nice kicheri dinner waiting."

"Mother, I won't be home for a while. I have something important to tell you and you must listen and do what I am going to ask you ... please. You are my only hope."

"What do you mean? Where are you?" Sipra's voice rose in panic but the serious tone of her daughter's voice told her she must listen. "What is it? Is this thing with your American professor bothering you? Whatever it is, you are better off dealing with it at home. Remember what we talked about last night."

"Please listen to me, Mother. I am going to tell you something awful ... and it involves father."

"What do you mean? He is fine. He is in the library."

"Father is responsible for the kidnapping of Professor Donovan."

"Don't be ridiculous," Sipra said, "Who has been filling your head with such nonsense? Your father has no reason...."

"He does have a reason."

"What is it then?"

"I have had a relationship with Professor Donovan for the past few years." Meniu could not use the word "affair" with her mother. "Father must have found out somehow, and this is his way of getting revenge."

As Sipra listened, she thought of the letter that had come in the mail a few weeks ago that had so infuriated Chingmei. Chingmei had never shared that letter with Sipra and he had been acting different lately. She had thought it odd that he did not let her come to the airport to pick up Meniu and her professor. And then of course, there were all those secretive discussions with Abhi Chandra.

"You know how father is about my being with any male outside of our clan."

"That is because...."

"That is because he wants me to live by the old ways, but how can I? He told me never to see Henyong again, but we have always found ways to see each other."

"Meniu, I don't know what to say...."

"You must help me."

"How? I can't believe your father would do this." Sipra heard the words that came from her mouth but in her heart she knew better. Since returning from Lok Sabha and coming home to Mon, it seemed the pull of the past had taken a greater hold on Chingmei.

"You must tell Father that I know he arranged Professor Donovan's kidnapping. Tell him I know the particular underground group that did this is the one calling themselves the Naga Liberation Army."

"How have you learned all of this?"

"I can't tell you that. It is not important now."

"What do you want him to do?"

"Tell him he must have Professor Donovan released unharmed within two days, or I will give the information I have to Captain Ghosh in Kohima."

"Meniu!" Sipra's voice rose as she envisioned the possible outcomes of what Meniu was threatening. "This is your father we are talking about. You can ruin him."

"I don't care. Professor Donovan has done nothing to deserve this. He is a kind and generous man. If he is released, I will tell no one what I know. I promise that."

"When will I see you again?"

"That depends on what happens. I will call you at this same time tomorrow night to learn his decision. Please answer the phone. I don't want to talk to him."

"I will do as you ask but I can't promise anything ... Meniu, please take care of yourself."

"I will, Mother. I love you." Meniu hung up the phone and, badly shaken, she left the booth with tears streaming down her cheeks.

"They are boarding," Henyong said to her. The ride to Dimapur was another two hours. Here they stayed overnight in a small hotel by the airport. They took a morning flight to Calcutta where they would wait until evening to learn Chingmei Konyak's decision regarding the fate of Robert Donovan.

23

Abhi Chandra learned of Robert Donovan's kidnapping on the front page of the *The Times of India*. He immediately recalled the threatening tone of his earlier telephone conversation with Chingmei Konyak. There was never a moment of doubt in his mind that the true facts behind the American's kidnapping were different from those being reported by the international press.

For two days, Abhi's telephone calls to Mon were answered by a servant who said the minister was away, nothing more. Abhi thought it best not to ask to speak to Sipra. Finally, on the third day, Chingmei answered to Abhi's considerable relief.

"Chingmei, I have read about the kidnapping. Are you alright?"

"You needn't worry, Abhi. Meniu and I are both fine. The army authorities detained us for two days with the usual interrogations. They even brought an investigative team from the American Embassy. They don't know where to begin to find their beloved professor. They think I can help."

"Obviously, they don't know the way you feel about Professor Donovan."

"Nor will they," Chingmei enunciated his words slowly, for

emphasis. "Just the opposite is true," Chingmei continued. "They asked me to use the connections I have in the district to find out what group has Donovan and what they want with him."

"You already know where he is, don't you?" Abhi Chandra thought he knew the answer to his question before he asked it.

"You will be surprised to learn that I don't have that information. The rebel group that is holding Donovan trusts me, but not with their lives ... but I can communicate with them at any time."

"To tell them what to do with the American?"

"Yes, this of course, is in return for some later favor."

"What are they going to do with him?"

The hesitation and the silence that accompanied it was palpable. After a moment Chingmei replied. "I have not decided yet. The rebels are growing impatient with me. They tell me that Donovan will make a statement in support of their movement if they release him. But that is not the reason I had him taken. Also, Meniu continues to be emotionally upset. She insists that I can do something to help."

"She is correct. Does she suspect anything?"

"No, I never told her that I knew about their relationship."

Chandra sensed from the uncertainty in Chingmei's voice that there was still an opportunity to intervene, to possibly save his friend from making a grievous error in judgment, a mistake from which, once it was made in all its finality, there would be no turning back.

"Don't do anything," Chandra pleaded, "I will come to you on the first flight from Bombay. When I arrive, sometime tomorrow I expect, we will talk as we did so often in Delhi. Wait until I get there; we will reason things through just like before. Things will be clearer; we are a good team together."

The last words Chandra heard before he hung up were Chingmei's protest, "You do not have to...."

The next day, after flying from Bombay to Calcutta to Dimapur, now driving the same mountain climb to Chingmei's village of Mon, Chandra began to have second thoughts about his hasty decision to come to Nagaland. After all, it was not as if he had been invited; rather he had invited himself, presumptuously relying on the strength of the relationship the two men had forged in years past to justify his intervention.

Perhaps Chingmei had changed, reverted back in some atavistic way to his childhood upbringing. After all, Chingmei had ordered the brutal abduction of Robert Donovan somewhere on this same wilderness road which was now being swarmed over by Indian army squads. The soldiers, dressed in their tropical khakis and red berets all carried automatic weapons which made them threatening beyond their years. They stopped and questioned the occupants of every vehicle, opening the trunks of cars and paying special attention to trucks in which a person or body might be hidden.

Chandra knew this intensified military presence would continue until the American was released or found dead. The pressure exerted by the United States State Department could be very persuasive in these situations. Additional army patrols would be futilely searching the jungle between Mon and the Myanmar border, all this to give credibility to the Indian prime minister's statement that "no resources of the Indian government would be spared in order to bring about the safe release of Robert Donovan."

How had it come to this and why should he, Abhi, expect Chingmei to listen to him now? Chingmei had already ignored his advice once and committed a savage criminal act. It may already be too late. By now, Chingmei may have taken revenge in the old Naga tradition. No, this was not the same man who, as a young representative in Lok Sabha had come to understand the give and take of politics, and had also learned that disagreements were not to be taken personally.

Despite these misgivings, Abhi Chandra knew he was doing the right thing in coming to Mon. An intellectually disciplined man with strong philosophical convictions, he believed Chingmei was no different in his essential self from any other human being. Chingmei was engaged in the old struggle between good and evil, brightness and darkness. Abhi had fought the same battles throughout his own life and believed this to be part of the human condition. What set Chingmei apart from most other people was his background, the fact that he had overcome the most primitive of upbringings to become a successful person in the modern world. Abhi respected that, and it was this respect that overcame his apprehension about his visit to Mon.

That the two men had gotten along so well and became such steadfast friends still amazed Abhi. They were different in so many ways. Abhi was the son of Tarun Chandra, one of the most influential bankers in Bombay, the financial center of the country. Bombay attracted visitors from all over the world, giving the city its cosmopolitan character. Abhi grew up in a comfortable home in the affluent Malabar Hill residential section. He studied international finance at the University of Bombay and, after graduation, worked for his father's bank. When he later became interested in politics, his father supported his effort, astutely reasoning that the years in Lok Sabha would allow Abhi the opportunity to develop contacts that would be valuable when he returned to banking. The friendship Abhi had with Chingmei Konyak was not the kind of new contact his father had in mind, so Abhi wisely did not discuss Chingmei with him. Tarun Chandra held the same prejudice towards the "savage" Nagas that was shared by so many of his countrymen, if they cared at all.

Chingmei Konyak's upbringing could not have been in greater contrast. Born the son of a headhunter, his formative years were spent on the opposite side of the country from Bombay in the primitive village of Mon within the protected territory of Nagaland. Except for Indian civil servants and the military, visitors rarely came to the Naga Hills. It was even rarer then for Nagas to leave the hills. Chingmei lived in the thatch-roofed hut whose portals were decorated with the trophies of recent headhunting raids led by his father. But it was this same father, who others would call a savage, who allowed Chingmei to begin attending the Baptist schools where education awakened him to the fact that there was another world outside of the Naga Hills. A gifted student, he was one of the very few Nagas of his generation to study and graduate from the University of Delhi.

The two shared some similarities as well. Both men were the same age, born in 1944, and both came to Lok Sabha as first year legislators in 1974. Both were married with one daughter, and their wives, Sipra and Pia, got along from the first meeting as if they had been friends from childhood. During legislative recesses, they visited each other's homes and, for both couples, the visits were cultural awakenings. It was during the visit to Mon that Abhi first met Meniu. That had been a happier time when the quiet and shy teenager was just entering adolescence.

Chandra remembered how their colleagues in the parliament had jokingly referred to Chingmei and himself as "the odd couple." In their case, the old tenet that "opposites attract" seemed to apply. Chingmei learned much about the world outside of the Naga Hills from the more sophisticated Chandra who, in turn, was attracted by the power, the natural authority that people felt in Chingmei's presence, however primitive his origins might have been.

Chandra had resigned from the Lok Sabha in 1987, anticipating correctly that the Congress Party's long-held domination of Indian government was about to end. With his father's help, he secured a position with an international bank, splitting his time between Bombay and Los Angeles. The two couples stayed in regular contact, with the Chandras traveling to New Delhi a few times each year when parliament was in session.

Meniu grew to be an attractive young woman and made the decision to attend university in the United States. When Chingmei asked Abhi for assistance, he was happy to help in small ways by periodically transferring her living expenses to her, telephoning her, or taking her out to lunch or dinner on his occasional business trips to Boston. Abhi had to admit he had become quite fond of his friend's daughter. There was something about her personality, a certain lonely vulnerability, that made her endearing.

"We are here, sir, the Konyak plantation." The voice of the driver roused Abhi from his reverie as the car turned into the winding driveway that led to the main house. At once, Abhi sensed a difference from his only other visit to Mon six years ago. Then, he and Pia had been given a welcome befitting a head of state. All the lanterns illuminating the driveway to the great house had been lit in honor of their arrival. A corps of servants stood at attention on either side of the doorway framing the host and hostess who greeted them with expressions of delight.

This time the long driveway was dark and foreboding. Two servants greeted Abhi at the doorway to the house, one to open the car door, the other to carry the light bag he had quickly packed. Neither Sipra nor Chingmei were anywhere to be seen.

"Where is Mister Konyak?" Abhi asked as he stepped into the front hall.

"Sir, the Minister apologizes he was not able to greet you. He is upstairs talking by telephone. He said it is important. He will be down shortly and explain all of it to you. He asks that you wait for him in the library."

Ten minutes passed while Abhi waited in the library, his mind once again filled with doubts about whether he was too late to help or whether he should have come at all. It was unlike Chingmei not to have been at the door to greet him. And where was Sipra? Or Meniu? As he paced the library floor, he paused to study the Naga artifacts that were displayed throughout the room. He came to a cluster of photographs, among them, one of himself and Chingmei posing with the late Rajiv Gandhi and other Congress Party leaders. It occurred to him that Chingmei's world had changed entirely and, yet, in some ways, it was still the same.

He turned away from the photographs when he heard voices outside in the hallway. Chingmei entered the room, closed the door behind him and, without a word, came to embrace his friend.

"Good to see you," Abhi said, patting Chingmei's back as if to give reassurance that everything would work out. "I hope you don't mind my coming. I thought you might need to talk."

Chingmei hesitated, his face a study in anguish and helplessness.

"Abhi, I am glad you are here. Thank you for being such a

true friend. I should have paid attention to your earlier advice. I have made a terrible mistake and I badly need your wise counsel."

Thinking the worst, Abhi immediately blurted out the most important question – "Is Robert Donovan still alive?"

"Yes, he is still at the camp. Nothing has been done to him."

"Then, you can still make things alright. Tell me everything."

Chingmei motioned to the two armchairs that faced each other in front of the bookcase which held the Naga artifacts. The lights in the room flickered briefly. Chingmei's eyes filled with tears as he began his explanation.

"My daughter Meniu knows everything that happened, that I arranged the kidnapping of her professor, and that the rebels are holding him captive until they receive orders from me. She has left our home and told her mother she does not want to be with me anymore. She says the underground must release her professor in two days or she will tell the military authorities what happened. I don't even know where she is or how she learned this. But I know I have lost my beloved daughter."

The telling of the bad news and all that it portended was too much for Chingmei who covered his face in his hands and sobbed. Abhi rose from his chair to comfort his friend. He had never seen Chingmei cry before. He was stunned by what he had heard, but he needed to learn more before he could be of any help.

24

Rajiv Gandhi had once said of Abhi Chandra that "for one of the youngest members of Lok Sabha, Abhi had an unique ability to analyze a situation from multiple perspectives. Chandra made decision-making easy," Gandhi added, "by providing a range of alternative actions to be considered along with the likely outcomes of each possible choice." This uncommon skill served Abhi well throughout his life. Indeed, in politics and his years as a banker, people sought him out to help them solve their most intractable dilemmas. Now, having traveled across the breadth of India from Bombay to the village of Mon in the Naga hills, he faced his biggest challenge.

The central, inescapable fact was that Chingmei Konyak had arranged the kidnapping of Robert Donovan. Regardless of anything else that Chingmei might do, or plan to have done, this was a serious criminal act motivated by the need to exact revenge. As far as Chandra knew, the American professor had not been harmed further, but this did not mean he wouldn't be.

Now everything had been complicated by Meniu's discovery that her father was responsible for Donovan's disappearance. Should she carry out her threat to turn her father over to the Indian authorities, it would destroy Chingmei. By denying responsibility, he would brand his daughter a liar or worse. Besides, the underground could not be relied on to accept sole blame without some significant benefit to the movement. As it was, Meniu's leaving home had shattered the family and the hopes the father had for his daughter. Even if Chingmei had the American released, a reconciliation between father and daughter would be very difficult.

All of this had happened because an older man had been attracted to a beautiful, young woman. There must have been reciprocal feelings on Meniu's part for the affair to have lasted as long as it did. These things happened every day all over the world. A number of Abhi's married banking colleagues in Bombay kept younger mistresses. Even he, this very year, had spent pleasurable time with Barbara, his thirtyish administrative assistant in Los Angeles. It was easy for Abhi to understand why Robert Donovan had this affair with Meniu.

And what about Donovan? The trauma of being kidnapped and held prisoner in the Naga hills certainly was enough punishment. Perhaps he could convince Chingmei that he already had taken revenge. From what he understood, Donovan was a serious scholar. Now that his kidnapping had the attention of the international media, perhaps some good could yet come out of this situation.

Abhi mulled all these things over in his mind during a fitful sleep as he waited for morning to come.

The problem that he kept coming back to was that Chingmei Konyak was not thinking in ways that Abhi considered logical and rational. If Abhi were to have any hope of persuading Chingmei to do what was right, he must remember that Chingmei was not the same person he had admired in New Delhi. It was as if the move back to his village of Mon had not just been a physical journey but also a psychological return to the culture of Chingmei's youth.

The sound of roosters crowing from the village heralded the dawn. Abhi arose slowly from his bed and went to the window. Chingmei's fields were still dark and morning mist mixed with the smoke of cooking fires from the bungalows below created an unearthly panorama that lasted just a few brief minutes. At the outskirts of the village, the shadowy outline of the Naga hills dominated the skyline. Abhi thought of all the horrific acts that had been committed in those hills by Chingmei's ancestors and members of the other tribes. These hills and the things that happened there had helped mold Chingmei's essential character. That same character contained extraordinary strengths as well as traits that were potentially monstrous.

The night sky above the tree line of the hills began to brighten with soft pink hues as the sun began its long climb. Abhi began to formulate a plan, the specific things he would say to his friend at their morning meeting. Then he would leave the Naga hills, perhaps for the last time, and return to Bombay. The rest would be up to Chingmei.

Down the darkened hallway, at the other end of the house, Chingmei slept alone since Sipra had chosen to stay in Meniu's room as she sometimes did when he was upset or agitated. She herself was devastated by Meniu having left their home, and the strain of having to tell her husband what his daughter knew about Donovan. Even after she brought him Meniu's ultimatum, Chingmei had not told her how he had learned of Meniu's involvement with the professor or his plan to take revenge.

Chingmei had left Abhi agreeing to meet in the morning after his friend had a night's rest following his long trip. He returned to the master bedroom and sat in a chair, unnerved by what had happened. He sat unmoving, staring straight ahead at nothing in particular while he gathered his composure. After a half hour or so, he stood and walked to the wooden desk in the corner of the room. His demeanor was calmer now as if he had come to terms with the difficulties he faced. He moved a framed picture of his father to the front center of the desk and knelt down on the floor in front of it. Though he had been converted to Christianity in the Baptist schools, that declaration of faith by the school children had been less a statement of belief and more an expression of collective appreciation for all that the missionaries had done for them. When Chingmei prayed for guidance as he did now, it was more often to his ancestors, especially his father.

This picture of his father was his favorite. Set against a backdrop of mountains with banks of white clouds resting on their peaks, the photo had been taken from a lower angle creating an unearthly effect in which his father's head appeared to stretch into the sky. The expression on his father's face was serious as he gazed out over the Naga hills, as if trying to fathom the world that was changing so rapidly before him. Somehow, for reasons Chingmei could not articulate, the picture made his father more accessible, easier to talk to in prayer.

"Dear father," Chingmei said out loud, "I need your wisdom to help me do the right thing. Tell me what to do with this man Robert Donovan who has violated my beloved Meniu. Help me get my daughter back to her family where she belongs." Chingmei bowed his head in silence waiting for an answer to his entreaties. He shut his eyes and concentrated, but no voice came to him.

"Father, I know it is not fair to expect you alone to solve this awful thing so I pray now to all of our ancestors for their guidance. Together, your counsel will steer me to the right course."

Again, he closed his eyes and this time, the voice of his father came in all of its venerable wisdom, giving him the counsel he so badly needed, erasing the doubts he had in his mind. His father's voice was no surprise to Chingmei. It was not the first time he had prayed to him and received a response. Reassured, he got up from his kneeling position, moved his father's picture back to its original spot, and went back to his bed where he soon fell into a deep sleep.

The two men met for breakfast in the dining room of the great house. Sipra was conspicuously absent, but Abhi made no comment about her. He was tired and, in an effort to revive himself, he drank black coffee and ate the warm wheat buns that the servant had placed before him. He was unshaven and the khaki shirt and pants he wore were still rumpled from the trip.

By contrast, Chingmei looked well-rested, once again in full control of his emotions. "We will go to the library to conclude our business after we have eaten," he said to Abhi, signaling that he did not want to talk in front of the servants. He ate heartily and talked about prospects for his next tea crop as if it were the primary concern in his life. Abhi wondered what it was that was responsible for the transformation of his friend. He seemed to have put the turmoil of the night before behind him.

In the library, Chingmei motioned Abhi to a pair of armchairs by the window. "We should be comfortable here, my friend," he said. "I have asked the servants not to disturb us." They sat across from one another, each waiting for the other to begin. Abhi spoke first, if only to fill an awkward silence.

"You look your old self again. You must have had a good night's sleep."

Chingmei nodded in agreement. "You are right. I did sleep well. But before I slept, I prayed for guidance in this difficult matter. After that, sleep came easier."

Abhi Chandra, a Hindu, assumed Chingmei's prayers had been directed to the Christian God he had learned about from the Baptists. Chingmei never thought to say otherwise. His prayer and his father's response to his prayer was entirely a private matter.

"I did not sleep as well as you," Abhi said, "but lying awake as I did allowed me time to think about your hardships. If you wish, I will offer some thoughts though I do not presume to have all the answers. I am not even sure there are a set of answers that are entirely satisfactory."

Chingmei shifted in his chair. "Of course, I want your counsel. As I said last night, you have always been wiser than I. Tell me what you think I should do."

Abhi leaned forward in his chair to state his case as forcefully as he could. "The first point I want to make is that this Professor Donovan has already suffered considerably as a result of his being kidnapped. Depending on the type of person he is, he may never be the same, never get over the experience. If your intention was to punish him, you have already succeeded. Nothing more is needed."

Abhi paused to get a reaction. Chingmei stared at him, his face hardened, his eyes steely.

"Reports from the camp indicate this depraved man is quite healthy. No one has harmed him. He is well enough to have written a statement about the Naga struggle for independence which the rebels want to tape and send to the media. No, Abhi, on this point you are wrong. Professor Donovan has not suffered enough."

"I am not here to disagree with you, Chingmei," Abhi said, "only to offer ideas that you might find helpful."

"Continue. Do not think I am not listening because I take issue with what you say."

Chingmei had not meant to dismiss Abhi's suggestion so abruptly. He did not want to offend the man he admired so much. Besides, that would be contrary to his father's counsel.

He thought back to the night before to the sound of his father's voice, to the words of his father in response to his prayer.

"Be open to all possibilities so that you can adapt to the changes that will certainly come. Welcome the new, the new that is better than the old." That is what his father had said. Who could dispute it? But his father had said more. "Realize there are some things that never change. Those laws that govern the great universe we live in and all that we do; these are unchangeable. You know these laws. I taught them to you as my father, your grandfather, taught them to me. Be true to these laws. That is all you need in your life."

Chingmei knew what his father's words meant, but Abhi was talking again.

"My second thought concerns your daughter, Meniu, who I have known since she was a young girl. Here I am very sensitive that this is a personal, family matter in which I hesitate to interfere."

"You are not interfering. You know I think of you as a brother."

"And I you ... I thank you for saying that."

"Meniu has told her mother she does not want to be part of our family because of what I have done to her Professor Donovan."

"Perhaps it is not too late to change her mind. To do that, you must give Professor Donovan his freedom."

"Why should I do that?" Chingmei's voice rose. "I prayed last night and asked what my father would have done."

"But this is not your father's time. You are a modern man. Each generation changes. You risk all that you have accomplished in your life if you do not release him."

"I am the Great Ang, with the blood of my father and my father's father in my veins. This man seduced my young daughter. It is he who is responsible for shattering my family. None of this would have happened if it hadn't been for him."

Chandra decided not to mention that Meniu had been of adult age when she had the affair with the professor and was as responsible as he for what happened. It was clear that Chingmei was adamant about further retribution against Robert Donovan.

In his methodical way, Abhi had prepared for this eventuality even though it was not the outcome he wanted. What he was about to propose was personally distasteful to him, but when he considered the possible things Chingmei might do to Robert Donovan, his proposal became the lesser of two evils.

"I have an idea," he said, "an idea that may satisfy Meniu so that she will consider returning to her father and mother. This idea will also put Professor Donovan to a test which, should he fail it as he likely will, he will suffer consequences for a long time to come."

Chingmei nodded knowing that whatever Abhi was about to say had been carefully considered. "Go ahead, Abhi," he said, "I will not interrupt you."

"The first thing you must do is to authorize Professor Donovan's release as soon as possible. Let this statement that he has written serve as the reason to release him. You must send a message to Meniu that this is happening and that you never intended to harm her professor."

"And what of this test you spoke of?" There was skepticism in Chingmei's voice but he continued to listen.

"This test is about giving Professor Donovan the opportunity to," Abhi raised his voice for emphasis, "'hoist himself with his own petard.' Do you know the meaning of this expression?" Abhi asked.

"I must admit I do not know its meaning."

"It means using an opponent's cleverness so that he brings about his own downfall."

"Ah, yes," Chingmei's face brightened with recognition, "is it the same as letting someone hang himself with his own rope?"

"You have the idea. Let me explain."

Chingmei listened carefully as Abhi outlined his plan. Though there was no guarantee the American would fall into the trap that was to be set, Chingmei believed that Donovan lacked the willpower to resist the bait that was to be offered. "My father would approve that you have studied your enemy's weakness and you intend to use the element of surprise," he said.

Abhi accepted the comment, satisfied that Chingmei was going along with his suggestion, even though it meant giving Robert Donovan his freedom. The plan he had proposed was better than anything Chingmei would decide, and it allowed Donovan the chance to leave unharmed should he have the inner strength to do so.

"What do you think?" Abhi asked when he was done.

Chingmei glared at his friend long enough for Abhi to feel uncomfortable. "I accept your plan because there is a chance it may bring my daughter home. This evil man will most certainly choose the path that will bring harm to himself and to his family as he has to mine. Justice will be done."

Abhi suppressed a sigh of relief at Chingmei's response. "There is much to be done. How long will it take to make arrangements? Are there any problems?"

"No. I will make the calls to set these things in motion immediately. I do not anticipate difficulty. The underground fighters will welcome the news that they can release the American and give his statement to the media. Meniu told her mother she will call this evening to learn my decision. Sipra will tell her of the professor's release. As for the preparation for Professor Donovan, I have people who can handle that."

Abhi Chandra stood up, his work done as best as he could have under the circumstances. It was time to leave. "I will say good bye, Chingmei. All I have to do is pack the few things I have brought. Your car will take me to Dimapur?"

"It is ready and at your disposal." Chingmei shook Abhi's hand, holding on for an inordinately long time. "I know you are not entirely happy with my behavior," he said to his friend, "but you must understand that we come from different worlds, and sometimes we must do things for reasons that are difficult for the other to understand."

It occurred to Abhi that he had ended up working as a banker because his father wanted him to be a banker. But that wasn't the same thing that Chingmei was saying, or was it?

"Thank you for coming," Chingmei added. Abhi walked out of the library and up the stairs thinking he might never see Chingmei Konyak again.

Chingmei closed the library door, went to his desk and picked up the phone to make the necessary phone calls. It took four calls to make all the arrangements he and Abhi had discussed.

When he finished, two questions still troubled him. What if Meniu still refused to come home? What if the American resisted Abhi's scheme before he was released? If he made a statement for television, he would end up a heroic public figure. For having done what – having violated his daughter and damaged the harmony of his family. The American would have defeated Chingmei – the enemy would have won. This was not acceptable to Chingmei as it would not have been acceptable to his father. He picked up the telephone and made one more phone call.

25

Robert Donovan had long ago given up the formal practice of religion. He and Paula only went to church for weddings and funerals and, if the spirit of the season moved them, they might go to mass on Christmas or Easter. "Skipping the middleman" was how he put it in spirited discussions he had on the current state of the church.

Despite his and Paula's distrust of the church as an institution, both of them still believed that a God existed and, though they tended to be ecumenical in their thinking, Christianity was their belief system, the one they had been brought up with, the one in which they were most comfortable.

As a teacher of sociology, Donovan regularly confronted his own religious philosophy in the classroom. It usually happened when he was explaining the difference between religious faith, agnosticism, and atheism. Where was he on this continuum of choices? Over the years, he had developed a two-part answer to his own self-questioning. The part of him that had been deeply influenced by years of Catholic education accepted the old Thomistic idea that the universe had to have a final cause and that the first cause was God. In modern terms, God was the original "Big Banger." Since most of his students had not and never would read Thomas Aquinas's *Summa Theologica*, Donovan also turned to a pop culture explanation, one offered by Johnny Carson during a Tonight Show monologue. "You may as well believe there is a God," Carson said, "because if there is, you have picked the winning side, and if there isn't a God, it doesn't matter anyway."

Donovan recognized the line as Carson's spin on a seventeenth century argument written by Blaise Pascal as to why people should believe. Carson's version was simpler and yet it contained the same logic. Robert Donovan used it when he needed to say to others, "yes, he believed in God."

Because he still believed, he still prayed. His prayers were not as frequent as they once were, nor were they the same rote communal exercises as when he was under the supervision of nuns, brothers, and priests. Now his attempts at prayer tended to be personal and private conversations with God. His prayers were rarely selfish, never materialistic. Usually, they were in reaction to someone else's crisis, some national tragedy.

But this situation was different. He was awake on the morning of his fifth day in captivity and, without any response about how his videotaped statement had been received, he was falling deeper into despair. And so he prayed. He didn't try to bargain; instead he made a promise. "Please God," he prayed, "let this man Nllamo succeed in giving the tape I have made to those who will decide to set me free. That's all I ask. When this is done, I will return home to my wife and, with your help, I will do what I can to help the Naga cause."

Donovan had been so depressed when he awoke earlier that he had remained on his cot. Now, the act of praying had picked up his spirits, given him some hope. He pulled himself upright and went to the table where his breakfast had been left. The morning sun shone through the walls of the hut, casting panels of light across the dirt floor.

When he had eaten, he opened the door of the hut to ask the guard if he could be escorted to the latrine. Neither guard was at the regular post. He adjusted his eyes to the brightness of the sun and looked across the clearing which served as his exercise area. What he saw was no less than a miracle. Marching across the square was Captain Nllamo with the two guards at his side carrying his slacks, shirt, and shoes. It was the clothing, the broad smile on the captain's face and the festive mood of the crowd that trailed behind him that told Donovan his prayers had been answered.

"Oh, Professor Donovan, I am happy to see you are awake. We have good news for you," Nllamo called out. He motioned to the two guards as he spoke. "Lowang and Ato have brought your things as you can see. You are going to need them."

The two guards bowed and presented freshly washed clothes and recently cleaned shoes.

"Does this mean that I...."

"Yes," Nllamo interrupted, "You are to be released this evening." He stepped forward and embraced Donovan who was too elated to feel awkward in the arms of the camp leader. "Come, let's go back inside and I will explain."

Donovan heard murmurs of approval from the crowd as Nllamo put his hands on his shoulder to lead him to the hut.

"How can I thank you for doing this for me?" he asked, barely able to contain his excitement.

"Your thanks are contained in the videotape you made for us. My superiors greatly admire the statement you have written, and how you spoke the words you wrote. Copies are being made and sent to different media. We marvel at how quickly you have understood our history and the justice of our struggle. You speak as if you are our Gandhi."

"Tell your leaders that I will find other ways to tell the Naga story when I return to my home."

Nllamo beamed his approval. "I want to tell you, Professor Donovan, that I have come to like you. I wish you a safe and happy life." Once again he stepped forward to celebrate the emotion of the moment with an embrace. This time Donovan returned the hug, patting the captain on the back as he said, "Thank you, my friend" over and over again.

With that, Nllamo moved towards the door. "We cannot leave until it is dark. You will be told the plans at that time. In the meantime, do what you have to do; exercise, clean yourself, shave, rest, whatever you need to prepare yourself."

Donovan nodded, thinking that, in the excitement, he had entirely forgotten he had been on his way to the latrine.

"One more thing," Nllamo said, "this afternoon we have a surprise for you. It is a going-away gift, something we think you will like."

The man who had been Donovan's captor for the past five days bowed as he closed the door. Alone again, Robert Donovan fell to his knees on the floor of the hut to thank God for hearing his prayer.

Later, in the early afternoon, Donovan lay on his cot thinking of his impending freedom and of going home to his wife. He had never before experienced the range of emotions he felt since learning the decision to release him. In a matter of minutes, he had switched from a deepening depression to a feeling of such joy that he had to fight an urge to shout his happiness to the entire camp. At the same time, he was profoundly grateful to Nllamo and whoever else was responsible for his deliverance.

He felt no anger at his captors. From what he had learned, their cause was just.

His kidnapping and release would bring him a certain celebrity, however short-lived that might be. Perhaps he could use that celebrity status to gain financial support for his work. He envisioned himself as becoming an American spokesperson of the Naga cause. Nllamo's characterization of him as the "Gandhi of the Nagas" was an overstatement, but he liked the sound of it.

Above all he would work hard to rebuild his relationship with Paula. He knew a distance had come between them, but he didn't quite understand how or why it had gotten there. He would make it well again. A place to begin would be to show his affection for her more often. His affair with Meniu would be over now. She needed to be with someone her own age, perhaps even her young Naga lover, the one she had told him about that night at the Boston Marriott. Of course, to do that, she would have to circumvent her father who had struck Donovan as a man of strong conviction.

Had Chingmei Konyak been instrumental in negotiating his release? Donovan thought it likely that he was. Eventually he would learn how it all had been managed.

A banging at the door of his hut interrupted his thoughts. He assumed it was the young woman coming to clean up his lunch bowls, but he was wrong. Instead it was Nllamo again and behind him, two women that Donovan had not seen before.

"I have brought you the going-away present I mentioned earlier, two companions to entertain you and make your last hours at our camp more pleasant." As he spoke Nllamo's smile changed into what Donovan thought was a leer.

"This is Shanta, and her friend Selima. I hope you find them agreeable. I will return after your evening meal to help you get ready for your departure." Without another word, Nllamo closed the door behind him leaving a puzzled Robert Donovan alone with the two women who entered the hut and stood smiling at him expectantly.

Both wore green blouses over black pants along with straw hats that Donovan associated with images of Vietnamese peasants working in flooded rice paddies. He had not seen those hats worn in the camp before. He sensed immediately that the women were not from the Naga camp. They were both taller than the women he had seen in the camp and they seemed older. He guessed them to be in their late twenties. They wore bright red lipstick and rouge and moved with a certain assurance that came from experience. If they were not Nagas, where were they from? Why were they here?

The one called Shanta carried an oblong bamboo mat which she unrolled on the floor of the hut. She arranged the mat so that it was squarely in front of Donovan who remained seated on the edge of his bunk. "This is so you can see our performance well. We hope you will like what we do."

"What kind of performance?" he asked.

"You will see," Shanta replied. Her companion carried a sack full of small black pillows. She arranged the pillows neatly in each of the corners of the mat. "There, we are ready," she said.

The two women stood side-by-side in front of Donovan, removed their hats and bowed in unison. Unsure what the proper response was, he hesitated, then half-bowed in response. Selima retreated to one of the corner pillows, turned her back to him and began to rearrange her clothing. Shanta stood upright in the center of the mat as if awaiting the playing of an overture and the rising of a curtain.

Donovan felt totally flustered. Was this some type of farewell ritual in his honor? If so, where were Nllamo and the others from the camp? Why had he been left alone with the women? Fearful of committing a cultural blunder, he did nothing. "What do you call your performance?" he asked quickly trying to understand better what was about to happen before it began.

"We call it Kama Sutra," Shanta replied with a smile that was both innocent and suggestive at the same time. "Do you know this love book?"

He knew the reference immediately. Kama Sutra, the Hindu classic which was an early "how-to" treatise on the important goals in life. Chief among these goals was men's right to experience sexual pleasure in moderation. To do that, men and women had to learn a variety of sexual techniques in order to be able to better satisfy one another. Over the years Donovan had perused with some curiosity a number of "Kama Sutra" texts, many of which came with illustrations depicting different sexual positions.

'Where do you give these performances?"

"We have performed in many places. We once performed in Calcutta but now we are...." Selima interrupted her by saying something in Hindi. Donovan did not understand what was said but he understood that further conversation was being discouraged.

He had been right; the women were not Nagas, not part of the camp. What was the purpose in their being here?

"We must begin now," Shanta said.

She started by matter-of-factly removing her blouse and pants. There was nothing sensual about her disrobing. She moved demurely, folding her clothes neatly and placing them on the floor of the hut. She wore nothing underneath. Naked, she stooped to pick up one of the black pillows which she used to rest her head on as she lay prone on her stomach in the center of the mat. As she did so, Donovan noticed a tattoo of a small red dragon on the side of her right breast.

The other woman, whose back had been to Donovan turned now to approach her partner on the floor. She had tucked her black hair under a red cone-like hat. She stood over the other woman who now rolled on to her side and reached up her hands in invitation. Selima stepped out of her pants and blouse. Underneath she had covered and flattened her breasts with a maroon silk scarf. On her bottom, she wore a garment which resembled an athletic supporter. She had stuffed it with fabric to give it heft. At first Donovan didn't get it. The scene was more comical than sexual to him. Then it dawned on him. Selima was playing the role of the man in the presentation of the "Kama Sutra" that was about to unfold.

Shanta turned towards Donovan. "Usually we have music," she said, "and sometimes we have message boards that show you the names of the Kama Sutra positions we will demonstrate. Is it okay if we only tell you the name of the position?"

"Yes," Donovan smiled, "of course." He hadn't had a good laugh in quite some time, but he suppressed his hilarity understanding that the women were serious about their act.

"These are the five Kama Sutra love positions," Selima announced. "The first is called Uttana-bandha." She sat down on the mat in front of her partner who raised both her legs and placed them upon her shoulder. The two began to move slowly in rhythm with one another simulating sex. Their emphasis was clearly on what they perceived to be an artistic presentation of this position. No attempt was made to actually stimulate each other.

No one will ever believe this happened, Donovan thought. He took the performers' efforts to be exactly what they appeared to be, an entertainment, however unorthodox, for his enjoyment.

Evidently, Selima was the spokesperson for the act. "This is Tipyak," she said. The second position was more involved than the first. Shanta, the "woman" shifted to her side while Selima, the "man" lay between her thighs, one under him and the other thrown over his flank.

"That looks like it hurts," Donovan joked. He felt more relaxed now that he could see that what was happening was harmless. He reminded himself how great cultural differences can be.

"This do not hurt," called out Shanta, "this feel good."

"My apologies," he said.

The third position "Upavista," required the women to change positions. Shanta stood for the first time while Selima sat cross-legged on the mat. Shanta then sat on "his" lap and began to rock peacefully.

For the first time, Donovan saw that Shanta had an exquisitely shaped fanny, the sensuality of which was enhanced by her movement. Still the overall effect of the performance continued to strike him as more farcical than sexual. He recalled an essay explaining how the western aesthetics of dramatic presentation differed fundamentally from eastern aesthetics making it difficult for one to understand and appreciate the other. Hadn't Henry Kissinger fallen asleep during a performance of the Beijing Opera?

Unaware of Donovan's lack of appreciation for their art, the performers continued on to the fourth position which was announced as "Utthita," a word which Selima had difficulty pronouncing, adding to the humor of the situation. "Utthita" required considerable strength from both women. First, Selima stood and took a moment to stabilize her feet. Her partner then put both hands around her neck and, with a little jump, came off the ground wrapping her legs around the "man's" waist. Selima staggered under the weight, and when Shanta began to simulate intercourse, it became too much and the two began to collapse. Donovan quickly came off his cot to gather the women in his arms to prevent them from falling. Apparently, this had happened before. Neither woman was upset by the breakdown of their act and shooed Donovan back to his seat on the cot, laughing together with him.

"We have one more position to show you. This one is called Vyanta-bandha. The English called it the cow position."

"The cow position," Donovan laughed out loud, "I don't believe it."

"You should believe it. Kama Sutra teaches there is much religious merit in this form." Having put him in his place, Shanta bent over to the floor, spread her legs and supported herself on her hands and feet. Selima approached from behind and proceeded to act out the role of the bull.

Donovan clapped long and enthusiastically as this wildly improbable scene wound down to what he thought would be its end. He clapped so as not to laugh at the two women performers. It had all been merry and great fun, this bon voyage gift from the Naga elders. And then it all changed.

As the act called "Kama Sutra" acknowledged his applause by taking a bow, Donovan stood up saying, 'Thank you ladies, thank you, I enjoyed your show."

Selima quickly pushed him gently back on to the cot. "We are not done yet. Now it is your turn to learn Kama Sutra."

"I think that was enough; you were wonderful."

"No, there is more."

"I have to get ready."

It was hot in the hut and the women were sweating from their exertions. They retrieved a basin of water from the table and placed it on the mat in front of Donovan. Where had the water come from? He didn't remember anyone bringing it.

The women sat down on the mat and took turns washing and drying one another. Selima took off her hat and let her black hair hang freely. She removed the scarf that had covered her chest. Her breasts were so perfectly round that Donovan thought she might have some sort of implant. He noticed a small scar on the side of her face and blemishes on the tops of her legs. Shanta, the one with the red dragon on her breast, was more slightly built than her partner. Her black hair was streaked with red coloring. Her breasts were small, and she seemed to emphasize the movement of the lower half of her body in all her gestures.

Once the two women were dry, they approached Donovan, offering to wash and dry him as well.

"No, thank you," he said, raising his hands in a defensive gesture. "You did all the work." They persisted, crowding around him, touching him with their hands, and rubbing their legs and breasts against him. He felt himself becoming aroused and stood up, taking the towel just to appease them. "Please, thank you, that's all I need."

The women seemed surprised that he had stopped them, refused their offerings. They returned to the mat. "Please sit down again and watch. Then you will want Kama Sutra." Donovan returned to the cot again weighing what he should do next. It was clear now the women expected him to join them in their sexual play. That was part of the Naga culture, wasn't it? But these women were not Nagas. Something was wrong, but he couldn't pinpoint it exactly. As he tried to analyze and understand the situation, he was becoming increasingly excited watching the women on the mat so close in front of him.

Selima lay back on the mat pulling her partner down on top of her. She then wrapped her legs around Shanta's waist in a scissors grip.

Donovan was mesmerized by what was happening in front of him. Suddenly, the two women ended their erotic embrace and rolled apart from each other on to their backs. Both held out their arms to Donovan. "Come join us," Shanta said, "we will see if you have learned the lessons well." He looked at the women who were flushed with excitement. It would be deliciously sexy to join them, he thought. Wasn't it a cliché that every man's fantasy was to be in a ménage a trois? Besides, who would ever know?

But would it be safe? He didn't even know where these women were from. As if sensing he needed more coaxing, the women began to touch each other again. Then, seemingly from nowhere, there came the words he had last heard in Calcutta, at Mother Teresa's, from Sister Frederick. "God works through weakness," she had said. He thought he knew what she meant at the time. But now, maybe those words could mean something else. It wasn't as if he actually heard the words. They weren't audible, but they came to him nevertheless.

He got up from his cot and walked to the door of the hut and went outside. The women looked up in disappointment as he left, one of them saying something to him that he could not make out. The guard seemed surprised to see him.

"Please tell the captain that I want the women to leave now. I want to be alone."

Donovan walked slowly around the edges of the clearing as his physical arousal subsided. It was another hot day in the jungle with rain clouds building above the tree line. Before long, Nllamo returned with the guard. They entered the hut and, after a few minutes, came back out with the two women who were now fully dressed, their straw hats protecting them from the sun. They seemed to be explaining something to him. He waved to Donovan as he passed. The two women did not see him, so intent were they on what they were saying to Captain Nllamo.

26

Captain Nllamo was as troubled as he had ever been during his twenty-seven years of commitment to the Naga resistance movement. Ever since 1964 when, as a teenager, he witnessed the shooting of both of his parents by Indian army soldiers, he had been steadfast in his devotion to the cause of independence. It was true that this unswerving dedication sometimes caused him to do things he didn't agree with, but he understood that to be the only way the underground could function successfully. And so he had accepted his role of carrying out policy, not making it. He obeyed orders, and he was not about to change in the case of Robert Donovan. However, there were a number of things that bothered him.

To begin with, he found it odd that following the successful kidnapping, days passed without any clear orders as to what to do with the American. It had been Nllamo who suggested that a video statement by Donovan might help the underground cause provided he was then released unharmed. Why hadn't that idea come from his superiors? He received more direction as to how the prostitutes should be presented to Donovan than he did about the making of the tape. And why did he have to immediately report back whether or not Donovan had sex with the whores from the brothels that served the Indian military? Why was that important? As far as he was concerned, the American had used good judgment. The probability that the women were diseased was high.

Nllamo was also concerned about the arrangement that had been made for Robert Donovan's release. The site chosen was remote and wild, a place where, in the dark of night, many things could go wrong. The captain's affection for Donovan was genuine, and he wanted the American to get back to his family safely. He deserved that after the powerful and eloquent statement he had made about the Naga cause.

Night had fallen when Nllamo and the two guards came for Donovan. As Donovan looked around at the simple hut that had been his cell, he was overcome with emotion.

"I can't explain what joy I feel," he said, "thank you for helping me."

"You already said thank you this afternoon."

"I know, but I didn't realize then what it would actually be like when the moment of freedom arrived. It is like nothing I have ever experienced before."

"That is because you have never been without your freedom before."

Donovan shook his head in agreement. "You are right. You're very right."

"Perhaps now you can understand even better the situation the Naga people are in. We are captives in our own land and, like you, we yearn to be free."

Donovan put out his hand to grasp Nllamo's. "I will remember you, my friend," he said.

"And I you. But we must go now and, before we do, you need to listen carefully to what I am about to say."

Donovan smiled. "You have my full attention."

Nllamo's tone of voice changed as if he were giving a military briefing.

"The first thing we need to do is to blindfold you. Lowang will see to that, and he will be more gentle than when you first were brought to our camp.

"It is important you understand the reason for the blindfold. Once you are picked up, the Indian army will want to interrogate you intensely. The less you see, the less you will be able to report."

"So far all I have seen is the inside of my hut, the square in the compound, the latrine, and the river."

"It would be better if you forget having seen the river."

"I understand," Donovan replied.

"The guards will lead you for a walk of some distance as there are no roads that are suitable for vehicles to reach our camp. This is intentional for our own security. A truck will meet you and you will sit in the back with the guards. You will remain blindfolded for reasons I have explained. The truck ride is lengthy. I will not say how long. You will be dropped at a pre-arranged spot, and the guards will undo the blindfold. You will be directed to walk about a kilometer on a rough path that we sometimes use. You will be left alone in order that the guards and your driver can return undetected."

"How will I know when I have walked the right distance?"

"You will know when the dense forest you are walking through opens into a clearing at the base of a small hill which will be facing you directly. It is here that the narrow path you are on widens to a rough road which is passable for some vehicles, though not without difficulty."

"Do I continue over the hill?"

"No. The transfer arrangements are very precise on this point.

You are to wait in the center of the clearing at the exact spot where the path becomes a road. The army vehicles assigned to pick you up will go no farther than the top of the hill. From there, they will be able to scan the area to see you are there as promised and to be sure they are not walking into an ambush."

"Will I have any light?"

"No, but you will be alright if you stay to the path."

The thought of walking through a narrow path without a guiding light bothered Donovan. "What kind of night is it?" he asked.

"Unfortunately for you, it is as black as it gets. There are no stars, no moon, just cloud cover. Just stay to the path."

Other questions troubled Donovan, questions about wild animals in the vicinity, but he didn't ask them. He could tell the captain was concerned about the timetable. Nllamo motioned to the guards who put a cloth over Donovan's eyes.

"The moment has come," Captain Nllamo said. "You soon will be free."

"Thank you for that."

Ato opened the door and Lowang led Donovan out of the hut into the clearing. Although Robert Donovan could not see them, a group of men and women from the camp had gathered to witness his departure.

"I will say goodbye to you now," Captain Nllamo said. Donovan thought he detected some emotion in his captor's voice as Nllamo's hand rested on his shoulder for the last time. A soft murmur of voices rose up from the people gathered as the two guards led Donovan away. Each of the guards held him by the elbow to steer his walking. Still the sensation of walking any distance blindfolded was strange, and his hesitation caused him to stumble.

Gradually he adjusted. The voices subsided and were replaced by the silence of the forest. Donovan could feel the thickness of the growth around him though he saw nothing.

The walk to the truck seemed longer than he expected. Fatigued and stressed from the difficulty of walking, he was relieved to hear the sound of a motor running.

The guards had been talking to each other in a native dialect. "We are at your truck, Professor Donovan," Ato said.

"Thank God. I need to rest."

They stopped walking and the guards released their grip on him. Donovan heard additional conversation and then the clank of a tailgate being unhooked and let down.

"We are going to lift you up and put you into the truck," Ato said. With that, two sets of arms hoisted him up, turned him around, and sat him down on the back edge of the truck. Donovan felt the guards climbing on the truck beside him. They stood him up and led him to a wooden bench where he was able to sit. He leaned back against the inside wall of the truck. Someone below put the tailgate back up and hooked it. A moment later, the truck left for the transfer spot.

Donovan estimated the speed of the truck to be no more than ten miles an hour. The vehicle bumped and swayed over the uneven terrain. At one point, the truck entered what must have been a particularly deep rut, causing it to lean precipitously to one side. All at once, Donovan became disoriented. He broke out in a cold sweat and for a moment, felt nauseous. The last time he felt this way, he and Paula had taken a helicopter ride into the Grand Canyon. When the pilot banked to give the tourists a better view of the canyon walls, he had an attack of vertigo whose symptoms were identical to the ones he felt now.

The truck righted itself, restoring Donovan's sense of balance.

"You okay?" Ato asked. Donovan nodded and the guards returned to their own conversation. Another hour passed before the queasiness left him, and he felt normal again.

The ride was the most uncomfortable of his life, his body continuously jarred as the truck bounced from one hole to the next. Still, he put the discomfort aside as he thought of all that had happened and all that was about to happen. Would Paula have come to India? Probably not. There wouldn't have been time for that. If not, the first thing he would do is call her to tell her he was free. Of course, there would be the interrogation by the Indian army. That was to be expected. He didn't have much to tell them. Nllamo had seen to that.

Then there was the issue of the videotape he had made. Would that have been released yet? Broadcast? Published? By whom? If the tape had been made public, Donovan had to prepare himself for the negative reaction of the Indian government and its soldiers. Of course, the American state department would protect his rights.

What was it that Nllamo had said? Something about appreciating freedom more now that he had experienced the loss of it. That was true of so many things in life. He remembered how, as a child when he became ill or, worse still, had a toothache, how he longed just to feel his normal self again, something he took for granted and didn't appreciate when he was healthy.

Captain Nllamo was right; it did help you value something more once you were without it. Perhaps he would write something about this. He wondered if all Nagas felt the collective loss of freedom or was it just those in the underground resistance movement? He needed to learn more, much more.

He was deep into a semi-conscious state, when the truck began to slow. He could not tell how long the trip had taken. His best estimate was three hours. His watch had never been returned to him, but he thought it to be about 10 o'clock in the evening. His blindfold had loosened and slipped, but it didn't matter at this point. The truck came to a stop, and the guards jumped into action.

"We cannot stay here long," Ato said as he removed the blindfold.

The guards unlatched the tailgate and jumped off the truck first. Donovan stood up, stretched, and then took the hands of the guards who lowered him to the ground. There was a new urgency in the movement of the guards.

"Here," Ato said, pointing in the direction Donovan was to walk. "This is the way as Captain Nllamo told you. We must leave right away ... Good luck."

Donovan fought a rising panic as the guards climbed back on to the truck. As the truck backed away to turn around farther down the path, he watched the driver light his way with the help of a hand-held spotlight which cast eerie shadows on the narrow path before them. In a matter of minutes, the truck disappeared leaving Robert Donovan alone in the Naga Hills.

He stood for a moment letting his eyes adjust from the total blackness of the blindfold. Though the night was as Nllamo had described it, moonless and starless, Donovan could make out the shapes of the trees which loomed around him and the outline of the narrow path where he had been left. He began to walk trying to put out of his mind all the possible dangers in the woods around him.

Ten minutes passed before he heard the snorting sounds of what had to be a large animal coming from the trees to his left. He quickened his pace and, as he did, a loud crashing noise came from the same direction. Perhaps it was a wild boar or something more dangerous. Terror took over, and he began to run and, suddenly, he stepped into a hole on the path and fell to the ground, striking his head hard enough to be momentarily stunned. He lay on the ground, vulnerable, half expecting some beast to attack him. But nothing happened, and he heard no more sounds from the boar or whatever animal it was.

He stood up and continued walking. A soft, warm breeze picked up just as the road widened and he walked into the clearing Nllamo had described. This was the spot where he was to stop and wait. He knew this because not twenty yards ahead, he could barely make out the shape of a small hill at the other end of the clearing. He began to pray, a prayer that asked his God to deliver him from this terrifying moment safely.

More time passed. He estimated it was between 11 and 12 o'clock before he heard the sound of a truck motor on the other side of the hill. He heard something else as well, a clanging noise as if the truck was pulling something behind it. This was it. The noise drew closer and suddenly the twin beams of the vehicle's lights appeared at the top of the hill pointing skyward. The beams penetrated the cloud-covered sky as if it were an airport searchlight searching for an incoming plane. The truck stopped at the top of the hill and then inched forward until the beams of light first dropped over his head and slowly lowered until the twin spotlights caught him directly in their glare.

Donovan could make out the shapes of the two men who stepped down from the front doors of the truck.

"Robert Donovan?" one of them called.

"Yes. I am Robert Donovan."

"Is there anyone with you?"

"No. I am alone."

"Stay right there. We will come to get you."

The two men started down the road. Both wore Indian army uniforms and carried rifles. Donovan was surprised there were not more soldiers or more vehicles.

"Are you the only soldiers who have come?" he asked.

There was no reply.

As they came closer, Donovan noticed something wrong with the uniforms the men wore. They were the right color, but they were incomplete, things were missing.

The soldiers approached, their rifles trained on him at all times. He looked at them close up and, for the first time, he suspected something was wrong. He had expected Indian army soldiers, young men perhaps in their twenties. These men were older, and they were Nagas. Now, as they talked to each other, they spoke in the same dialect used by Ato and Lowang.

The soldiers grabbed him roughly, one on each arm, and urged him forward.

"Walk," one of them ordered.

"Is there some misunderstanding about who I am?" Donovan asked.

Again, no reply.

The soldiers stopped. Above them, the truck idled, its headlights now directly in Donovan's eyes. He raised his hand to shield his eyes from the glare. As he did, the back door of the truck opened, and another figure slowly emerged. At first the lights prevented Donovan from seeing details other than the fact that the man was not wearing a military uniform.

The man stepped forward to stand looking down at them from the edge of the hill. He was short but powerfully built, covered only with a green cane belt and blue loin cloth. Fresh white markings striped his face and chest. Feathers attached to a headdress made him appear taller than he was.

He held a long spear in an upright position in his left hand. He removed a dao from the sheath on his back and held it loosely in his other hand. For a moment, the figure remained still, outlined in the stance of a warrior behind the lights of the truck and the dark sky above him. An animal roared from the rear of the truck.

Robert Donovan recognized the face of the warrior and understood immediately why he was dressed as he was and what was going to happen. The soldiers tightened their grip on his arms, but frozen by fear, he did not try to move.

As the figure advanced menacingly down the hill, Donovan thought of the beautiful dream of freedom he had earlier in the truck. It was clear now that it had all been an illusion, something he would never experience again.

Chingmei Konyak did not hesitate. As he raised the dao to strike the first blow, Robert Donovan saw a conviction in Chingmei's eyes that what he was about to do was the right and just action to take, the only thing left that he could do. The last thought Donovan had was of his wife, Paula, and how sad all of this would make her. His scream of terror filled the silence of the black forest as the blade of the dao flashed towards his head.

EPILOGUE

May 1992.

Chingmei Konyak sits alone in his library worrying about his wife, Sipra, and how their relationship has changed over the past year. Sipra stays with him, manages the household affairs, and still comes to his bed though not as frequently as she once did. Things are not the same, and they both understand that. She is present physically, but spirit and vitality have gone out of her. He doesn't know how to make things the way they were. What's done is done.

The telephone rings. He considers ignoring it but then decides to answer. Perhaps some good news for a change.

The caller is Abhi Chandra whom he has not spoken to since that fateful night last June. He is startled to hear his friend's voice and needs a moment to compose himself. Abhi, always gracious, apologizes for not having contacted him sooner.

"You have had many burdens this past year, and I felt I already had interfered enough," Abhi says.

Chingmei is cautious. He trusts his friend, but Abhi knows things others don't. "It is good to hear your voice again," Chingmei replies.

"And Sipra, how is she?"

"Sipra has not been the same since Meniu left. I am very concerned about her."

"Time is a healer."

"It has been a year."

"And Meniu. Is she well?"

"I know only what my wife tells me. Meniu has gone to the United States with a young man from the village. She works for the university she graduated from as an international admissions representative. The young man is a student there."

"I read that the university has named one of their academic programs after the American professor."

"Yes. Meniu was at the announcement ceremony. She had to meet his wife."

"That must have been difficult for her."

"The woman has remarried."

"She didn't wait long."

"Everything is done differently these days." Chingmei senses Abhi's questions are coming closer to the real point. He has to be more guarded. He has already said too much.

"You were pleased with the investigating commission's findings?"

"The commission had no other choice, Abhi. The soldiers reported animals at the body when they arrived. The medical examiner supported their conclusion."

There was silence at the other end.

"All these foolish interrogations; a waste of time and money," Chingmei continues. "There was a mix-up about the time he was to be transferred. The underground doesn't trust the army enough to hang around, and shake their hands. They fear they would be arrested, and they are probably right. Both sides blaming the other – a waste."

Abhi Chandra hesitates and Chingmei knows the question will come now, and it does.

"Was the commission correct in its findings, Chingmei? Was it an accident?"

"Of course I agree with the findings of the commission. What I also believe is what my father taught me, that there are no accidents, only things being set right, balance restored."

There is silence as Abhi considers what he has heard. In exasperation, Chingmei continues. "I tried your way. It didn't work." He stops himself. He has gone too far.

More silence. He hears a click on the other end as Abhi Chandra hangs up.

Chingmei looks out the window at the field he had planned for Meniu to manage. That would never happen now. She has contaminated the bloodline and the royal clan status will not be passed on through his daughter. He cries when he thinks how painful that must be for his dead father. So many things have gone wrong.

Rumors of what he did to the American professor circulate through the Naga hills. The underground no longer trusts him, and he may be in danger. They foolishly glorify the American because of the statement he made defending the independence movement. The videotape did draw some world attention to the Naga cause, but it is all forgotten now, an old news item overshadowed by whatever is happening today.

What did the American know of the long fight for freedom? Nothing. Did he realize that independence would lead to chaos, a likely civil war, and bloodshed among the different liberation groups? And yet, the people make a hero of him, even a martyr.

Chingmei worries that his ministerial position will soon be given to another. Even in his own village, his stature is no longer what it once was. Others challenge his power. He can't really blame them. After all, why should others respect him, if his daughter disobeys to run away with a man he had forbidden her to see.

He prays to his father and his ancestors to forgive him for what has happened. He knows that he, Chingmei, would never have thought of disobeying his father. But that was in another time, long ago, when the world made more sense, before everything changed.

AFTER WORD

While *An American in Nagaland* is a work of fiction, the ongoing struggle for independence in Nagaland, a sub-theme of the novel, is very real. BBC news periodically reports on the struggle which it characterizes as "the forgotten war in Nagaland" and "the world's longest running conflict."

During the past ten years, advocates have presented the Naga story in world forums as varied as the US House of Representatives and the United Nations Commission on Human Rights. The Naga Vigil Human Rights Group continued its work to "highlight the silent plight of the Nagas by informing the international opinion of the prevailing situation in Nagaland." The National Socialist Council of Nagaland signed a new cease-fire agreement with the government of India in 1997. Since not all of the underground separatist groups signed the cease-fire agreement, there is considerable skepticism among the Naga people that the present agreement will last.

T.J.F.

Tom Farrell served as the dean of the John Hazen White School of Arts & Sciences at Johnson & Wales University from 1992-2001. He is the author of a novel, *Nantucket 1970*, several textbooks, as well as articles in newspapers and academic journals. He earned degrees from the University of Notre Dame and the University of Rhode Island. He divides his time between Narragansett, Rhode Island and Nantucket Island, Massachusetts.

Acknowledgments

Many thanks to Donna Laporte, Norman Brooks, Mary Lou Gardner, and Erin FitzGerald for their help in preparing the manuscript. I also appreciate the ideas and suggestions offered by James Anderson, Ph.D., Maureen Farrell, Ph.D., Saiyeda Khatun, Ph.D., Robert Olmstead at the Charleston Writer's Conference, Angela Renaud, Ed.D. and Veera Sarawgi.

I relied on the following books: *The Naked Nagas* by Christoph von Farer-Haimendorf Ph.D. and *Nagaland File – A Question of Human Rights* by Luingam Luithui and Nandita Haksar. Also helpful were *Tribes of Nagaland* by Sipra Sen, *The Naga Tribes of Manipur* by T.C. Hodson, *Peace in Nagaland* by M. Aram, and *Baptist Missions in Nagaland* by Dr. Joseph Puthenpurakal.